It was huge. A grotesque, irregular, twisted skeleton of barbed bone and pitted metal shot through with bands of stretched sinew and muscle. An amber glow emanated from deep in its rib cage and then it opened its alloy mouth to reveal rows of chipped teeth.

The lunge came suddenly. Elspeth manage to side-step the strike, but the force of it knocked her off her feet. She was up in a second. With numb fingers she hoisted her greatsword. The blow caught the creature between the eyes, but the bright blade glanced off, and Elspeth had to fight to keep it from flying out of her hands. The creature lunged again. Elspeth twisted away. She regained control and whispered the words she knew so well. White fire leaped momentarily from her sword's tip. Elspeth stepped forward and brought her blade down in an overhead sweep. The moment before impact a white light filled the room and thousands of flashing blades blurred the air. The strikes seemingly came from all angles at the same time. Venser rubbed his eyes and looked again at the creature's body where it lay hacked as though by one hundred swords.

Venser would have asked Elspeth about her sword right there and then if not for Koth. The vulshok ran to the wet rumple of his mother's skin and dropped to his knees. His tears smoked as they ran down his cheek. "Mother," he wailed, holding the skin in his large hands.

But there was no time for grief, and less for tears. A shadow moved in the next room. Venser sensed it first, of course . . . the creature from the dark doorway, the one who had been controlling Koth's mother through the wire she dragged with her. But no sooner had he detected its brain movement in the next room than it exploded through the wall. A hulking creature with long, filthy claws and a dark metal head shaped like a gigantic, battle-chipped spear tip. Most of it was grown of black, chipped metal and burned bone, and its jaw extended well past what was typical on any plane Venser had ever traveled to, and only the end of the jaw was toothed and vicious. It brought its head down and charged Elspeth, who swept up with her sword and caught the creature in the jaw, slicing it delicately in half.

The horrific thing reached up and took hold of its bisected jaw and tore the parts loose with a wicked chortle. The black blood ran down its stretched muscles and soon a torrent of fluid was splashing from its gullet. It tossed its jaw pieces aside, turned, and charged Venser. The artificer waited until the creature was almost upon him before disappearing in a sudden blue flash and reappearing on the other side of the room. Meanwhile, the creature continued in its charge, running headlong into the house and driving its head blade halfway into the metal of the structure. Thus trapped, Elspeth ran, screaming at the beast, chopping it until it breathed no more. She kept hacking with tears running down her own cheeks and froth collecting at the corners of her mouth, until Venser's yelling stayed her hand and she stood blinking in the flickering lights from the magma lamps.

Walk the Blind Eternities . . .

Discover the planeswalkers in their travels across the endless planes of the Multiverse . . .

AGENTS OF ARTIFICE BY ARI MARMELL

Jace Beleren, a powerful sorcerer and planeswalker whose rare telepathic ability opens doors that many would prefer remain closed, is at a crossroads: the decisions he makes now will forever affect his path.

THE PURIFYING FIRE BY LAURA RESNICK

The young and impulsive Chandra Nalaar—planeswalker, pyromancer—begins her crash course in the art of boom. When her volatile nature draws the attention of megalomaniacal forces, she will have to learn to control her power before they can control her.

TEST OF METAL BY MATTHEW STOVER

Beaten to within an inch of his life and left for dead by the psychic sorcerer Jace Beleren, Tezzeret has lost control of the Infinite Consortium—an interplanar cabal he commanded with a power and influence few in the Multiverse have ever achieved.

ALARA UNBROKEN BY DOUG BEYER

The fierce leonine planeswalker Ajani Goldmane unwittingly uncovers the nefarious agency behind the splintered planes of Alara and their realignment. Meanwhile, fellow planeswalker Elspeth Tirel struggles to preserve the nobility of the first plane she has ever wanted to call homeand. And the dragon shaman Sarkhan Vol finds the embodiment of power he has always sought.

ZENDIKAR: IN THE TEETH OF AKOUM
BY ROBERT B. WINTERMUTE

Nissa Revane, a planeswalker and proud elf warrior, is witness to what the Eldrazi can do when she stumbles into the vanguard of their monstrous brood. What she doesn't know is that they are merely pale reflection of the titans that spawned them. But the ancient vampire planeswalker Sorin Markov knows all to well the power of the ancient Eldrazi titans. He was among the original jailers of the ancient scourge and he has returned to Zendikar to make sure they do not escape.

And revisit these five classic planeswalker tales, repackaged in two volumes

ARTIFACTS CYCLE I
THE THRAN BY J. ROBERT KING
THE BROTHERS' WAR BY JEFF GRUBB

ARTIFACTS CYCLE II
PLANESWALKER BY LYNN ABBEY
BLOODLINES BY LOREN L. COLEMAN
TIME STREAMS BY J. ROBERT KING

MAGIC
The Gathering®

SCARS OF MIRRODIN

THE QUEST FOR KARN

ROBERT B. WINTERMUTE

Wizards OF THE COAST®

Magic: The Gathering
Scars of Mirrodin:
The Quest for Karn

©2011 Wizards of the Coast LLC

Published by Wizards of the Coast LLC

Magic: the Gathering, Scars of Mirrodin, Wizards of the Coast, and their respective logos are trademarks of Wizards of the Coast LLC in the U.S.A. and other countries.

Printed in the U.S.A.

Cover art by Jason Chan

ISBN: 978-0-7869-5774-3
ISBN: 978-0-7869-5916-7 (e-book)
620-30693000-001-EN

U.S., CANADA,
ASIA, PACIFIC, & LATIN AMERICA
Wizards of the Coast LLC
P.O. Box 707
Renton, WA 98057-0707
+1-800-324-6496

EUROPEAN HEADQUARTERS
Hasbro UK Ltd
Caswell Way
Newport, Gwent NP9 0YH
GREAT BRITAIN
Save this address for your records.

Visit our web site at www.wizards.com

κάλλιστον μὲν ἐγὼ λείπω φάος ἠελίοιο,

δεύτερον ἄστρα φαεινὰ σεληναίης τε πρόσωπον
ἠδὲ καὶ ὡραίους σικύους καὶ μῆλα καὶ ὄγχνας·

Finest of all the things I have left is the light of the sun,

Next to that the brilliant stars and the face of the moon,
Cucumbers in their season, too, and apples and pears.
                              (trans. Bernard Knox)

—Praxilla of Sicyon

CHAPTER
1

They scuffed over a small rise from the south, with the blinding rays of the Sky Tyrant in their eyes and the heat of the other four suns burning at their backs. Underfoot, the hills themselves creaked and popped as their metal sides expanded in the hot morning sunlight. Venser of Urborg pulled off his helmet and surveyed the rusted horizon before casting a wary eye at the two beings walking ahead of him. One towered over the other and both dragged their feet over the tarnished hill.

"I would have come on my own if you'd only asked," Venser said.

The large one stopped and turned. In the almost blinding light of the five suns the iron spikes growing from his shoulders looked dull and tired. But not his teeth, as a sly smile spread over his face.

"Would you really have come, artificer?"

"Venser is my name."

The muscular vulshok shrugged as if to show just what he thought of a name like *Venser*.

"And yes, I would have come," Venser said.

"Well, this is my world and my people," Koth the vulshok grunted, bringing his foot down on the metal floor. "I do not have the luxury of pleasantries." He looked out over the jagged razor of mountains jutting against the horizon. "We should arrive at my village by nightfall," he said. "Be ready for meat and drink served by those with fire in their veins. We will find the one who will know what has become of the situation."

Venser watched the vulshok walk away.

"I can hardly wait," he said.

As the rest of the day passed, the suns switched places in the sky and a far range of dun-colored, symmetrical mountains grew closer. Their chipped tips of jagged metal thrust at uniform angles, and the round clouds that massed around their serrated tops reflected the rosy brilliance of lava in the valleys below. The vulshok stopped walking.

"Why have we stopped?" Venser asked. "We should keep walking. I haven't had enough walking."

The third companion turned away and Venser thought he heard a stifled laugh from under her hood.

"Kuldotha, the great mother of thunder and fire nears," Koth said.

"What? In there?" Venser said, pointing to the valleys between the lumbering mountains.

The vulshok turned slowly to look at the young artificer. "You have fear in your heart?" Koth said. It was more of a statement than a question, but Venser held Koth's gaze.

"No," Venser said. "I was simply saying that canyons are perfect for ambush."

"And you are a leader now, as well as a prodigy?" Koth said. "Elspeth, what do you think?"

The other figure raised her hands and pulled down her hood.

"I think he is right," she said, adjusting the greatsword strapped at her hip. "You brought him here against his will. The least you can do is listen to him," she said.

"Well," Koth said, flustered. "There is no other way to Kuldotha but through the canyons of the Oxidda Chain."

Elspeth squinted at the near mountains.

"That is true," Venser said.

"How would you know truth in the Oxidda Chain?"

"I have been to this plane of yours." Venser slipped his helmet back on his sweaty head. Through its eye slit he watched as Koth scowled at him. "A clockwork planet," the artificer said. "Karn brought me here." He stopped short. The geomancer was watching him intently and when Venser did not continue speaking, Koth's eyes widened.

"Karn?" Koth said.

"An old friend," Venser said, looking away.

Koth's mouth tightened. "I know nobody by that name," Koth said.

"Do you know every being on Mirrodin?" Venser said, still looking away. He showed an uncharacteristic tightness around his eyes and mouth. Koth's eyes narrowed in suspicion.

"We are here to see if the stories I have heard are true," Koth said. "If they are, we will fight. This is why we brought you here. You will perform."

A wry smile appeared on Venser's face. "You do your world no good by threatening those you wish to recruit. You attack me, suffocate me, and expect me to do as you instruct. You are mad if you—"

A squeaking sound was blowing on the wind, and Venser cocked his head to the side taking the sound in. *How far, three leagues or just over the next hill?* It was hard to judge distance in this steely place . . . without vegetation sound could echo and travel great distances unobstructed. But Koth appeared not to have heard the sound. He was absolutely red in the face and taking shallow breaths as he stared at Venser.

"Are you well?" Venser said.

"It is *you* who will follow me and do what *I* suggest on *my* plane."

"I think it may be time to separate the boys from the women," Elspeth interrupted, her own head cocked, listening to the sound that had caught Venser's attention.

Venser followed the white-clad woman's gaze. Far off, over the heat-bent air, a form was clearly visible. As they watched, it lumbered and jerked closer on four sprawled legs. As they watched, the thing suddenly came to an abrupt stop and its legs pulled into the main body. A tube came out of the top and turned until it was pointed at the three of them. No sooner than the tube had pointed at them, the creature hopped to its feet again and began scurrying toward them at an alarming speed. They watched it come.

"Is it a machine?" Elspeth said.

"A biomechanical entity, I would think," Venser said.

"A *biomechanical entity*," Koth said in a mocking tone.

"What do you think it is?" Venser said.

"You are both fools," Koth said. "It is an artifact creature."

"A biomechanical entity, as I said."

The leveler sped over the dun-colored hill toward them. As it came nearer they could gauge its size better: larger than an average human and double as wide, with a dome-shaped turret on its top that spun with large, spiked metal balls affixed on chains. Its old, jagged metal sides squeaked as it glided across the space between them on small legs.

Venser stepped forward and took a deep breath. When he exhaled, the beds of his fingernails glowed a dull blue. Elspeth drew her sword and Koth fell into a squat. The creature shot directly at Venser, who was farther to the side than the others. Venser put out his hand. As fast as it was moving, the machine came to an abrupt and jarring stop at Venser's touch, and the balls spinning around its turreted top jerked free and spun away to clatter over the metal hill. The machine stood still.

"Well, let's take a look," Venser said.

He rapped twice on the side of the creature and the rivets holding one of its panels in place popped free. Venser whispered a word under his breath and the panel snapped to his palm as though magnetized. He placed the panel carefully at his feet. Then, to Elspeth's surprise, he pushed his head into the hole and began taking deep breaths.

Koth glanced at Elspeth. Venser suddenly jerked his head out of the hole.

"Fascinating and good."

"What is fascinating?" Koth said.

"This creature, of course. It has never had any synaptic taint . . . ," Venser said.

Elspeth slipped her blade back in its sheath.

"That *is* good news," Koth said.

Venser waited. "That means no taint of, uh, infection."

"Superior," Elspeth said. "One machine we don't have to send to the scrap heap."

She sounded confident and angry, Venser thought, but there was something else in her tone—some slight tremble in the upper ranges that did not sound confident in the slightest.

Koth knocked carefully on the artifact's thick side. "What do we do with this?"

"We will leave it and my spell will eventually wear off and this marvel will continue on its way."

"Why not dismantle it now so we do not have to fight it later?" Koth said.

"Because it has done nothing to us," Venser said.

"Except try to destroy us."

"Let us keep walking," Elspeth said, ignoring them both. "This heat tires me greatly."

They kept walking. Soon the mountains they'd seen in the distance were upon them. Their dull iron sides shot up at right angles never seen in nature . . . at least never seen in any kind of nature that Venser had spent time in.

"The Oxidda Chain," Koth said reverently.

The Chain seemed to be composed of corroded, notched slab iron run through with winding conduit tubing. Dark caves and holes abounded in the tight valleys between the peaks. Unaccountably, walkways of metal welded to the sides of the mountains wound away through the valleys. Venser smelled oxidation in the air and something else . . . rotting meat maybe. Nothing moved. No tree limbs stirred in the hot breeze. There were no birds. No sand blew around the cornice of a hill. The view appeared as still and remote as a painted picture.

They pieced their way through the jagged debris that had corroded and rolled off the higher peaks and came to rest deep in the valley. Eventually they reached the base of one of the raised walkways and clambered up its side. The walkway's metal gang-planks were buffed to a dull sheen, but many were oxidized through and derelict.

"Enough of this," Koth said. He put his two sizable hands before him and made a seizing motion, as if to grab one of the huge iron boulders lying in the bed of the valley. To Venser's momentary shock, three of the chunks rose off the ground and floated toward them, guided by Koth's glowing hands. The chunks stopped, one in front of each of the Planeswalkers. Koth stepped on his, and soon Elspeth and Venser were on theirs. Koth's boulder began to float out over the valley floor, a bit higher than the stature of a man. Venser was next. When it was Elspeth's turn, she shot her arms out to her sides to steady herself as her chunk glided forward.

The heat seemed to increase as they moved deeper and between the riven spires of the Oxidda Chain. There was no noise save the wind skittering the loose metal flakes along the valley floor.

Koth had to maintain a lifting motion as the slabs flew. For a moment Venser considered teasing the geomancer for the pose, but then thought better of it and looked out over the raw landscape. He thought about how it had appeared when he visited all that time ago. The same. Just as harsh and, to his eyes, unforgiving. He remembered Karn's pride in Mirrodin. He would go into great detail explaining how many days it had taken him to create a certain ridge, or sculpt a peak with just the right sheer. As Venser looked around at the tortured aspect of the Oxidda Chain's brown and orange mountains, he wondered . . . where the creator of Mirrodin was. Where was Karn?

"Where are the living things?" Elspeth said.

"I too would have expected to have encountered a border patrol by this point," Koth said.

"Perhaps the situation on this plane is not as dire as we had thought?" Elspeth said.

"Do any of these suns ever set?" Venser said, gazing upward at a low red sun. "I mean, one falls and another rises, and so on and so on."

Koth glanced up at the sky. "They pull into alignment, and then fall. This will happen soon and quickly—and by that time we should be in the safety of my village."

"Why?" Venser said.

"It is not safe to wander through the Chain at night. The dangers of falling into something sharp or striking metal is enough."

"But there are creatures, as well?"

"Oh yes, there are many creatures."

Venser let the comment hang in the air before turning to Elspeth.

"What is Bant like, fair knight?" Venser said to Elspeth, with only the barest lilt of jest in his voice.

The corner of Elspeth's mouth turned down.

"It was beautiful," she said.

"But there is sadness, now. Is there not?" Venser said.

Elspeth was looking down the canyon. She did not shift her gaze at Venser's words.

"There used to be only honor, bravery, and perfection," Elspeth said. "In my dreams it is still as it was, and people serve for the greater good."

Koth let out a gruff laugh. "Service?" he said. "I have never heard something so . . ." he stopped and turned to Elspeth, who was staring at him intently. "I have never heard of anything so . . . foolish. The strong lead. The weak follow or die."

"Foolish?" Venser said. "Strength comes in all

forms. Sometimes working together is the only way to achieve an end. You may be required to cooperate to save your precious Mirrodin, by the end."

Koth growled at Venser before gliding away on his rock.

The suns lined up in the sky as Koth said they would. They fell in a line toward the craggy horizon. Their light was almost extinguished by the time the village came into view. Sunset found them floating above a high precipice looking down on the quiet village.

"It is too still," Koth muttered. How could a village that had been bustling when he left Mirrodin be completely still now? *Where are the fires?*

The suns sank still farther in the sky. It would be dark soon. Almost all the light had drained from the sky, and their view would be in question.

Except for the wind, the silence that lay on them as they floated through the village was unbroken and total. They glided along the road that passed between a rough huddle of huts made of rolled-up lengths of metal hammered into tubes. Some of the tubes were wide and some were narrow enough to fit only a body. Elspeth noticed some structures composed of rolls piled together into triangles. There were metal mesh curtains that acted as doors, but most curtains were thrown back to reveal the darkness within the tubes. Many of the curtains whipped and snapped in the wind.

They stopped above the well that marked the center of the village. An iron bucket that acted as the village dipper creaked on a chain in the wind.

"This is a warm reception," Venser said. "Are vulshok homecomings always so lively? If so, I have to make a point of attending more of them. They remind me of home on Dominaria."

But nobody laughed. Even Elspeth did not chuckle. The white warrior had droplets of sweat on her top lip, Venser noticed. Her right hand, resting in what she undoubtedly hoped was a casual pose on her sword hilt, was clenched in a fist.

Koth closed his eyes. Lines began to glow red along his ribs until his whole body was as an ember might be. His eyes popped open suddenly, as red as the tracer lines on his body.

"Be ready," he said.

Elspeth, at least, was ready. She drew her sword in a clatter of steel, her eyes wide. "I smell something strange," she said.

Venser smelled it as well. It could be anything, but he knew what it was just as he knew a million compounds from their smells alone. One could not be an artificer without knowing the smell of things. How could you tell old oil from new or solid metal from corruption without smell? No, he knew corruption when he smelled it, and called deeply to siphon mana from the lines he could feel pulsing deep under the metal surface of the plane. Oh, there was mana in this place. Much mana. *Hopefully we will not need it. Hopefully we will find Karn easily and leave Mirrodin to its own devices.*

"Something is watching us from the huts," the geomancer said.

From behind them came the sound of metal scraping metal, coupled with a low moan. The scraping sounded like many fingernails dragged across flaking iron. It had been some time since the hairs on Venser's back stood, and he was not altogether happy to be visited by that feeling again. "I think we should move," he said.

"Yes," Koth said. "I think that is a good idea." Venser and Koth's slabs moved forward.

But Elspeth did not move. She had put one of her feet on the iron ground. Her wide eyes slowly narrowed.

"Elspeth? This is the time now to find my friend on the outskirts of the village. He will be able to tell us what is happening here."

"The knights of Bant do not flee, ever."

"Of course they don't," Venser said. "Nobody would ever ask you to do that. To flee. Koth here is suggesting we visit his friend."

Koth nodded.

"Do not patronize me, artificer."

"How do we know there are enemies out there?" Venser said. "And if they were, don't you think our position here is not the best? Strategically, I mean. We are as vulnerable as plucked pullets, and whatever is making that noise has many in its party." *You only just kidnapped me here. I can't die yet*, he added to himself.

Elspeth blinked.

"Yes, this is low ground. Let's repair to a better position," she said, taking her foot off the ground and putting it back on the slab, which floated to catch up with the other two.

"A wise choice," Venser said, when she was floating next to him. If she'd waited more than a second longer he would have snapped a submission spell on her.

They moved very quickly after Koth who led them over more tube huts.

The scrabbling sound they had heard earlier continued behind them. Elspeth was reminded of another time she had heard a similar sound: fleeing a certain prison as a child. When she had run, the beasts had screeched and clawed at their own bars.

She remembered the smell of them in that moment and brought her gloved hand up to pinch her nose as she floated along on the slab.

Koth moved them over the land. They saw not a single living thing, except a strange mechanical bird which alighted on the ground and turned its one good eye to stare at them as they passed. Soon the huts became fewer and fewer, and they were away from the village. Elspeth sheathed her sword.

Soon a different type of hut came into view. It was composed of a series of large tubes welded together and nestled in the valley between two vast iron hills that leaned toward each other.

"Is this your friend's house?" Elspeth said.

Koth said nothing for a time. He glided his slab to a stop near the entrance of the hut.

"We'll stop here a moment. This is where I was raised. My family has gel-fruit orchards," Koth stepped off his slab. "And beds."

"Good, I think I might fall down," Venser said. He had taken his helmet off sometime earlier, and had it under his arm.

"You will watch your mannerisms around my mother," Koth said to them. "She has yet to meet one such as yourselves."

"What does that mean?"

"A being of only flesh," he whispered. "Flesh is distrusted by many Mirrans. You must do your people credit."

"My people?"

Elspeth eyed the house surrounded by its low, metal trees. The noise that had been behind them seemed to have disappeared, and she felt more at ease. The dark was on them, and she could see lights in the window of the large hut and smell roasting meat. The night was silent. She realized suddenly that she did not like this plane for its utter silence.

"What is your opinion, my lady?" Venser said, the half smile that played frequently across his face in evidence. Koth was already moving past the twisted metal tubes that made up the gel-fruit trees around the hut.

Elspeth nodded as she watched Koth, thinking Venser was talking about the vulshok. "I watched the vulshok fight in the pits at Urborg. I fought him there as well."

"And what is your impression?"

"He is as good a fighter as I have ever seen, and a strong mage, but . . ."

"But?"

"He is given to the foolishnesses of all men, and one of those is impulsiveness."

Venser straightened a bit. "Excuse me? Am I not a man?"

She looked back at him. "Yes, and what of it? I am sure you are as thickheaded as the rest of them."

Venser bobbed his head in agreement. "You are probably correct."

"Now that that is settled," Elspeth continued, "we should follow him before he does something foolish that gets us all throttled."

And they did. They caught up with Koth just before he reached the house. The smell of roasting meat was strong. And there was something else in the air as well, Venser thought. Koth pushed the mesh aside and walked headlong into the largest tube of the dwelling.

The interior was brightly lit with sconces welded to the wall and holding globs of what looked like bright molten metal. A fireplace cut out of a chunk of iron stood at one end of the room.

"Hello," Koth said. He walked to the hearth, turned, and looked around the room. "Hello?"

Elspeth put her gloved finger to her lips. "I am not sure that we should . . ."

"Look who has arrived at long last."

The voice came from the dark doorway next to the hearth. A woman's voice, made by a woman who sounded as though she needed to clear her throat, Elspeth thought. A form moved in the shadow and Venser found himself sucking mana through his eyes and temples in anticipation of an emergency teleport. He wasn't the only one concerned—he noticed that Elspeth dropped her hand to her sword's pommel when the woman spoke.

"Mother?" Koth said. "Is it you? Come from the shadows, Mother.

"It is I, Son. None other."

There was more shuffling in the shadows but nobody came out. Koth took a step closer.

"Mother we were being pursued . . . by something making strange *sounds*. We must leave this place and take to the mountains. Mother?" The vulshok took another step closer to the form in the darkness. Venser snatched a deep breath and thought, *do not step any closer.*

The figure in the darkness shifted and stepped forward a bit. "You always were a coward. Afraid of shadows and sleeping alone."

"But Mother."

The figure in the darkness stepped forward and into the flickering light from the sconces. Elspeth's hand left the pommel of her sword. The being standing before them seemed as harmless as could be: a vulshok mother in a simple robe, with spiky silver hair and forearms of alloy that glimmered in the dim light.

But Koth seemed bothered. He cocked his head at the woman. "You have changed, Mother. You are thinner. Your hair is different."

The mother's expression did not change, though. Her face remained impassive, plain somehow, as though emotion had never occurred to her.

"You have nothing to fear, I am the same as I have always been. It is I, your mother."

But Koth's unease increased by the second. The tracer lines along his wide chest began to glow red, as did his eyes.

"Where is Father?" Koth said. "Collect him and we must flee."

"It is not time for that," she said.

The woman went to the hearth. She snapped her fingers and a lick of flame ignited in the firebox. The smell of food, of roasting meat, was suddenly overpowering. Venser's stomach turned as he realized he had not eaten in days.

"Perhaps she's right," Venser said. "Surely we have time for a snack before we flee."

Koth set his teeth together and scowled at Venser.

Just then someone screamed outside. The cry echoed off the mountains. It came from far away, Elspeth thought, and was soon cut short, but it was a cry of utter fear and despair.

"That cry will have to do with whatever is pursuing us," Elspeth said.

But Koth was staring at his mother, who was looking into the fire she'd created in the fireplace.

"There is no need to fear," she whispered to herself. "No need to fear. No need to fear. No need . . ."

Elspeth felt a tug on the sleeve of her tunic. She looked and Venser pointed at Koth's mother's feet. It was hard to see in the dimness of the room, but there seemed to be a snake on the floor at her feet. The smell of roasting meat was strong in Elspeth's nostrils, too. She squinted and looked again at the thing on the floor. Venser leaned in close, so close that his helmet touched her ear.

"Tube," he hissed.

Tube? Elspeth looked again, and now the shape she thought was a snake looked more like a conduit that went from under the woman's robe and into the dark doorway she had stepped from.

"Koth," Elspeth said casually.

The vulshok turned to her.

"Let us be off, we will come back for your mother as soon as we've found a secure place in the mountains." It was a desperate move, but worth trying.

Koth's mother remained unmoving. Her expression had not changed since she came from the doorway.

"Come give your mother a hug," she said, and lurched toward Koth with stiff knees. "Then we will go eat your father, he is roasting in the other room."

She opened her mouth wide and something shot out with an audible *snap*. Then a metal mouth was clamped on Koth's face. The event only took a fraction of a moment and the vulshok was rolling on the floor pulling at the writhing metal creature attached to his face. A thin tube extended from it and lolled in a wet loop into the mother's mouth.

Elspeth drew her sword and in a decisive slash severed the tube. Koth's mother stood still next to the hearth, her eyes staring blankly ahead. A moment later a crease appeared on her forehead and down the middle of her nose and chin, down her throat and farther. Then a *click* and blood appeared at the seam, and in the shocked silence her skin suddenly peeled back to reveal dark sinew. Jagged bones began to push out, followed by a great maw of serrated teeth and the mandible that held them, and then a whole face of jags and two black eyes unfolded itself from within.

As the creature opened up like a puzzle to stand as high as the ceiling, Elspeth felt the blood in her body drop a degree. The creature unfolded more, sloughing off the body of the vulshok like the peel of an eaten fruit.

It was huge. A grotesque, irregular, twisted skeleton of barbed bone and pitted metal shot through with bands of stretched sinew and muscle. An amber glow emanated from deep in its rib cage and then it opened its alloy mouth to reveal rows of chipped teeth.

The lunge came suddenly. Elspeth manage to side-step the strike, but the force of it knocked her off her feet. She was up in a second. With numb fingers she hoisted her greatsword. The blow caught the creature between the eyes, but the bright blade glanced off, and Elspeth had to fight to keep it from flying out of her hands. The creature lunged again. Elspeth twisted away. She regained control and whispered the words she knew so well. White fire leaped momentarily from her sword's tip. Elspeth stepped forward and brought her blade down in an overhead sweep. The moment before impact a white light filled the room and thousands of flashing blades blurred the air. The strikes seemingly came from all angles at the same time. Venser rubbed his eyes and looked again at the creature's body where it lay hacked as though by one hundred swords.

Venser would have asked Elspeth about her sword right there and then if not for Koth. The vulshok ran to the wet rumple of his mother's skin and dropped to his knees. His tears smoked as they ran down his cheek. "Mother," he wailed, holding the skin in his large hands.

But there was no time for grief, and less for tears. A shadow moved in the next room. Venser sensed it first, of course . . . the creature from the dark doorway, the one who had been controlling Koth's mother through the wire she dragged with her. But no sooner had he detected its brain movement in the next room than it exploded through the wall. A hulking creature with long, filthy claws and a dark metal head shaped like a gigantic, battle-chipped spear tip. Most of it was grown of black, chipped metal and burned bone, and its jaw extended well past what was typical on any plane Venser had ever traveled to, and only the end of the jaw was toothed and vicious. It brought its head down and charged Elspeth, who swept up with her sword and caught the creature in the jaw, slicing it delicately in half.

The horrific thing reached up and took hold of its bisected jaw and tore the parts loose with a wicked chortle. The black blood ran down its stretched muscles and soon a torrent of fluid was splashing from its gullet. It tossed its jaw pieces aside, turned, and charged Venser. The artificer waited until the creature was almost upon him before disappearing in a sudden blue flash and reappearing on the other side of the room. Meanwhile, the creature continued in its charge, running headlong into the house and driving its head blade halfway into the metal of the structure. Thus trapped, Elspeth ran, screaming at the beast, chopping it until it breathed no more. She kept hacking with tears running down her own cheeks and froth collecting at the corners of her mouth, until Venser's yelling stayed her hand and she stood blinking in the flickering lights from the magma lamps.

"I think you have done him to death," Venser said. What was left of the thing was gashed and raw and lying in a clump of black reek on the floor of the house.

Venser glanced at Elspeth as she wiped her eyes. *A disturbed individual.*

"What do you feel?" Venser said toeing what was left of the creature, which was mostly claw and tooth. Worthy of investigation, if he only had the time.

The white warrior was staring at the wall. Venser's words took some moments to register. Finally she turned to him. A bit of black fluid was spattered on her forehead, but Venser thought it would not be the right time to point that out to her.

"I feel nothing."

"Do you feel fear?"

"I will admit that I have felt fear in the past," Elspeth said. "But heroes shed no tears. And I will fight these *things* with every fiber of my being until I've drawn my last."

"But my lady, I saw you weeping," Venser said. It was out of his mouth before he knew it. So many times he'd encountered that type of person who claimed not to *feel*. It made him sick. One could not understand how machines and biotic creatures worked without empathy. Parts of Dominaria were full of those beings who claimed not to feel.

"I feel only hatred," she said. "They will all pay and I will not rest until this happens. Any who stand before me will feel this wrath." With that she turned and walked out of the home.

Koth was standing at the far side of the room staring at the dead creature. He made no sound as Elspeth threw the steel mesh curtain aside and strode out. "I hoped it wasn't true. Not here," he said.

"So you kidnapped me and brought me here to fight this infection?" Venser said. "Knowing that now I cannot leave, or I risk spreading the contagious oil to any other plane I visit?"

"Are you afraid?" Koth said, standing as tall as possible.

"Am *I* afraid? I would be a fool indeed to not feel trepidation on a plane that seems to be freshly infested with Phyrexians. Your mother would have killed me if left to her own devices."

"That was not my mother."

"She looked real enough for me. Part of her at least."

"Not my mother," Koth repeated decisively. The vulshok's tone of voice warned against further pursuit of the subject.

"Since our worst thoughts proved true, and Phyrexia has reached this metallic shore, then our only hope is to find Karn."

"Karn?" Elspeth said. She'd moved into the doorway so soundlessly that Venser had not detected her. *Very nice.*

"His friend," Koth said. "Who brought him to Mirrodin. Some *unknown* Mirran."

"He created Mirrodin," Venser said. "He is the artisan who made this plane. The Silver Golem himself."

They said nothing for a time. "That is not true," Koth said. "We vulshok have our own stories."

"It is true, I assure you."

"Venser," Elspeth said. "Why would he be here? And if he is, then he has surely been consumed. And in that case, we do not want to find him."

"Last I heard he was traveling here. He sent a message that none should follow him. He is my friend and I would have followed him."

"Eventually?" Koth said.

"Yes," Venser said, staring darkly at Koth.

"What is our next course of action?" Elspeth said.

Venser turned to her. "We don't know just how badly this place is infected yet. I have not seen many of the telltale signs of septic infiltration. He could be somewhere fighting the Phyrexians even as we speak."

Elspeth nodded once to acknowledge that that was indeed a possibility. Koth, on the other hand, frowned.

"Silver golems and Phyrexians are both foreigners and will be expelled as soon as possible," Koth said. "You will see that Mirrodin does not stand alone. Her children will fight for her. People like my comrade Malach. We will find him. He can tell us how bad the infection has become." Koth walked out the door.

CHAPTER
2

They moved though the darkness on Koth's iron slabs. Koth stopped to whisper words of power and wisps of light danced in the air, lighting the surrounding walls as they made their way deeper into the canyon.

Without warning, it started to rain so hard that Koth could not see the outline of the mountains silhouetted against the sky, and the group had to stop. They laid up in a small draw under a slag overhang as the rain fell hard, spattering the rust mud over their boots.

When the rain stopped, they rode the iron boulders again.

"Where does the water go?" Venser said. "It is gone, all that fell. There are no pools."

Koth cocked his head to the side and spat.

"What do I know of water?" he said.

"I heard gurgles."

It was Elspeth who had spoken. Venser turned to her in the darkness. Only a white form gliding behind.

"Yes, it must drain," he said.

"Hush your nattering," Koth said. "We are here."

The sky had a slight greenish tint, Venser thought, as the boulders came to a stop. For some reason it was brighter there, as if the suns were about to rise. It was bright enough, for instance, to see a small hut soldered to the side of a peak that shot straight up and high into the air. A light burned in the hut and Koth stepped off his boulder and made for it.

"Why is the air green?" Elspeth said.

Koth stopped and looked up. Then he looked down at the metal ground. Long blotches of darkness were clearly visible on the metal, even in the low light. "It can't be," Koth said.

He ran the rest of the distance to the hut, and into the doorway. A moment later he was back out again.

"Malach!" Koth yelled with his hands cupped around his mouth. The noise echoed off the cliffs and boomed back at them.

"Koth," Venser said. He was standing away from the hut, behind a small heap of iron rubble, his eyes looking at something on the ground. He bent. "I'm sorry, but I think I found your—" Venser was turning a corpse over by the shoulder, when the limp form gave a violent shudder and lunged for his neck.

Venser recoiled and the creature came away with only air. It struggled to its knees and lashed out with its misshapen claws. Half of it was pocked metal and the rest was twisted meat, Venser realized in horror. A plate of metal covered its face where its eyes would be. And its stretched skull ended in a grotesque, fang-packed maw that it jacked wide in a silent scream.

Suddenly there were four more of the monstrosities, charging out from behind a hill—their rotting bodies sticky in the green air.

Elspeth drew her sword and in one fluid motion separated the skull from the nearest one. Black fluid spattered against the side of Venser and the creature's body crumbled with a dull thud to the metal ground. Instantly the others were upon them. Koth put up his arms and narrowly escaped having his face bitten as he pushed the thing back with his stony forearm plates. He brought his fist forward in a ruthless blow that crumpled the thing's face plate and sent it spinning back.

Two zombies tackled Venser and the three rolled over each other. They came out on top and pressed their gaping jaws at Venser's neck. The disgust and effort showed on the artificer's face as he struggled to shove them away. Their jaws snapped as they began to press closer.

A slight blue tinge began to glow around Venser, and in the next moment all three forms were suddenly gone, leaving only a wisp of blue.

Venser and the bewildered zombies appeared in the same position high, high above the glimmering expanse of Mirrodin. The next instant they all three began to fall. The creatures thrashed as they fell. But a blue glow appeared around Venser again and he blinked out of existence . . . and back to the ground, where he stood up and brushed his clothes off.

Elspeth heard a sound and turned as a large form lumbered toward her. Its snags of teeth were as long as her head. It towered above Elspeth, dripping dark slime as it squeezed between two large boulders. Elspeth moved her greatsword to her left hand and then to her right, judging how to attack. From her indecisiveness, it was clear to Venser that she was not altogether sure she could best the adversary.

Koth stepped next to him. The geomancer brought his hands together in a decisive motion. The boulders on each side of the thing slammed together, crushing the beast and sending a spray of black ichor over them all.

Just then the two that Venser had teleported into the stratosphere came crashing to the ground and burst into wet pieces.

By the time Elspeth had cleaned and sheathed her greatsword, Venser was looking closely at the dead, if, indeed, they had ever been alive enough to be called dead.

The pieces of them that had been made of flesh did not bleed, so dried out was the meat. Their metal parts were pitted and corroded. The articulating metal plates, like fitted armor, covered where their eyes would have been. A series of tubes thrust out of the ribs. The larger of the creatures had more tubes.

"What are those?" Venser said, prodding one of the tubes with a gloved finger.

"They are vents," Koth said, looking out into the green vapors swirling around them. "They release this necrogen gas, which is what creates more of them. They are called nim."

"Nim," Venser said. He pressed on the seam where a nim's metal arm grew onto its misshapen body, where one of the roped muscles of its back transformed into a conduit of metal that wound up its bicep. "Fascinating."

"Not how I'd put it," Koth said. "And it is very bad that they are here. The Mephidross has reached its dark fingers far indeed if the nim are on our doorstep." He stared down at the crushed giant nim.

"If I were them I'd be hiding."

"Why," Elspeth said.

"Because the Phyrexians are coming for them as well," Koth said. "They will take them away and experiment on them, just as they would any of us."

Elspeth nodded, as if seeing the truth of the statement. But in her mind she could feel a cold shackle on her own ankle, and hear the howls of pain coming through the barred window at the top of the door to her cell. She suddenly smelled the odor she'd detected in Koth's mother's house—the tinny, dry reek of Phyrexia. A deep chill ran up her spine.

"What do you think?" Venser was saying to her.

Elspeth sniffed and looked down at her ichor-spattered feet, half surprised not to see a shackle attached to her ankle.

"Should we make for the Vault of Whispers?" Koth said. "It must surely be there that the phyresis starts." When Elspeth said nothing, the vulshok stamped his foot in the murky water. "This place was part of the Oxidda Chain when I left this plane. It must be the Phyrexia's doing. We must cleanse them at the Vault."

Venser looked up. "It spread that quickly?"

Koth nodded, not deigning to answer Venser's question directly.

"Yet I see no Phyrexia on it," Venser said, looking back to the nim's parts, half submerged in the filthy water.

Once again on the boulders, Koth turned them north and led them above a small path into the rougher country. Soon the metal under them became steep and they made their way to a higher plateau. Elspeth held her sword close to her chest, still shivering at the thought of the shackle she'd imagined around her ankle.

Koth was down with his ear against the ground. "There are sounds," he said finally.

"How far are we from the Vault?" Venser said. He was standing nearer to the wisp lights that he had brought out to light their way, looking closely at an area in the side of the Oxidda, where jags of metal were jutting out.

"Perhaps ten angles of the sun," Koth said with his ear still to the ground. "Perhaps less."

"I smell smoke," Elspeth said.

"We are near the hut of a shaman," Koth said. "It is her fire you smell. It is a good sign. It means she is not gone to the nim or Phyrexia, but I will not stop there."

"Why?" Elspeth said.

"She is mad, that is why."

"And what are the sounds you hear?" Venser said.

"It is hard to say," Koth said.

"And their numbers?"

"Twenty at least. Accompanied by something I have seen in a nightmare, I think."

"Nim, Phyrexians, villagers?"

"These are not villagers. These are creatures. They drag parts as they wander."

Venser went back to looking closely at the metal cliff face they were standing next to. Then he said, "Come help me with this."

Venser had them scrape at the metal cliff face, which crumbled easily. . . . Koth with his igneous forearm growths and Elspeth with a boot knife. Venser used the edge of his helmet. A strange, crumbly material sifted down as they scraped. A bluish brown hue.

"Irrenphor," Venser said. "A byproduct when certain metal alloys are heated and cooled. This material grows on slag. It is part mineral and part mana life."

Just then Elspeth made a small spark when her knife caught some of the iron as she scraped. Venser stayed her hand with one of his.

"It is part metal, part life, and all *explosive*," he said. "Work carefully."

Elspeth and Koth chipped, digging out chunks and culling them with the edge of their gloved hands into small piles, which they moved into larger mounds. The whole time Venser stood back, watching the process and making small marks with a thin metal quill on a wad of papers he kept tucked away, as a breeze ruffled the hem of his tunic.

Finally the piles were painstakingly pushed together into a single as high as a man's shin. Venser carefully tucked his papers away before he got down on his knees beside the pile. It glowed slightly in the dark night. Venser began crumbling the thicker chunks of material between his fingers. When the others stooped to help, Venser motioned them away. When he was finished a pile of gritty powder lay before him.

"This will give them something to remember," Venser said.

A long, guttural sound, like an animal being choked, cut the night. So shocking was the cry that a group of small mouselike creatures on metal legs burst from a hole in the mountain and fled disturbed into another hole. Koth ran to the edge of the plateau.

"Where will they come?" Venser asked, calmly. "And how?"

Koth did not move his gaze. "They will come here," the vulshok pointed to his left. "And here."

"I have not seen much of Phyrexia," Elspeth said. "Their numbers are surely smaller."

Venser looked up briefly. He was separating the pile in to many smaller piles again. "Do not think what you see reflects the extent of the phyresis." He shook his head. "We could all be surprised."

Venser stood and brushed his hands down the front of his leather and metal tunic.

"Will it work?" Koth said.

"Well," Venser said. "I do not run fast. On the other hand, I don't have to run faster than them. I only have to run faster than you."

Koth looked at Venser before chuckling. Venser smiled.

"Well, I am quick like ionized lightning," Koth said.

"Then help me move these piles to the edge."

They could hear more strangled sounds and a strange grinding scream in the darkness as they moved the piles. There was a sudden metallic clambering.

"Quick," Venser said.

There were three piles, each the size of Koth's foot. They stood near the precipice. A moment later two claws topped the edge and a head followed. Red eyes glowed in deep sockets as the creature jerked and convulsed for better purchase. Black oil streamed over a face composed almost entirely of mouth, with huge, looping fangs jutting at strange angles. It shuddered and regurgitated a jet of blackness at Elspeth who raised her foot for a kick at its head. The Phyrexian snapped open the mechanism of its mouth, which popped to double its size and caught Elspeth's foot and jerked back. She fell, but managed to bring her sword down and split the creature's skull in half.

"Back," Venser yelled. Elspeth crabbed backward just as the creatures, with eyes of blood, began clambering over the edge of the plateau.

What scrambled over the edge was terrible to view. Koth inhaled sharply with the shock of the moment.

Venser fought to keep from fleeing. At the head of the Phyrexians was a creature double the size of a man but stooped and with massive skeletal shoulders of metal and stretched skin. A black spine twisted through its body, and rough jags jutted out at irregular intervals from the grotesque twist. The thing's huge claws and teeth dripped with black vomitus and it shook as though caught in the throes of a most violent fit.

"I never thought," Venser managed to say. "That they would be so . . ."

"Awful?" Elspeth said.

Venser nodded. Before this sojourn on Mirrodin, he had never seen a live Phyrexian, had seen only their artifacts and remnants, and with the handful of the beasts that stood before him, he wished he could still say that. They were more haphazard than he thought they would be. And they appeared smarter than he would have believed. Their dark eyes glittered in their deep sockets. He turned his head in disgust and stepped back.

But none of the Phyrexians moved. Their red eyes stared until the large one raised its mouth and began to make the noise they'd heard earlier: the sound of choking and screaming. A moment later the others joined in, and then farther away another chorus. Then another, very far away. Soon the Phyrexians were gargling their black oil in unison all around. At that moment Venser realized fear. It came slowly to the artificer. But when he heard the full extent of the infection echoing around them, how many of the scourge frolicked freely in the surrounding terrain, he felt a deep grimness settle on him.

Elspeth was shaking in her own right. But it was not from fear. When Venser glanced to his side, he saw that she could barely hold herself back. Sweat had broken upon her brow, her eyes were wide and wild, and the promise of deep violence surrounded her. He noticed, as he had in Koth's mother's house, webs of spittle at the corners of her mouth. Her blade was drawn in the shining blackness. Elspeth started forward.

"Wait," Venser hissed. For one dire moment he thought the white knight would charge, and they would all be lost. But she stopped.

Irrenphor was known even on Dominaria as one of the most powerful naturally occurring explosives. Venser tugged a thread of mana into him, and flicked a spark at the feet of the Phyrexians. The effect was instantaneous. Colors popped and flashed and everything jumped together and burned. A moment later Venser appeared with a *snap* on a distant precipice. Teleporting always left him with a slight queasiness, but that time it was worse.

A concussive blast shook and the side of the plateau where he had stood a moment earlier.. There were no more gargled calls. There was nothing except the aftermath sound of falling bits of metal. The hole opened by the detonation was as dark as a maw and about the same shape. Koth and Elspeth were alive and struggling to stand at the other end of the high plane.

Venser teleported back onto the plateau to help Elspeth and Koth stand. "They are coming for us even now," Venser said.

Elspeth was still holding her sword, which didn't surprise Venser who had seen how hard she was gripping it before the explosion. Silhouetted against the dark sky was a dark, twisted mountain. Venser turned toward it. "This way," Venser said.

Koth was brushing himself off. "We travel that way

anyway, little artificer. The Vault of Whispers lies at the bottom of that mountain."

"That is good. Perhaps Karn is there. Our hope is with the Silver Golem."

"But where does one find this silver golem?" Elspeth said.

"Don't know and don't care," the vulshok said, the red slits at his sides flaring briefly as he followed Venser.

"I knew I had to come long ago," Venser said. "When Karn sent that cryptic message, 'Don't follow me'."

They walked for a time before anyone spoke.

"So you spared no moment to get here," Koth said.

"No, I thought it would be a bad idea to come here," Venser said. "I still do."

"But you feel duty-bound to find your comrade, Karn?" Elspeth said.

Venser was silent a moment. "Yes."

"Even though we kidnapped you?" Koth said.

When he reached the hole created by the explosion, Venser fell into a crouch. He stared at the hole for a very long time, running his hand along the edge and gauging the thickness of the metal exposed. There was a strange, acrid smell—and right next to Venser lay a dark arm composed of stained metal with claws and hanging flaps of greasy flesh. Koth walked carefully around the Phyrexian arm as he approached the edge. Blackness lay in the hole, unbroken blackness and no sound.

"Mirrodin is composed this way. A shell over whatever is underneath." Koth said, carefully sitting on the edge. He could feel a slight draft of warm air rising from the hole. It smelled like a machine.

"What is underneath?" Elspeth said, standing next to Venser.

"I do not truthfully know. As a youngling we would break rules and sneak below, but never too far. Our ore came up to the surface for us and we rarely had to go below to find it."

Venser nodded. "What about other parts of the plane? Do other Mirrans venture below?"

"Who can tell with those types? In the Tangle, the elves huddle in their steely trees, damn their eyes. And the leonins of the plains stay in the air and sleep in burrows just beneath the gleaming flatlands—there are no males of note in this race . . . the ones they have are really just a group of female lovers. They may break one of their fingernails if they ventured under the crust. I have heard that the vedalken of the quicksilver sea *live* under the surface, experimenting on humans and eating eyeballs for power, and one look at those blue bastards and who would doubt it."

Venser smiled as he listened, but Koth did not seem to notice, and continued his tirade.

"And that brings me to the Mephidross, this stinking swamp. Who knows what happens in these fell lands. The rot has long ago taken away the brains of its denizens. They may live underground all the time . . . I have heard word that those squirrelly bastards do this."

"Your golem is down there?" Elspeth said.

Venser nodded. "Perhaps."

Koth noticed it, as well. "Each of the lacunae is only a great hole where the mana from the deep once punched through and spouted upward."

"You mean that lacunae must have a path down?" Elspeth said.

"I mean that you will not like it when you see the Vault of Whispers."

"Really?" Elspeth said seriously.

"Really."

"How far is the Vault?" Venser said.

"A day, maybe less if certain people would move faster."

Elspeth looked back at where the smoke smell she'd detected before came from. Back to where Koth had gestured that the shaman lived. Then she looked in the direction of the Vault. The memory of the shackle on her ankle made her leg seem heavy, and seeing the Phyrexians made her hands tremble so badly that she could not grasp her sword's pommel. She stopped walking.

"I am not going with you to the Vault of Whispers." Elspeth said suddenly.

"What?" Koth said. "Why?"

"I am going to find the shaman you spoke of earlier."

Koth and Venser stared at her.

"Why?" Venser said.

Elspeth looked at him for a moment. "Do you realize that you shake?" Elspeth said.

Venser raised himself up a jot. "That is not true," he said. But from the vehemence of his tone, Elspeth could tell that he knew exactly what she was talking about. He even shoved his shaking right hand into the tight space between his under robes and his tunic as she watched.

"I have seen you when you think nobody is watching," she said. "You shake, don't you? How long has it been thus that you have had this palsy?"

Venser turned away. "This is absurd," he said.

"I can perhaps heal you," she said. "But the truth is not that I will go to this shaman's place to find herbs to heal. I will leave you because I have been enough of a burden to you."

THE QUEST FOR KARN

35

"A what?" Koth said. "What is this rot you speak?"

Venser's face had drained of its color as he stared at Elspeth. Both of his hands were shoved into his tunic, and his lips were drawn tight in obvious embarrassment. "Go then," he said.

"I will," Elspeth said. She turned and walked in the direction of the wood smoke blotting the horizon.

Koth grunted. "I will go now to the Vault to save my people." He turned and began walking. He kicked at the wet ground as he walked. "And there is no decent ore. So we cannot ride boulders."

Venser followed. "What she said," Venser said. "About my shaking . . ."

But Koth said nothing, and Venser found he had nothing to say. He walked after the vulshok clutching one hand to the other.

In the darkness the tablelands stretched out to the edge of the known world, it seemed, but Koth led them back down into the dim valleys. The dark sky closed in as the walls narrowed around them to almost total blackness. With the blue lights of Venser's wisps he could see they were walking next to a slough of fetid water, along a mushy bank. Bits of tubes and cracked, buckled walkways littered the side as they moved through.

They had to be careful not to catch bits of themselves on exposed jags. Everything was sharp. Everything poked. Even the inhabitants of Mirran's insides must be metal, Venser thought. He was thirsty, but the filthy water of the Mephidross was dark and foul smelling. He would not touch it.

They walked until all five suns took the sky as a single line rose above the horizon. The world went from darkest dark to nearly blinding sun in a matter of minutes. The sunlight revealed a profoundly changed Oxidda Chain. A puce haze drifted in the valleys. The mountains themselves seemed more spiky and contorted, with edges sprung in wide, torturous curves that made Venser's stomach churn. There was not one sound to be heard in the utter silence. Each of their footfalls echoed loudly away.

Koth took in the new appearance of the Chain with his mouth pressed tight in a line. He stopped and squatted next to what had been a plantlike growth of oxidized metal, barbed thin, and stirring very slightly in the heated breeze. It had become a blackish green color, and sticky to the touch. And it stunk . . . smelling mostly like burned lead. Koth stood and spat.

"It is worse than when I left. I thought it was bad then."

Venser was squatting next to the metal plant. He took the frond between his fingers and tried to break it from the rest of the plant. It bent and he had to wipe his fingers on his leg before standing.

"Well,". Venser said. "It is not very good. I'll say that."

"And," Koth said in a lower voice, "I believe we are being followed."

Venser looked to the side before turning to evaluate the claim. Koth stared at the plant an extra moment before shaking his head and looking back down the valley.

"There is no life on this plane, it appears," Venser said. "I would take even the enemy rather than this vacant place."

Koth looked back the way they had come. He nodded once, and then looked down at his feet before speaking. "The Oxidda was not always as you see it. It had life once," he said. He took a deep breath before continuing. "Not too long ago in the annals of the vulshok, our elders disappeared. This happened all over Mirrodin, I am told. But other creatures lost their elders and segments of their people. The filthy goblins rebounded quickly, of course, as they had little-to-no knowledge to pass on. To us the loss was very great. Our skill with ore, and smelting too, was compromised.

"Then the metal failed altogether. A flaw found its way into the molten ore and the ingots lost their vigor. Conflict among the tribes erupted. Armed conflict followed.

"And you?" Venser said. "Where did your loyalties lie?"

"I am an alloy," Koth said. "And because of that I have always been . . . *apart*. But my bones ring with metal and I was able to drive from the ore the contaminants, but only in small batches. A day's worth at a time. This proved enough ore to give each tribe good metal to work, and they stilled their hands from fighting and took once again to working."

"That was before Phyrexia?" Venser said.

It was as though the word *Phyrexia* itself made the metal beneath their feet tremble. Each of them glanced around, half expecting to see scourge-beings materialize from the clear air.

Koth nodded.

Venser coughed. With a start he noticed that his hand was shaking. He stowed it in his tunic. Hopefully his tic wouldn't present itself, as it sometimes did in times of stress. He drove the thought from his mind and looked down at the ground.

"Here is why we cannot leave this place," Venser said. He ran his finger along the underside of the infected plant. Then he held his finger up. It dripped with dark oil of a slight greenish tinge.

"Oil?" Koth said.

"The spawn of Phyrexia . . ." Venser said, "seethes with infection." Venser wiped the sticky substance on his breeches. "Only one drop can yield legions of Phyrexians."

Koth took this information in without expression.

Mirrodin is lost, Venser thought.

"We will win," Koth said.

Venser did not look so sure. He turned toward the path. "Only Karn can stop the Phyrexians, if such a thing can be done here. He created this plane of yours."

"When I am leader non-Mirrans like Phyrexians will be first against the wall," Koth said.

Koth stood and started walking. When Venser heard Koth's words he stood. "I will be sure to be gone by that time then."

<hr />

Elspeth took the blacksmith's tongs the woman offered. Clasped in the tongs was a crucible full of steaming soup. It had roughly the look and consistency of molten lead, and Elspeth's stomach did not welcome its arrival. "My thanks," Elspeth said, eyeing the soup uncertainly. She put the tongs and the soup down on the table where she was seated.

The woman sat opposite, her eyes lingering on Elspeth's armor, which was carefully laid out on the metal floor.

"It is well wrought," the woman said, her eyes still on Elspeth's armor. "I would not ever take it off."

"Truthfully, I do not feel fully clothed without it," Elspeth said. She pulled her robes tighter around her and took in the surrounds of the hut. Chunks of various rocks swayed on lanyards from the hammered ceiling. The bones and full skeletons of metal creatures were posed and welded to the metal walls around the hut. The air smelled of lead solder and brimstone.

The woman took a fire tool and poked the dung fire in the middle of the floor until flame licked up. "I am Vadi," she said.

"Elspeth."

"Well, Elspeth," Vadi said. "You are paler than any auriok should be. You had better drink my ore stew."

Elspeth looked at the soup, but did not move to pick it up. "How long has the Mephidross swamp been advancing?"

"Who can say? Forever."

"But faster lately?" Elspeth said.

"Yes."

"Are you concerned?" Elspeth said.

The woman shrugged. She was not old, as Koth had made her seem. She was wide-beamed and robust. "Why be concerned?" the shaman said. "I lived through the advent of the green sun, and the disappearance of our elders. What can hurt me now? We are vulshok. We adapt."

Elspeth felt the blood rising to her face. "You will all die, you know."

For the next day the suns above Koth and Venser's heads moved in their prescribed paths. Night was punctuated by the desperate screams of the Phyrexians wandering the rank canyons. But Koth kept their path on small byways known only to him, he said, and they saw none of the enemy for that day. That night they slept in the nostril of an immense statue of metal buried to the top lip. Venser asked who the statue was modeled after and Koth shrugged. "I have never seen its like on Mirrodin," Koth said. "Ours is not a plane of monuments."

"I could teleport us to that mountain," Venser said, gesturing to a distant gas-chimney. Koth fixed him with an even gaze.

"I don't teleport well," Koth said. "I tend to be detrimental to the teleporter's health."

Venser shrugged. "Can I wait for you at the next rise?"

"Without Elspeth I think we should stay close, don't you?"

Again the shrug.

By that time the water situation had become dire. As they drew nearer to the leaden horizon where Koth said the Vault crouched, the air had become more toxic, burning their lungs and the water was not potable in the extreme. Late afternoon found them collapsed in a high crevice. Returning to the valley long after sunset. With visions of choking Phyrexians in the backs of their minds, they prowled until Koth dropped into a low crouch behind a jagged boulder. He pointed ahead.

"Be very still," the vulshok said quietly.

Ahead the valley widened slightly and approximately thirty small treelike forms shown in the crepuscular light. They had been wrought, that much was obvious to Venser, but how long before? The whole plane had been made by the hands of Karn, and so the tree forms must be the same. From their hard boughs hung large white balls that glowed with a greenish tinge.

"Gel fruit," Koth croaked, walking around the barbed boulder and toward the trees in a low crouch. "Water."

Venser was unsure if they should eat the fruit from a Mephidross gel-fruit tree, even if it had been part of the Oxidda Chain recently. It looked sick. Its form had begun to twist and effect the torturous aspect of the Mephidross. Off to the right, Venser heard the skittering of something. He crouched and ran behind Koth. Whatever had made the sound had quieted. Venser and Koth reached a scattered pile of tubing and stopped.

"Something is afoot," Venser said. "There are sounds I have not heard before."

"What do they sound like?" Koth said, his voice little more than a whisper.

"They scratch."

"Do they whine?" Koth said.

"I did not hear them make that noise. It was a dry metal noise."

Koth was silent.

"It could be blinkmoths," he said. "There are still a few around. Or ink moths, their Phyrexian version."

"I like the first one better," Venser said. He had found the metal carcass of some creature with the articulated back plates of an insect. It was lifeless and limp, but he held it up, flopping before Koth's eyes.

"Could it be one of these?"

"A dung disposer?" Koth said, glancing momentarily at it. "You disgust me."

Venser dropped the small carcass.

Koth hardly seemed to notice, so intently was he gazing at the tree forms and their low-hanging fruit. "The sounds are not made by a dung disposer. But something is most likely watching us at this moment. Gel fruit groves are found in some of these canyons, and they are always dangerous places, even before the Phyrexians. Whatever lives makes its way to these. Either to gain water and food or to eat what comes here to gain water and food. I generally avoid these areas, but we need what they can give."

Crouched, they watched the grove until Venser's knees burned and his stomach was wound into a knot

ROBERT B. WINTERMUTE

of thirst so painful that he would have agreed to fight a legion of Phyrexians if it meant a drink at the end. He could hear Koth's stomach gurgling. But Koth did not move. A hot breeze rocked the fruits on their branches tantalizingly. Finally Venser spoke. "Let us make a move or whatever is watching us will soon hear my stomach and know our position."

"You are right," Koth said. "You go ahead. Now is the time for you teleporting."

Venser paused. "I will." He watched the trees, thinking how to move into the grove.

But Koth thought better of it. "I will have no more of this sneaking around," he said. And with that he began striding to the trees.

He stopped at the first tree and picked a head-sized fruit, which he carried back toward Venser. It happened when Koth was about halfway between Venser and the tree. A momentary whistling of wind and Koth dropped the fruit, drew his fist back, and lashed it out. Something fell from his fist and banged off the ground. There were two more whizzing sounds, Koth swung twice, and two more small forms fell clattering.

Koth seized the fruit and started walking back to the crevice. Venser blinked into being next to Koth and had to immediately duck one of the vulshok's bright fists.

"Say something next time you are to appear, young artificer."

Before Venser could reply another whizzing cut the air and he put out his hand, a blue miasma appearing around it from which only his fingers poked. The metal form flying toward them slowed and began to waver in its path, until it floated lazily past and bumbled away into the dimness.

"You should see what it's seeing it its mind's eye," Venser said, nodding as the small dartlike creature moved past them. It was long and thin, with a beak pursed to a sharp needle as long as a man's arm. Fluid dripped from that sharpened tip. A finlike appendage extended out its back. "We look like tall reeds to it, and it hungers for our flesh."

Venser leaned close for a look, and at that moment was pierced by another dart flying from behind. The pain was instantaneous and searing. So much so that Venser found he could not concentrate enough to teleport away, and a moment later felt the world fade into blackness.

When he opened his eyes again, the land of Mirrodin was moving slowly past and the heat around his face was as if he were standing near a blast furnace. He closed his eyes and when he opened them again he was slumped against the metal side of a small cave. The metal burned his back, but he could not stand, could not make his limbs cooperate with his brain's commands. The best he could manage was to slip over and fall on his side. He closed his eyes again.

When he opened his eyes for the third time he was floating again, bobbing as the land fell away behind. He found he could raise his hand and he did so. He scratched his matted hair and spoke.

"Where is my helmet?" he said.

"He lives," Koth said. Koth turned to Venser, who he had strapped to his back.

"Well," Venser croaked. "I feel just wonderful."

He felt so bad that when Koth untied him from his pack, Venser cried out. Moving his limbs felt like the worst pain imaginable. As if they were being ripped free from their joints. Koth stood him on his feet.

"There is nothing wrong with you," Koth added. "Stinger mechs like the one that found your neck offer paralysis serum, but movement does away with its effects."

Venser nodded painfully.

"So move," Koth commanded.

He took one excruciating step, and then another. It felt as though sand had found its crafty way into his joints. But soon the pain lessened and after an hour of walking in circles it felt only as though he were walking on fractured bones. Koth threw Venser his helmet and he greedily slipped it on. The familiar smell of his hair was in it and he relaxed a bit.

"Where are we?" Venser said.

Koth stepped dramatically back and extended one arm.

"Your body they will harvest," Elspeth said to Vadi, her bowl of cold soup long forgotten. "They may even keep you alive for a time, letting you heal, occasionally taking strips of your flesh and sinew for fuel or musculature. You'll begin to recognize your own body parts stretched and fused into the skeletons of your captors.

The vulshok watched Elspeth without expression.

In her mind Elspeth watched helplessly as three Phyrexians lifted a human in their meat-hook hands. *The screaming . . . the screaming.*

"But your mind will be left to its own sad devices. They don't understand the mind or its needs. Your mind will fall away, or you will scream yourself to insanity. Be ready for this. This is the harvest you shall reap."

Vadi looked at her suspiciously. "How do you know?"

"I know," Elspeth said. "Because I survived them." 45

The vulshok's hand went out, but instead of touching Elspeth in consolation she took the hefty handle of a battle spear lying propped against the low table.

"I do not have their infection, if you think that," Elspeth added, noticing how the Vulshok held her spear.

"You are not auriok. You are a troublemaker and liar like that upstart Koth. Speak now or I will lay you low." The vulshok kicked her stool back and brought the head of her greatspear up so it hovered at Elspeth's throat. "You are a spy for the Hammer tribe. Speak doomsayer!"

"I wish I had a confession for you," Elspeth said. She looked down at the sharp tip of the spear. She scooted her chair forward toward the spear tip. "Knowing what I know about our mutual enemy, I wish you would end my days now."

Vadi lowered the spear, the scowl still on her face. "You are no auriok. You're no spy. You are none of these things. You are something much worse." The vulshok spat a dry splotch at Elspeth's feet. "You are a coward."

"You do not know what I know."

"You say you left your friends. You say they are better off without you. You say there is a great enemy. You say, say, say. All talk. All words. And words are wind."

"They are better off not depending on me," Elspeth said.

"So you will hide, is that it?"

ROBERT B. WINTERMUTE

CHAPTER
3

Behind the vulshok loomed the tremendous mountain they had seen on the horizon. Green gas swathed it in the bright light. It appeared to be made of corroded lead.

But Venser stepped forward and brought his hands together in a surprisingly loud clap. Koth could see the shockwaves from the clap bend and distort the air, as hot gases escaping a vent, and he felt the metal in his body stiffen momentarily. Then Venser disappeared and reappeared at an outcropping not far away. He teleported back a moment later.

"Did you see it?" Venser said. "A small metal form, smooth and shiny? Does that description match anything you know?"

"Yes," Koth said in a low voice.

Venser cocked his head at the vulshok.

"But not exactly," Koth said. "It is probably a myr. They are harmless little things," Koth pronounced.

"I mean, they are generally harmless," he said, sounding less sure.

"The question remains why is this small creature following us?"

Koth turned to Venser. "How do you know it is following us?"

"I have heard it," Venser said. "In the outer dark last night."

"So have I," Koth admitted.

"I wonder," Venser said, staring out to where he'd heard the creature.

"Enough of this," Koth said. "Come, let us walk."

By nightfall of the next day the mountains had begun to fall. Koth, grumbling, walked toward where the suns seemed to go when they fell from the sky. The smell of rot was what reached them first. It was a type of rot smell Venser had not experienced before: the putrefaction of metal and meat as if from a derelict slaughterhouse.

The deeper they got into the swamps the more the mountains started to cut free from one another and slide slowly into the dark murk of the Mephidross. Koth shook his head and said that the ore had destabilized . . . every day the swamp and its green, necrogen fog bit deeper into the Oxidda Chain. Venser stopped to investigate how that could happen. He looked closely at the way the oil of the swamp suffused the metal of the mountains, until the great hulks of the Oxidda took on a crumbly consistency.

At one point they witnessed a mountain sliding into the swamp. The ground shook and in its immenseness a slab from a mountain creaked and suddenly fell with a great crash. Liquid from the swamp rose up in a wall many times taller than a man, and the green haze enveloped the slab.

The land began to smooth. By the second day they gained the big sky and all that lurks in that high place. Koth's eyes were always on the sky. Once he saw a dark dot moving across its open sweep. They stopped to watch, but the dot moved away.

Their boots sank deeper in the black ichor of the swamp. Caught in the lowest places, the sticky material reached to their ankles. They slept on whatever high ground they could find, and only when they were so exhausted that they could not lift their scum-covered feet. They slept where they fell, in fireless camps. In that way, they escaped detection for a time.

At the end of the second day they found a corpse of a sort laid out in a twisted pose that left it half in and half out of the murky water.

Venser turned to Koth. "Phyrexian?" Venser said.

"Nim," Koth said solemnly.

The nim looked a bit different from the others they had fought near Koth's village. It was more skeletal, for one. There was little or no meat left on its body, and the meat left was rotting off the shiny bones. Its forearm had simply rotted off, and only a stub at the elbow remained, with rags of flesh where the limb had once been. Its skull had fused onto its body and the teeth of the maw had fused and grown together into a tangled mass that looked like sharp antennae. Its limbs were longer than those of the other nims, as well.

"It walks partially on its hands," Venser said, looking up from his investigation of the creature. The artificer's eyes were shot through with red and he appeared aggravated, Koth thought. He watched his hand shake slightly. He'd seen him like that before

THE QUEST FOR KARN

over the last days, and the trembling always disappeared eventually. He decided to keep an eye on him.

"There is oil on it," Koth pointed out.

"Yes," Venser said absently. He stood and almost tripped.

"Are you wounded?" Koth said.

Venser smiled absently. "No, I haven't been." He looked first one way and then another. "I only need to sit down."

He found a small boulder that was out of the swampy murk, and seated himself on it. From his left sleeve he drew a small bottle filled with turquoise-colored fluid. He uncorked the bottle and took a small sip. He carefully replaced the stopper and slipped the bottle back into his sleeve.

"What is that?" Koth said.

Venser swallowed the fluid in his mouth before turning to the vulshok with a small smile.

"Nothing," he said.

Koth did not seem convinced. "Well, whatever it is there is not much of it left."

"That is true," Venser said, straightening the fabric of his sleeve over the pocket holding the small vial. "I did not have much time to pack for my journey to sunny Mirrodin."

"What if you don't get it?"

Venser stood.

"This is our way, I believe," he said, and started walking.

"So, we're done talking about whatever is in your sleeve?" Koth said.

Venser said nothing.

They moved through the wet of the Mephidross only in the daylight, and slept as little as possible. By the third day each of them was stumbling in their tracks and had to sleep. They did so under the other's close guard. They encountered in their wanderings other nim lurching and sniffing, and mostly avoided them. Once Koth found a small enclave of the wretches and tore their parts loose from their bones, which he then wished aflame and left smoldering on a high place for the entire known world to see.

Soon they made out the ghostly shapes of distant hills in the green haze. As they neared, the hills became more pronounced and especially a hill in the middle of all the others. Its torturous aspect was clearly the focus of this derelict land, yet they made for it.

"The Vault of Whispers," Koth said. They were stopped in a stinking dell very near the tower, and all around them the calls of creatures unknown clinked in the failing light. The tower itself loomed overhead.

"Has it always looked like this?" Venser said.

"Yes. Always," Koth said. "That middle section has always been rotted out."

"But what keeps it from toppling when the middle has a hole as it does?"

"That network of strings. They are lead. There is much lead in this place. The lead holds the halves together. That and the power of the Black Lacunae."

"What is that?" Venser said.

"The Black Lacunae?" Koth said. "It is where the dark power under the surface of Mirrodin shoots upward as a geyser of water might. There was no stopping or slowing the flow at this place, and those that have given themselves to dark foolishness come to this place for power. We vulshok have a saying, 'Steel is hard, but a fool's head is harder.'"

Venser chuckled at that. He looked back at the lead and iron mountain that held the Vault, and the smile fell from his face. It really was an amazing thing to see. It seemed to be constructed of dull gray veins wrapped around struts of melted lead. The green gas that floated ominously out of the chimneys of the other mountains did not float as much out of the top of that mountain. Rather, a powerful dimness rose as heat waves might and moved up into the air before mushrooming out over all of the land. The top was corroded away to such a degree that only fingers of lead remained. The very air seemed to be breaking down the mountains, and despite himself Venser had to wonder what his own lungs looked like after breathing the air.

"What does this air do to us?" he said.

Koth was squatting out of the hot winds, sitting back on his haunches and poking absently at the ground with a long sliver of iron. "It turns us into nim." He said. "If we stay long enough."

Suddenly Venser cocked his head. "Do you hear that?"

A roaring echoed off the mountain.

Aware that the vulshok was watching him, Venser hardened his face into an expression he hoped conveyed a sense of command. Truth be told, he had not felt in command at all lately. With the vulshok constantly undermining him, and the uncertainty of the mission they had kidnapped him to accomplish, Venser was not altogether sure any of them would make it off of this fascinating plane. He had already resigned himself to die before he could planeswalk away, spreading the spawn of phyresis to other places. As he looked out over the vista, he wondered if the others had the same commitment.

The green necrogen gas suddenly swirled around in a dense shroud. Through the mist, coming over the rise, the outline of a monstrosity materialized. A huge, vicious-looking Phyrexian lumbered into view. Roughly snake shaped but with bare ribs and articulated metal cabling, the smell of rotting flesh preceded it, and long appendages ending in sharp spikes swung as it loped forward. Its eyeless head turned toward them.

"We are close now," Koth said. "Let us destroy this beast and be done with it."

As the creature had not detected them yet, Venser and Koth lay sheltered in a raw divot next to a slough and awaited its arrival. When the beast had moved between them the Planeswalkers attacked. But it was stunningly fast, and snapped around in an instant, extending an appendage Venser had not seen from its belly. The segmented limb shot at Venser's head, knocking him out of the aura of blue he had wound around his head.

Koth wasted no time in extending his arm and shooting a column of rock from his forearm in a loose stream. The Phyrexian knocked the javelin of rock aside and in the same motion swiped Koth off his feet and into an outcropping.

It was Koth who woke first. Blinking in the low light, he struggled to remember the events that had brought him there. He appeared to be lying on a table. The unconscious form of Venser was on a similar table next to his. The vulshok turned to move, only to realize that he was bound at the wrists and ankles.

The room around him was lit only in faint patches and from unseen sources, but what he could see did not fill him with joy. The walls were made entirely of many coils of fleshy tubes and dull metal pipes held flat by webs of pale sinew.

Koth began pulling at his restraints. He turned his face so he could see the thick metal shackles. Well constructed, they did not budge. Out of the corner of his eye he suddenly made out a strange shape, small and human in form, but perfectly smooth and silver, as if made entirely from the most perfect chrome. The figure was squatting in the corner, regarding him with the utmost calm. When the creature had Koth's attention, it stood and beckoned him with one hand before squeezing between some pipes and disappearing.

Koth had no time to think about the strange creature. Around him, the horrible walls dripped with black oil and the ceiling appeared to be held up with curved columns constructed of the twisted bodies of vaguely familiar, yet unknown creatures. Dark fangs and exposed ribs intermeshed with die-cast iron plates and shards of whitest bone.

Koth closed his eyes. He pulled the power from the earth into him. Smoke rose from his head, his fists balled, and his craggy forearms began to animate. Sharp spurs stabbed outward, shearing the shackles. He sat up and yanked on the shackles binding his ankles until they gave way with a tremendous snap.

He was free.

"Venser!" Koth said. He was off his table and shaking the artificer in a moment. "Venser!" The artificer could teleport out of his restraints, Koth knew, if he could just wake him.

But he would not wake.

A clank cut the air behind him: the sound of something banging metal against metal, and he knew something was there, that something was coming. Koth cast his eyes around for a place to hide. The walls seemed to be almost alive—the intestinelike pipe work glistened green-black in the low light. He did not relish the idea of hiding in the wetness of the pipes, but he was able to spread open a void in them and in the next instant he slid within.

From between the pipes, Koth watched as a section of the wall on the far side of the room split. Two Phyrexians stepped into the room. One of them had huge, gruesome meat hooks for hands, which it held up before it as it stumbled toward Venser. The other smaller Phyrexian had dozens of small arms, each ending in a filthy, bent syringe. Both of the experimenters' bodies were nothing more than metal skeletons wound around and through with fleshy swaths. Their too-small or too-large limbs gave them an unsettling, off balance appearance that made Koth want to gag. Or maybe it was the wall, which was dripping on his neck as he watched the Phyrexians approach Venser who lay strapped to a table.

They walked around Koth's empty table, seeming to make no note of its vacancy, and stopped to look down at Venser. Suddenly a space in the ceiling opened above Venser. A metal arm girded with pink muscles extended downward. A mouth apparatus with spines surrounding it hung at the end of the appendage. Ichor dripped over Venser's chest as the device centered itself on his neck. As Koth watched, the device opened like a nightmarish flower.

Koth felt the anger rush up like a geyser from his feet. And by the time the energy reached his shoulders he knew he would be absolutely unable to control it. The power reached his forehead and he exploded out of the wall, sending fléchettes of the pipes and metal substructure shooting out at the Phyrexians.

The experimenters fled backward, howling.

Koth ran to Venser. The device on the arm seemed to sense Koth's movement. It turned toward him and as he came near enough, clamped onto his neck with a metallic *snap*.

Venser's eyes fluttered open. Above him the sinewy arm of the device was extended into Koth's neck. The vulshok struggled, pulling against the device that gripped him.

In one fluid motion, Venser teleported to Koth's side, took hold, and began to pull at the clamper near its mouth pincers. Then he started snapping parts off the device in a mad attempt to disable it.

"I'm taking us out of here," Venser said. Koth's face was blue as he nodded.

Venser closed his eyes and took hold of Koth's upper arm. A blue mist began to filter out of his pores.

The device attached to Koth's neck clicked and a panel displaced in its side. A curved, armored syringe slid smoothly out of the panel and pointed its dripping tip at Koth's right eye.

At that moment the walls of the chamber began to tremble, and then shake thunderously. The right wall began to vibrate. Venser turned to the wall, a look of resignation pulling at his face.

A cut appeared, shearing off the conduit-work walls. Bright white light flooded in the dark room through the cut. Then another cut appeared and more light glinted in. With a deafening smash a hole appeared and the room became blindingly bright. In the light the forms of the two Phyrexian experimenters disintegrated to nothing. Silhouetted in the new entrance stood the shining form of Elspeth of Bant.

Dull gray hills showed behind her and Venser could smell the necrogen gas of the Mephidross around her as, with her sword shining like a rising star, she charged forward. Koth was motionless on the floor. With a sweep of her sword, Elspeth sheared the device in half. The two parts that fell away shrieked and writhed on the pocked metal floor, leaving Koth gasping and holding his neck.

Elspeth stepped back into a ready pose and surveyed the room. Seeing no other danger, she stood up and sheathed her sword.

"Elspeth," Koth choked. ". . . of Bant."

Elspeth pursed her lips and nodded. "There are more of these beasts near a cave on the outside. Let us end this now and see if we may hammer them once and for all."

"Where were they?" Venser said.

"There," Elspeth said. She pointed to one of many holes in the very center of the mountains, at base level.

"I have been here once before on reconnaissance," Koth said. "And that doorway seemed to be used more than most, but vermin creep out of any hole. You know how vermin are. Let us move closer," Koth said.

"They are here," Elspeth said. "Be ready."

They crept along a dell until it trenched, and then they crawled on hands and knees to a place close to the base of the mountain. They lay in the warm, scum-covered water until Venser finally spoke.

Then they felt it. The ground began to shake slightly. The filthy water began to ripple. Soon small waves were coursing its banks. The mountain above them began to groan. Venser sunk as deep as he could in the black water. Everything about his being said *fly.* But he mastered himself and did not move. The banging became rhythmic and strong, like a battering ram on the door of a castle, and then it turned to a deafening thunder. The ground trembled.

And the Phyrexians came. First one stumbled through a hole in the mountain and stood blinking in the open air. Then another came from another hole. A third appeared from yet another hole. More came after them. Soon a steady line of bulky, toothy beings of skeletal angularity with long tooth-crammed mouths were streaming out of each entrance. Then the flow increased again. Phyrexians were crawling out of the holes, one over the other, clawing forward. It stayed that way for a time, with the entrances pressing out shadowy, hairless beings like material through a sausage press. Some survived, and those stood outside screaming their guttural choking cries into the green murk, while other Phyrexians fell upon their wounded brethren in a mad feast.

"Is that all there are?" Koth murmured. "They are not a large force."

But there were more. Soon the cave entrances split at the corners and still larger amounts of Phyrexians came pouring out. Larger and larger beings emerged: twisted trolls with long bony faces, tiny eyes and huge mouths sheltering long teeth. They swatted other Phyrexians out of the way. Hulking great soldiers made of tattered metal and raw flesh with tiny, stitched together skulls lurched from the bowels with long fingers of glittering metal. Behind them a vast array of strikers that the companions had seen earlier, with heads formed into the notched tip of a spear, and broken, gnashed teeth chipped and bleeding black. At the head of the mass swaggered a herald with a grim standard held aloft: its own small head impaled on a spike. Wispy scouts hopped from head to head, and behind them all tumbled wave upon wave of massive brutes as large as three men with claws as long as legs, which they swung as they walked, laying open their own kind and themselves in the mayhem.

"We must get closer," Venser hissed.

Koth turned and stared at the artificer.

Venser leaned forward in the water, so his stomach scraped the bottom of the slough. The artificer walked himself with his hands along the slough. Reluctantly, the others followed. Soon they were close enough to the menagerie to smell the filthy reek wafting from their rot and rust in their moist folds. And the sound. They made the oddest creaking as they walked. It was an ominous sound that Elspeth remembered well. The sounds and the smells brought back such memories that she could not make herself move along the slough to join the others. As soon as she did, by touching her sword, she wished she had not. The closer she got to the Phyrexians, the more she felt again like a little girl, held captive in their oubliette.

The gross, twisted expressions that played across the Phyrexian faces were what affected her most. For something with half-sentience, at best, Elspeth thought, that leer was unnerving. It spoke of all manner of callousness . . . of slyness and cruelty. Of extreme, painful carelessness coupled with playful curiosity. She put her head under the filthy slough water and held it there until she thought she would burst.

When she raised her head the others were gone. She spied them sheltering in a raw divot where they must have crawled from the slough. They were not farther than two lengths of a human body, but she would not follow, not with *them* on the move.

She realized too late that she had risen to her knees to look for the others. That, coupled with her soiled white garb, made her easy to see. A single, garbled cry went up from a marching Phyrexian, and Elspeth fell back into the water. She walked herself backward along the slough and behind a slight turn, and dropped lower in the water.

A moment later the beast appeared. A brute trooper, as luck would have it, with tiny, glittering eyes set close together in a head stitched more than once it appeared. Layer upon layer of armor crisscrossed every part of its body so it squeaked as it fell remarkably fast to its knees next to the water. It smelled the slough and bit at the water until it ran out between its transparent teeth.

Another, rougher cry went up and the trooper stood and dashed back to the ranks. Elspeth rested her head against the metal bank and took deep breaths until her heart stopped feeling like it might beat up and out of her throat. When her breathing was normal, she carefully tore off her white tunic, so her tarnished armor showed.

And so it was. By later in the day the flow of Phyrexians had not lessened in the least, but the light from the suns had changed. Shadows appeared, and Elspeth was able to crawl to the divot the others were sheltering in.

". . . An invasion," Koth was saying.

Venser nodded.

"I am not going into the camp of the enemy. Our numbers aren't enough. Our battle is in the hills with the others, snapping off parts of the main force. This is how a smaller force . . ."

"I know how to fight a large force," Venser said, cutting off the geomancer. "But you cannot hope to save your plane with that technique. Not with a foe like this."

Elspeth agreed with Venser. But, to be fair, she was not altogether sure that any technique could save Mirrodin after the display of numbers and strength she was seeing.

Venser continued. "Only Karn has even the smallest chance of setting this straight." Now the artificer looked directly at Koth to speak. "Your people and all the beings of this plane will fall to this force. This number is larger than any I have ever heard of. They must have been spawning under the surface for *years*.

Koth squinted back the way they had come. The entrance Elspeth had hacked through the leaden side of the mountain was a small dark hole far behind. But in that moment Koth saw a shiny form standing in it.

"We should travel into the Vault through the room where Elspeth found us," Koth said absently, his eyes still on the silver creature. He blinked and it was gone.

"Why?" Venser said.

"I have just seen the creature that was following us, I think. I saw it in the room when I first awoke also." Koth pointed. "It is in the hole that Elspeth cut when she came for us."

Venser turned to look, but the creature was gone.

Koth stood in a crouch and began moving back along the slough toward the hole. Venser watched him go.

"You who are such tight comrades?" Venser asked Elspeth.

Elspeth watched as the Phyrexians continued moving. There *were* fewer of them than before, she noted. "Not that such things are your business in the least," Elspeth said. "But we met only days before he kidnapped you."

"Where did you meet?"

"Fighting for coin in a pit."

"You?"

She smiled. "Yes, me. I have need of coin as does anyone."

"Did you win against the geomancer?"

"As a matter of fact, I did," Elspeth said. "Does that surprise you?"

Venser shrugged. "A bit."

"There are other parts of me that you may find shocking."

"Such as?"

"I was imprisoned by the Phyrexians once."

"How did you escape them?"

Elspeth looked back before speaking. "Through despicable means," she said. "I am embarrassed to speak of it now. It was long ago."

"You were a child?"

"Yes."

"Children do not act despicably," he said. "They are simply children doing childish things."

Images flashed suddenly into Elspeth's head, images of blood and intestines strung across a large room. The length of the intestines shocked her as a little girl, but still they strung them across the room when a new prisoner arrived. They inserted their sharp fingers into the belly and out came a line of intestine, which they drew out as thread from a spool. And she, she moved from cell to cell, relatively free, pointing out the ones who would die soon to the Phyrexians, who lacked simple common sense. She aided them. Even though they did not speak, they followed her for some reason, maybe because she had been there so long that they saw her as part of the prison and not a fun toy to be experimented upon. But she saw it all. Every horrible thing that can be done to a human.

"Children are children," Venser said.

Elspeth blinked. If he only knew. Perhaps he should. It had been with her for so long, carried on her shoulders during all her travels so that, perhaps, with almost certain death approaching, she should relieve herself of the weight.

"When they became interested in me, I would divert their attention by pointing out better candidates to be experimented on. Sometimes women, even children. Old men. They all cried. They all wailed." She felt like covering her ears from the wailing she heard when she closed her eyes to sleep at night, the same sound she heard first thing when she woke.

Words had escaped Venser. He opened his mouth to say something, only to close it again.

She could tell by his shocked expression that he was expecting another story—perhaps the story of the brave child helping the other prisoners, only to end up the subject of experimentation herself. Truth was, she managed to evade being cut or molested in any way. Countless others took that burden for her. And the children were the cries that stayed with her the longest.

Sound came back to Venser's lips. "How did you escape?"

"I escaped," she gulped. "By cutting open a large corpse and slipping inside and staying still in its reek until it was tossed into the rot heap. I was small and still the fit was tight." She didn't tell him that it took many days for the Phyrexians to move the corpse; they were not good housekeepers. She lay in the corpse for at least two days, but it could have been more. She was almost dead herself of thirst when she finally crawled out. But the smell never left her. It was always in her nose, waking her in the morning and turning her stomach and making it difficult to eat.

"But you survived," Venser stammered. "You persevered. You were unbeaten."

"Unbeaten," Elspeth said hollowly.

Venser looked away, out to the darkness. She could see the evident disgust on his face. Still, there was a certain lightness building in her stomach. "I can tell you more," she said.

Venser shook his head. "I have heard enough." He turned back to the Phyrexians. They watched the revolting combination of decomposing metal and sinewy flesh of all shapes and sizes march from the holes. Elspeth found herself wondering where they all slept, and how. Were they able to talk to each other? Her time in one of their prisons had not left her with a strong impulse of find out more about the Phyrexians. They were the essence of cruelty, with a child's desire to experiment and play.

She glanced away from Venser's eyes at the Phyrexians. One tripped and fell and the one behind it stepped squarely on its head and laughed its chortling laugh. "It seems to me that their numbers are decreasing," she said.

Venser peered back over the edge of the divot they were sheltering in. The dark smudge of the main body of the Phyrexians was spread out in the green haze filling the large valley.

"Are you ready?" Venser said. Without waiting for an answer, the artificer began crawling down the slough after Koth.

CHAPTER
4

The experimentation room looked as it had before, with one exception. On the far wall as they entered was an area where the wet gut-works had been spread. A hole was revealed. Koth was squatting next to it with a smile on his face.

"Something is guiding us," he said.

Venser stepped closer, and suddenly a shake caught him. He put his hand out to the wall, and it sunk into the wetness. Venser lurched sideways and fell to his knees, shaking over half his body. From experience he knew to wait. When enough time had passed, and Venser could open and close his fingers, he struggled to his feet. The others watched him wide-eyed.

"We will not speak of this," Venser said. "It happens sometimes."

"But why?" Elspeth said.

"It happens because of my foolishness. Because of a great mistake I made."

They moved through the darkness, skidding their feet across the strangely smooth floor for a long time without the least sense of where they were going.

"Can we dare light?" Elspeth whispered.

Venser nodded.

It took Elspeth some moments to cull the mana she needed in that black place, but eventually her suit of armor began to glow slightly and they could see more of their surroundings.

"I hear its movements ahead," Koth whispered. "This is the way."

"It makes me nervous to follow something I've never met," Venser said.

A loud hissing sound broke the stillness behind them. Elspeth dropped the charm on her armor, and the light blinked out. Shadows were moving in a passage in front of them.

The passageway opened into a very large cavern. An eerie green light filtered weakly to the edges of the large space. At the far end a group of beings stood, tapping on the wall with their knuckles or whatever they had that passed for knuckles. They were Phyrexians, yes, but somehow different. They moved with the jerky, sudden movements of the Phyrexians—had the same frantic speed and carelessness as they bumped into one another, seeking something in haste.

"Are they sick?" Elspeth said.

"Vampires," Venser whispered. "Succumbing to phyresis."

Elspeth nodded at that, and tried hard not to let Venser sense her disgust.

Standing a bit back was their leader. The first thing that struck Venser was the size of the being. Its body was a massive shell of flesh and metal, one substance wound into another, with jags of metal jutting off the carapace. Two huge, tipped claws hung on robust arms at its sides. And the head, the head looked tiny atop the mountainous torso. A black line of hair ran from the front forehead in a crest to the back.

"Keep looking," the leader yelled.

Venser watched the leader very carefully—when he walked, his body jerked to the side and the head was momentarily sideways.

The creatures kept knocking on the walls and floor until at last one of the Phyrexian vampires found what they were looking for. They all bent around something on the floor, until the leader lumbered over. They moved out of the way and he looked down at the floor with eyes that glittered in the low light, even from where Venser was standing across the room.

"Pull it up," he said.

"Yes, Master Geth," one of the Phyrexians hissed.

It was a door, but one that had to be torn from the floor. Ragged, bloody flaps of skin hung around the door's circumference when it was raised.

"Get moving," Master Geth bellowed suddenly. "The silver one's temper makes mine look pleasant. Move."

The silver one, Venser thought. Was he making reference to the silver creeper they were following, or was it the silver golem Geth?

The Phyrexians dropped one at a time down the trap door. Geth kicked the last one, sending him careening through the hole. Before Geth stepped into the secret door, he looked around the room. Venser jerked his head back, but for a moment Geth's eyes froze in his direction. Eventually he turned and hopped down the hole.

Venser and the others poked their heads around the corner, just in time to see a small silver form slip down the hole, after Geth.

Elspeth spoke first. "It seems that is our direction," she said.

"Yes," Venser said.

"I'm not going anywhere," Koth said. "And neither are you." He turned to Elspeth. "Or you. You will stir up the enemy even more than you have already. Let us fight the force that just left the Vault. We must leave here and raise a warning."

Elspeth looked from one to the other before speaking. "I think this is not the place to argue . . . especially loudly," she said.

Venser and Koth stared at each other. The small space between them sparkled and cracked with mana.

"I have known the Phyrexians," Elspeth continued. "And they are cruel beyond measure." She paused to take in a deep, shaky breath. "I would like to kill each and every one of them, but the reality is that I cannot do that." The white knight was shaking, Venser observed. Whether in anger or fear he could not be sure. But her hands were clenching and releasing as she talked.

"How did you escape them?" Koth said.

But Elspeth was clearly not listening. Her eyes were raised and she was looking off into the darkness, caught in the dream playing in her head.

"I was only a little girl," she said. "And their experiments were . . ."

"Pointless," Venser interjected. "I have read that they are always pointless. Only so those beings can feel like they are experimenting."

Venser's words drew Elspeth out of her thoughts a bit. Her eyes focused and she looked down at her hands. "Only to cause pain in as many ways as possible. And terror," she said.

Koth said nothing. He looked at the patch of floor where Geth and his undead minions had pulled up the door.

"You saw our silver guide went down that hole," Venser said.

Elspeth was not done though. "They seemed to especially hate skin. My skin and skin of the others in the cells around me. They would remove it and stitch it onto their own bodies, along with appendages. There was one of them, a smaller one, who did the stitching. It had a long needle attached to its right wrist. With this needle it sewed the swatches of skin over the others. The sewer. Sometimes the skin took and stayed on them," she said.

"Should we be on our way?" Venser said, glancing uneasily at Elspeth.

The door had healed itself, and it lay without crease. They searched the floor and still could not find anything to grasp and pull. The walls of the cavern room were run with conduit and pillars of metal tubing, but the floors were generally smooth.

"Did they create it," Elspeth mused. "And then make it disappear when finished?"

"It was open when that silver devil jumped down it," Venser said. He ran his palm over the ground. Then he got down on his chest, put his cheek on the cold floor, and looked sideways at it. "That could be," he said. "But when they found the door, there were no incantations said that I heard." He looked up. "Did either of you hear anything?"

"No," Koth said, "but I have a better way." The geomancer put his hands on the ground. "I'd step back," he said, "if you value your boots."

Soon his hands began to glow red as did the floor around them. The slits along his ribs pulsed like a magma core. The glow in the floor spread, and soon covered most of it. Pink light filled the cavern and they could smell the soles of their boots singeing. The heat was nearly unbearable to Venser.

"I see something," Venser said, pointing.

One area of the floor was not the same color as the others. A perimeter of lighter color created the outline of a rectangle. At one end of the rectangle was a small divot of yet another shade of orange. Venser took a small knife from his boot. He bent down and carefully poked the tip of the knife through the loop hidden in the divot. "Got it," Venser said.

Koth nodded and removed his palms from the floor.

Their boots were smoking as they waited for the metal to cool. When the ring was cool enough to grasp, Elspeth and Koth took hold and heaved. Nothing happened. Venser bent down and pulled as well, and slowly, very slowly, the door began to tear free from the metal floor. It was a sound that made Elspeth's stomach turn—she'd heard it so many times when imprisoned by the Phyrexians— tearing flesh.

But they managed to open the passage. A foul smell wafted up the chute, and a ladder descended into darkness. Koth went first, his whole body glowing slightly as he moved. The walls of the chute seemed to be bored out as if by an immense drill. Under their feet a hard banging sound echoed up from deep below. After climbing for what seemed like hours, they saw a light. Every movement they made echoed, so none spoke but quickened their pace toward the light. Venser took deep breaths to keep from hurrying too much and perhaps slipping to his death. He was not overly predisposed to darkness. And after the long darkness of the chute, Venser would have welcomed a legion of Phyrexians as long as the hall they were in was well lighted.

The light was brighter underneath. Koth stopped when they were just about to climb into the room below. The banging noise was loud there, and the vulshok spoke in a normal volume. "Should we drop down and take them unawares? How many can there be? From what I saw they're all on the surface."

Next in line was Venser, but he said nothing. He was trying hard not to jump for the red light.

"Do you smell something familiar?" Elspeth asked.

"The reek is horrible, but not familiar," Koth said. "Rot, I'd say. Rotting flesh."

"Yes, that," Elspeth said. "And . . . something sweet."

"That is blood, unless I am mistaken," Venser said.

"Blood," Elspeth said.

The hot updraft blew past their faces. The pounding sound continued.

"Well," Koth said. "I guess we should just drop down."

"I'll teleport down and then back," Venser said.

"I cannot see any floor, my friends," Elspeth said.

"I can appear and then disappear."

When nobody said anything, Venser settled himself and took a series of deep breaths. He slapped himself on the cheek once and felt the mana in the lines he kept tethered to other places course blue like blood in the vein toward him. It rushed to his cheek and he took one final deep breath and held it. When he felt as if he would faint, he pushed in his mind and disappeared with a *snap*.

Elspeth counted one, two and then the artificer was back holding the ladder, gasping for air.

"Do you always hold your breath?" Elspeth said.

"No, but it helps for short ones."

"What is down there?" Koth said.

Venser did not replay at first. "It is a bad place, that," he said. "The enemy is there, working."

"Are they?"

"Yes," Venser said. "Very many of them, but lumbering ones. Fit for their work."

"That pleases me," Elspeth said.

"Nothing about this place pleases me," Koth mumbled.

". . . and there are some others that I could not identify. I was in the air only a moment. They are larger, I know that."

"What makes the hammering sound?" Elspeth said.

"I will let you see that for yourselves. It would cause you to question what we are about to do."

Koth looked up. "Jackass, you are not supposed to tell us that. You are supposed to tell us the hammering sound is nothing."

"I was never good at lying."

Koth shook his head.

"I will appear off to the side, and fight them from there," Venser said.

"I will slay everything in that room," Elspeth said through gritted teeth.

"Then keep in front of me, crazed one," Koth said. "Actually you are both cracked."

"You brought me here," Venser reminded.

"To fight the Phyrexians, not track down an old comrade."

"Right. Ready?" Venser said, he looked down at Koth and up at Elspeth, who nodded. The pounding continued, and something metal and large banged into a wall. "Go."

Koth pushed off from the ladder rungs and fell feetfirst to the floor, which was farther down than he thought it would be. He stumbled back a bit, and Elspeth landed soundlessly next to him.

The scene laid out before them took their breath away. The walls were splattered and the floor was covered, as were the slablike tables, with a bright redness. So bright, in fact, that it looked like paint. There were many of the metal catafalques in the room. Each had a body on it in the process of being butchered. Next to the table more bodies were piled. The meat pulled and hacked off the bodies was thrown in a cart next to the table, as were the organs. Everything else lay glistening and white. There was no drain in the floor, so the carnage was ankle deep. The reek was enormous, like a wall that hit them in the face.

Each table had a Phyrexian butcher. A huge thing with no face to speak of—only an immense mouth of long teeth crammed one over the others. Each butcher had a notched iron blade where its right hand would have been, and a hacked, gashed, fingerless stump for its left. Done with the meat, each butcher loaded the bones onto a creaky cart and walked them to an immense crusher, which Elspeth took for a machine at first. The bones were thrown into a basin and the room-high Phyrexian raised its boulder of a fist and dropped it on the bones. Every eighth pound or so, it brushed the bits left into a large hole next to the basin.

The meat went into another hole, but samples were obviously taken by the butchers, who had blood and material smeared around their mouths and over their wet teeth.

Elspeth and Koth stood stunned in the middle of the room. Venser was off to the side near the pulverizing Phyrexian. So still were they that the Phyrexians did not notice them at first, as the butchers had no eyes. But they had noise holes, Venser saw.

It was the pulverizer that raised the alarm. Its eyes were set spiderlike on a tiny head fused onto the trunk of its immense body. It had a toothless mouth hole, which began bellowing, with what must have been its tongue flopping around in its mouth. Its crushing hand stopped, and all the butchers froze. Dripping blood from their work, and from the flaps of skin hanging cut from their left hands, they turned toward Elspeth and Koth. Venser was nearer the crushing beast, but he had not been detected.

One of the bodies next to Venser moved and moaned. The artificer backed up. The body groaned and extended a bruised hand. It was an elf, Venser saw, or had been. He backed up farther, until he bumped something. He turned, and towering over him was a butcher. But the creature was facing Elspeth and Koth, and had apparently not noticed him.

Venser brought the mana to him. He felt it sparking the air around him and seeping into his pores. He reached out to touch the Phyrexian, who froze stiff in place.

Suddenly the other Phyrexians were running at Koth and Elspeth. She had her sword out and it reflected the red glare of the place. Koth was positively red, with his fiery slits wide and the furnace of anger within him blazing in his eyes and at his fists. He struck the first Phyrexian, and that creature burst into flames and fell flailing off to the side. Koth ducked the swinging cleaver hand from a Phyrexian that had moved in from the back. Crouching, he planted one of his hands and swept the thing's leg with his own. It fell with a loud thud. Then another was trampling it, swinging its own cleaver down on Koth's head.

Elspeth cut a Phyrexian's head from its body, but still it fought with black oil spouting out where its neck had been. She leveled an overhand smash on the body, cleaving the left arm off, but still it did not fall. Thrusts and hacks to the torso had little effects either. Her sword was there to block each blow, and soon the butcher's cleaver was notched almost to its handle, and after another blow the pocked top of it fell off. The Phyrexian hunched its headless and armless body but still stood.

Elspeth took two steps back and lowered her blade. She took some deep breaths until her heartbeat slowed a bit. The opponent was disarmed. She could not normally attack a disarmed opponent, but the Phyrexian did not seem to know it was disarmed, and she cut it as it advanced, oil still bubbling out its neck and streaming down its body and arm.

Koth stepped between Elspeth and the Phyrexian and cast a column of fire from his hands, which ignited the hulking creature. Burning, it still charged. Koth waited until it was almost upon him, then he dropped to his hands and knees, and the lumbering beast fell over him and went sprawling. With only one arm, it had trouble getting up, and after a short while it stopped trying and burned.

Koth and Elspeth stood and turned to the other butchers. They had crowded into a loose circle around them. Venser was behind somewhere. Koth tapped Elspeth's shoulder, and when she turned she saw even more butchers staring at them. Their stillness was unnerving. She tried counting them but stopped at sixty. And there were plenty more than that.

The Phyrexians began rocking. From leg to leg they rocked. Then they started making the frenzied, mad sounds Venser had heard before. He glanced around until he located the ladder they had descended. Another quick look yielded the hole where the Phyrexians threw down the meat. Behind it was the hole where the bones were dumped. Across from him Elspeth was still breathing hard from her fight. Koth was doing a bit better, but even the vulshok looked exhausted. Venser cast his eyes over the enemy, front to back. Ninety-three, not including the huge ones. Odds were against them, based on how much they had worked to slay only four.

"Bones or meat?" Venser said.

His head down as he caught his breath, Koth looked up and then back down. Elspeth understood immediately.

"I cannot retreat in this case," she said, matter-of-factly.

"Retreat?" Venser said. "Nobody's asking for that. Retreat would be to the ladder we climbed down, right? We simply have to find our next path."

By then Koth understood. "Meat is softer," he said, between breaths.

"Very true," Venser said. "We need to move over to our right, past the one with the dung slipping down its leg."

Koth swallowed hard. "I see it."

"Shall we?" Venser said.

They all waited for Elspeth to speak. When she said nothing, Venser started to move.

Luckily the Phyrexians had not moved forward, but continued to rock back and forth making their retching sounds. The moment the party moved they stopped rocking, put their heads down, and charged from all angles, their cleaver hands slashing.

"Go," Venser yelled.

The Phyrexians converged on them when they were still a zanda beast's-length from the meat hole. Elspeth rushed forth and she and her sword became a blur as the sword attacked from every angle at one time. Six Phyrexians fell with thousands of slices crisscrossing their wizened sinew and metal.

At the rear, Koth caught a downward chop from the first Phyrexian's cleaver in a sticky pillow of fiery plasma, yanked the beast off balance, turned it, and threw it into the others. Venser teleported to the lip of the meat hole. It was so slopped with viscera that he almost lost his footing. It took him a second of flailing before he steadied himself. Then he turned and took three deep breaths of mana and blew out a thick cloud of shimmering air. Venser's gusted breath enveloped the Phyrexians caught in the back near him and suddenly their sinews leaped off their bodies and began to dance a mad jig amidst the gore. So surprised were the butchers that they stopped to stare . . . and were cut down by Elspeth as she moved like a flashing blaze through them.

Still more butchers shoved and rocked in from the edges, running surprisingly fast in a convulsive frenzy to cleave the intruders' skulls and, Venser assumed somehow, drink their brains.

They were a stone's throw from the hole when the far wall quaked and a large portal in the shape of an iris diaphragm blossomed and out of the conduits and gutlike wetness of the hole stepped two massive Phyrexians. They were near the size of the Phyrexian machine that had been crushing bones with its one huge hand. But their hands, unlike most Phyrexians, had no sharp tipped fingers. Each hand was as large as their torso, and made of some metal wrapped with thick bands of sinew. The monstrous Phyrexians moved over the crowd of butchers, crushing them as they planted their knuckles on the floor and swung their bodies to catch up.

The smell of the place was already rot and old blood, but with these crushing creatures, the smell of singed hair joined the mélange.

Elspeth stopped swinging her sword. She turned to Venser, but the artificer was not looking at the crushers or the butchers. His eyes were fixed on a place at the far end of the room.

"What is our plan with this large foe?" Elspeth yelled to her comrades. "Will we choose this point to continue on our path down that hole?"

The meat hole was within their reach. The few Phyrexians left that stood between them and the hole had stopped fighting to watch their huge cousins.

"I wonder," Venser said, ignoring what Elspeth had said. "If that is what I think it is."

Koth ran toward the hole. He reached down and seized a huge section of spinal vertebrae. He hurled the bone and it took the first Phyrexian in the eye and knocked it back and over. As the Phyrexian struggled to get up, Koth jumped on him and drove an ember-red hand down into the beast's chest, stilling its efforts. Another Phyrexian charged forward and swung. Large gauntlets of metal snapped out of Koth's forearms, which he raised as a shield. The Phyrexian's cleaver bounced harmlessly off the growths.

Koth's hands went black, and the seams where his fingers bent glowed a bright red. He dived forward and plunged both hands to the elbows into the

ROBERT B. WINTERMUTE

Phyrexian's body, instantaneously melting through the thing's metal framework of supports and bone shards. As he ducked the Phyrexian's swings, Koth lifted it off its feet and hurled it into the other butchers who had begun to advance.

The path was clear to the meat hole.

"Let's go," Koth said.

But Venser was not moving. In a moment the crushers would be upon them. Even Elspeth had begun to walk toward the hole.

"Oh, artificer, sir," Koth said. "You coming?"

At that moment Venser blinked out of existence to teleport to the bottom of the pit. Shrugging, Koth ran to the hole. The ground shook as the crushers advanced. They were just behind him, by the feel of it. Koth could smell their grim knuckles.

Elspeth was the first one down. Koth looked before he jumped. Darkness. The first crusher stopped and pulled back its huge fist for a punch that would surely have driven Koth back and into the metal wall. He jumped. The cushion of wind at the front of the punch whizzed past his head as he fell down into darkness.

CHAPTER
5

The landing was soft and wet. They lay in the dark, listening to the caterwauling screams echoing from the hole above them. When Elspeth struggled to her feet a voice broke the quiet.

"Be at ease," the voice said. "We are many and you are few. Do not struggle or we will gut and leave you and the twisted ones will work through your skins. We need you as you need us to leave this dark place."

"We are not leaving this dark place," Venser said.

"Oh, you are leaving," the voice said. "You are coming with us. Furthermore, you will *like* it very much. We will even take the vulshok, if he will agree not to run away."

"Show yourselves," Koth yelled, starting to glow red in the darkness.

"Loud as always," the voice said.

But many forms started to appear in the darkness at the edge of Koth's glow. They were of differing heights and sizes, but all carried weapons. There were thirty that Venser counted. An elf with etched copper arms stepped forward, with his bow half drawn and two cocked fingers holding an arrow in place. His skin was greenish, and the smell of him was odd, Venser thought. Perhaps it was the copper growing into his skin. But the elf's hair, which seemed to be made up of segmented sections of cable or some close substance, was sweat sodden and pulled back. Deep creases surrounded both his eyes and mouth, as if he had frowned for years.

Behind the forms, vast boulders towered.

"Are we saved by the elves?" Koth laughed.

The elf at the front of the group held up one finger. "Not entirely," he swept his hand back. The outline of a vulshok, with spikes at the shoulders and head, was clearly visible behind him.

"I am Ezuri and you are saved by Mirrodin. It is a place you may remember from the old days," the elf said.

Koth was quiet.

Venser noticed for the first time that the elves in the group, and the leader in particular, had small circular parts of their arm and leg metal that glowed green.

"What do you seek?" Elspeth said, standing tall and white in the festering filth around her. Her sword was unsheathed and laid across her left arm. Venser was suddenly very glad that she was a part of the group. Koth was seething . . . getting redder and redder the longer he stood. There would be a fight if the situation continued.

It was the elf who spoke. "We are here to lead you out of this madness," the elf said, "if you would come."

Koth brightened. "Yes, please," he said. Then he seemed to realize that he'd spoken too quickly. "Why are you helping us?"

The elf laughed a high, shrill laugh. "One, maybe two more rooms and you would be as this meat we are standing upon," he said. He looked down at the rotting flesh. "Some of this is elf. Perhaps some of these elves were from my tribe." He lifted his foot. "That might even be my wife."

Nobody spoke. After a moment Venser stepped forward.

"I am Venser of Urborg."

"It is I, Ezuri," the elf said. "And these are raiders against the fiends."

"Ezuri, we thank you for wanting to help us, but we must continue down from here."

"Why?" the elf said. "We have been tracking you for some time, and at every turn you seem to be uniquely able to choose the most dangerous path, and to take it."

Venser heard Koth stir next to him. He would hear from the vulshok later how they were not on the correct path, but it was time to make sure that the elf did not impede their progress.

"We search for a friend who was lost here."

"Who is this friend? I might have seen him."

"His name is Karn," Venser said.

Ezuri stared at Venser for what seemed like a full minute. "No, I have not seen anyone by that name."

"We must find him," Venser said.

"If he is any deeper than the meat room, you may forget you ever heard his name."

As if to prove the point, a chorus of gargled bellows cut the stinking air. Ezuri did not move his head, but his large ears pivoted slightly at the sound. His eyes never left Venser's.

"I cannot let you pass this room," Ezuri said. "You know this. I cannot let you stir those that tear flesh into a frenzy. We have been pressing them hard and making good progress against them. I cannot let you undo our work."

"You think you have them on the run?" Koth said. "We were just at the Vault of Whis—"

"And there were some Phyrexians around there," Venser cut in.

Sensing he was not getting the whole story, Ezuri cut his gaze from Koth to Venser, then after a quick glance at his troops, turned back to Venser before continuing.

"There are small pockets of the enemy there," Ezuri said. "That is known."

Elspeth picked up on the tone of the conversation. "Yes, some," she said.

"But what we saw come out of that mountain . . . ," Koth began.

"Koth," Elspeth interrupted. "Would you introduce me to your kin?"

Koth cast an eye at the vulshok standing behind Ezuri. "He is Shield clan." Then to the vulshok, "Come forward, Shield clan."

The vulshok stood where he was, and looked to Ezuri. The elf nodded and the vulshok stepped forward.

"Since when do the wrought follow the bidding of those of the forests," Koth said.

"Since we lost most of our tribe," the vulshok replied.

"Do you know Ranglif or Nagel?"

The man shook his head.

Venser seemed unconcerned. "You must surely know the Lyser?"

The vulshok nodded once. "He is dead."

The small smile faded off of Koth's face. "Is that so?"

"That is so," the vulshok said. "A battle in the Tangle did him."

"What was he doing in the Tangle, with the elves?"

Venser watched the vulshok shrug his shoulders. The shoulder shrug must be one of the worst expressions in existence, Venser thought. So meaningless and yet so insolent.

The artificer looked critically at the band of rebels, as Koth argued with the vulshok. They had spread their ranks as Ezuri spoke. They would be hard to flank or evade. Still, if they could get to the other side of that large rock behind Koth, it might be possible to run through the boulder field. With a little luck they might find an exit before Ezuri and his thugs caught up. It was worth trying.

But Ezuri had been watching Venser. When the artificer moved, three of Ezuri's elves had their bows up and aimed.

"Do not move, friend," Ezuri said. "You really are going to accompany us."

Venser took a breath. In his toes and ears he could feel his mana tingling and building. He had enough mana for a very small jump. It could perhaps take him behind the large boulder. But if he made that jump he would be completely without mana and fighting all of them.

"We have watched you disappear," Ezuri said. "Do not do that here." To make his point, Ezuri had his archers point arrows at Elspeth.

Venser nodded. "Mirrodin will continue to suffer unless we find this person," Venser said.

"Then we will suffer," Ezuri said. "And to be honest with you, Mirrodin's suffering has allowed me this position of leadership. So, let her suffer more, Mirrodin. I could not have risen as I have without the Phyrexians or the Vanishing."

"That is blasphemy!" Koth said.

"Oh, hush, Koth, son of Kamath," Ezuri said. "We know of you and yours. You have no standing with us. If, indeed, you have any with your own people."

"Mirrodin will find herself again soon, when all machinery has been cleansed from her face and bowels," Ezuri said. "Our decline started with vedalken tinkering. If they had left the inner working of Mirrodin a great, natural secret instead of mucking around and making her into a machine."

Venser yawned. "Mirrodin is metal, in case you haven't noticed."

"Mirrodin is *alive*," Ezuri said, and then a sneer crossed his face. "We have no need of artificers here, my friend. Tinkering has got us to this impasse. Phyrexians are tinkerers."

"They are not artificers," Venser said, unconcerned by the red face of the elf. "Artificers create."

Elspeth, who had been standing a bit back from the rest, stepped forward. She spoke simply, with no expression on her smooth face. "We are here in this place to help, for the good of this plane. If you force my hand, I will be compelled to slay you all. You are not thinking about the good of your plane, about what is good for all. Only for yourselves. So, for you own good, I will be compelled to teach you humility and discipline at the edge of my sword." She held her sword up, glittering, in the vast room of piled boulders.

All of Ezuri's force nocked arrows and pointed them at Elspeth. "Suit yourself," Ezuri said, but his voice betrayed a certain unease.

"This will not go well for you," Koth said offhandedly.

"What would a coward know?" Ezuri said. "You leave your people alone and undefended. Your home is overrun, rock man. Your people are scattered and they died calling your name, but you were away on your merry travels."

Koth was instantly bright red. "You might slay me, but I will kill at least three quarters of your numbers. And you first," he said, pointing at Ezuri.

"Oh really?" Ezuri squinted and spat at the nearest rock. He stepped forward.

"Shall we see?" Koth said.

Elspeth nodded. "Ready."

Ezuri turned to one of his men and seized his bow. He turned back to Koth and Elspeth.

"Gentlemen!" Venser bellowed. "Wait." The artificer opened his hand and a bright flash popped. Venser rushed forward and knocked the bow from Ezuri's numb fingers.

Taken by a sudden terror caused by Venser's magic, the other rebels turned and ran. Yet Ezuri did not run. He stood looking from Venser to Elspeth. "You will bring the Phyrexians storming up," Ezuri said.

"That has already come to pass," Elspeth said. She was gasping between words to keep her battle lust abated. "You should flee to your home and prepare for the worst."

But the elf did not seem convinced, Venser thought. As long as his hand did not stray to the sword on his belt he would live.

He stared at them a moment longer, before turning on his heel and following the other rebels.

Venser sat down hard on the nearest boulder. All of a sudden, he felt a familiar pinch in his brow. His stomach tightened. His skin began to shiver. He felt like he was succumbing to the onset of a sudden sickness, but he knew he was not. It was a familiar feeling and he knew its cure. He also knew what would happen if he did not cure it within the next hour.

He began patting the many pockets sewn into the leather tunic under his loose-fitting armor. His britches were similarly accoutered and he felt those as well. The vial was in a pocket sewn onto the back of his pants. Koth's eyes were fixated on Ezuri's last position. The vulshok was still as red as fire, and grumbling under his breath. Elspeth watched as Venser drew out the vial.

"Leave me," Venser said. "Let me have my peace."

"Why?" Elspeth said, forgetting all about Ezuri, who she had only minutes before been willing to kill.

Venser shook his head, his patience waning. His stomach ached and he could feel the mana on his brow bubbling and seething for what he was holding in his hand. As soon as the white warrior left he would be able to . . .

"You want what's in that bottle, don't you?" Elspeth said.

Venser said nothing.

"You should see yourself. Your skin has gone to the color of ash. Have you seen that your left hand is trembling?"

Venser knew that more than his hand would start shaking if he didn't have what was in the bottle.

"Leave!" Venser yelled suddenly. He did not know he would yell. Yet when he opened his mouth it was indeed a yell that came out. It didn't stop there. He continued to yell with such force, spittle came out of his mouth. "I will make that metal in your armor writhe like a snake and melt itself through your very flesh."

Elspeth blinked at his words. "What is in that bottle?" she said.

Venser's head was suddenly pounding. It always happened so quickly. "I will give you to the count of five before I begin working with your armor. I am an artificer—it is easy for me to talk to the metal in you. One, two, three."

Elspeth put up her hands and began walking backward. "What will happen to you when you use all that is in that bottle of yours?"

"I will use the next one." Venser mumbled, working on the cap of the vial.

Keeping their distance, Elspeth and Koth watched as Venser took a sip from the bottle. He tried not to be greedy, but when his need reached the point it was at, it became difficult to keep composed. One sip was enough. He felt the raw mana course through him and his senses tightened and then bloomed and he could feel the energy of the metal of that place pumping all around him. He felt as if the power in him was circling his head and tapering up toward the sky.

"I feel better now," Venser said.

Elspeth raised one of her eyebrows.

Venser put the small vial back in its pocket. He patted it and pulled a deep breath.

"What is that fluid?" Koth said.

"It's a personal concoction," Venser said.

Koth nodded.

"It contains the extract of the sap of a corkscrew tree from the plane of Zendikar," Venser said. "Plus minerals rendered from certain material pulled from a disintegration hollow I know of in Dominaria, and something from Mirrodin, as a matter of fact."

"Yes?"

"Moth extract, it is called."

Koth's mouth tightened. "Blinkmoths. There not many of those left on Mirrodin anymore. They were harvested to decimation, I have heard. But who knows these things—all I've heard are old stories. Rumors."

"Of what?"

"Of the vedalken, the indigo experimenters, who became obsessed with that fluid, and the power they believed it brought. They still exist deep in the Lumingrid where the Knowledge Pool ripples. But they delved too deep, the myths say. This was so long ago. I would not ever touch what is in the blinkmoth."

"You are not me," Venser said, patting the vial through his armor.

"Clearly."

CHAPTER
6

To the center of Mirrodin, down holes riven through solid metal, along runways both twisted and forgotten, moved Geth—commander of the Vault of Whispers. He scuttled in his bulky exoskeleton of barbed alloy, ducking low-hanging veinlike tubes that had torn free from the wall and hung varicose in the dim passage.

Geth's skull, surrounded up to his ears with a body that glinted and grew, turned neither right nor left. He knew the way to the throne room.

He imagined what he would report when questioned about the weekly progress. All fairly routine, a similar meeting to many of the others: good progress, pockets of resistance that will shortly be absorbed. Issues with furnace-level discipline, suggest harsh punishment. No significant problems encountered. Geth felt his mouth grin, a feeling that was becoming more and more difficult as his Phyrexian transformation continued. Skin is the thing he lacked. The skin that was left on his face was hard to move, leaving him with a permanent expression of stretched rage. He shrugged. It had always been his favorite expression anyway. It was what he'd become, and he was great.

Glissa the meddler would be there, asking him questions that she already knew the answers to, testing him. Imagine that he, the Lord of the Vault, would be weak to the words of the likes of her. A former elf. It was she who told him to find a solution to the problem they were having fully assimilating the red ones. Him? What control did he have over how phyresis overtook, or didn't, as the case was? Why didn't she turn her dripping eyes and ask the tinkers, the cutters in their halls of blood and blades? She was always consulting with them anyway. Ask them.

He was Geth—Lord of the Vault. His job was to bleed Mirrodin until she was pale and then fill her full of the black oil. Make her one of the chosen.

And his job was almost complete.

He neared the final passage, never his favorite. He struggled between the wet tube works, the barbs from his new body catching on stringy parts and stopping him until he found the part caught and freed his body. It smelled like emptied bowels. Glissa had designed the passage, he was sure. She had made it just for him. She made it impossible for him to arrive clean, without being covered in recyclate and stinking like a festering corpse.

Whereas Glissa was always clean and shining when Geth arrived, and that day was no exception. Geth was sure she had a special passage all to her own.

He entered the hall and fell to one knee and bowed to the nascent Father of Machines on his throne.

Glissa was in her usual place at the base of the high throne, and Geth did not look at her.

"Ah," Glissa said, projecting her voice so the golem would be sure to hear, if he was listening, which Geth doubted. "Our lord of the Vault has arrived." She clearly hated him at least as much as he hated her.

"I am here to give successful tidings," Geth said.

The chancellor minion scurried over to him, *tink-tink-tink*ing the metal floor with its claws. The creature's robe was still rotting off its miserable little body, Geth saw. The hood it wore was still low over its eyes, showing only its stubby, cleaverlike teeth. A book was clutched in its metal claws.

"Maybe, Lord, you are not familiar with the time The Father of Machines called this meeting?" It said, opening the book and moving one fingertip down the page.

Geth swatted the book from its claws. The minion scrambled across the floor to collect the book off the ground.

"If there was anything written in that book, anything but the scribbles you make with your bloodied fingertips, then I would pay more attention," Geth said.

It was the same every time. The little theatrical play they put on for the golem's benefit.

But it was somehow different. Geth could feel it. The minion scrambled but did not pick up the book. It stood over it without bending. Geth had forgotten why the little creature was always in the chamber.

A howling cry cut the air, making the very walls shake. The cry was filled with some of the most exquisite angst and pain Geth had ever heard. But for one severe moment Geth thought the chamber would fall in on itself.

His eyes went to Glissa, who was looking up at the throne.

The golem bellowed in frustration and anger as he tried to stand. Geth knew that the throne was bound to his metal spine, ingrown, but the golem was strong and pulled until the throne released him and he stood to his full height.

The minions that held his throne column on their backs readjusted their stances.

Karn crumpled into a crouch, sobbing. Then he tipped forward and tumbled off the top of the throne column. It was a high column, and Geth watched as the golem hit the floor with a tremendous thud.

Moments later Karn stood out of the dent and fell to his knees, raving in a language Geth could not hope to understand.

"Father of Machines," Glissa said, her voice as smooth as the oil dripping out of her eyes. "We have council with you today." She snapped her fingers at the minion, and the little creature scrambled over with the book, which it popped open and held up before Karn's wide-eyed face. The silver golem looked down at the book, his face jumping to an expression of pain and then to one of anger and then to tears.

Geth could clearly see the rivulets of black oil popping out on his brow. Glissa noticed it too, Geth was sure of that. More fuel to the fire for those that said that Karn was not the true Father of Machines, no matter how much Glissa wanted to make him thus.

His body was fighting the oil, that much was certain. More times than not Geth found him that way at their councils. He found him raving mad, teetering between clarity and instability.

The oil could do that as it was moving through the pathways of the chosen's neurological workings, Geth had been told. But that period in the transformation only took a couple of days at most. Karn had been volatile for months. His body was simply not accepting what they all were offering. At least that was what those in command said of Karn, when nobody was listening.

Glissa would not hear of it. Brothers had lost their hands and then heads. Sisters had disappeared. Since Glissa had become fully Phyrexian, with a right hand wrought and strong, and a dull scythe for a left, she listened to zero backtalk. She even refused to allow Karn his tantrums, if she could help it.

The minion, all silver and sculpted smooth, snapped his book closed and skittered away into a shadow. Glissa sauntered over to Karn and helped him stand straight. He looked down at her arm before peering around. "What is this place?" he bellowed.

"This is your throne room, Father," Glissa said.

"Who is that?" Karn pointed.

Tezzeret stood at the end of Karn's pointed finger.

"Father," Tezzeret said. "It is I, your Tezzeret. Here to counsel you away from these bootlickers." Tezzeret smiled and flexed his arm.

Geth wanted to look away. Truth be told, that arm with its bonelike claw caused him great worry. He imagined it crushing his skull when he was trying to sleep.

"Oh look, the toady of Bolas calls us bootlickers," Glissa said. "You are late as usual."

Tezzeret bowed slightly. "Guilty as charged. Please accept my most sincere apology."

Karn fell to his knees with a clank. "Machines," he said. "Machines."

"I can see that today we have filth," Tezzeret said. "This is Karn's weakness leaving his body."

"Father of Machines, I think you mean," Glissa said. She watched Karn kneeling on the floor. Then she turned to Tezzeret. "Your contributions on Father's well-being, one-arm, are both useful and valuable. Thank you." Glissa said icily.

"Only trying to help."

"What is a machine," Karn was whispering. He reached down to the floor and as easily as Geth might tear a human's skin from his body, Karn pushed his finger into the metal of the floor and tore out a head-sized sheet. He held it up before his face.

"This is flesh," he said. "But where is metal?"

"He is not himself today," Glissa said.

"Really, do you think not?" Tezzeret said.

Glissa ignored him. She bent down to help Karn to his feet, but he would not cooperate, and Glissa could as easily lift Karn as she could the Oxidda Chain. He remained on his knees regarding the flat metal piece.

"How do we fix him?" Geth said.

"He is not broken, dunce," Tezzeret said. "He is not a machine."

"But he is metal," Geth growled, his own exoskeletal framework swelling with anger.

"So are you, and nobody's been able to fix what's wrong with you."

Geth moved to swipe Tezzeret's neck with his huge claw. Tezzeret merely grabbed Geth's claw with his etherium hand and in a moment the claw was bent into the form of a five-petal flower.

Geth bellowed and raised his other claw.

Tezzeret held up one finger. "Attention. I will turn your other hand into something more, shall we say, anatomically correct for where I will insert it if you continue this."

It took Geth a moment to piece through what Tezzeret said. His anger seemed to swell even more when understanding bloomed on his face.

"Are you both done?" Glissa said.

"I have always dreamed of being flesh," Karn said. "Metal is cold. Flesh is a meat machine. Flesh is metal."

Tezzeret smiled at Geth, who was looking down at his one good claw.

"I have received word of a totally flesh being," Glissa said. Karn suddenly looked up at her.

"Flesh is a cage too," Karn yelled.

Glissa ignored him. "Would either of you have any idea how we could use such a freak?"

Both Geth and Tezzeret shook their heads.

"You'll have to be creative," Tezzeret said. "I would have no idea what to do with such an anomaly."

"You lie too well," Glissa said. "It gives you away. Your master sent you here to assist, I believe."

"That is what he said," Tezzeret said.

"I believe there is a certain caveat to this endeavor. She cannot be infected by our *gift*."

"Really?" Tezzeret said. "Perhaps she should be released to the rebel settlement."

Then Karn began bellowing. "Maybe what we think makes us free is nothing more than a symptom of our cage," he said.

All three stopped and turned. Karn was regarding his own steely hand very closely.

"I like that," Tezzeret said suddenly. "What he just said." He swept his arm toward the throne. "What if all this is holding us back?"

Glissa put her hand to her head and closed her eyes.

"I will give you more experimenters," Glissa said. "Find why this flesh creature refuses to be infected."

But Tezzeret did not acknowledge what she said. He stared keenly at Karn.

"We make our own cages," Tezzeret said.

"Did you hear, creature," Geth said, stepping forward.

Tezzeret raised his eyes slowly until they met Geth's. Geth stepped back.

"If there were worms on Mirrodin," Tezzeret said, watching Karn sink onto his knees and hands, and then begin walking on them on all fours. "He is at the point where he would begin eating them."

But Glissa would not be ignored, and she clearly had not the slightest fear of Tezzeret. "Do you understand your assignment, or do I need to have your arm taken off so you remember it?"

"You will need to have my arm taken off," Tezzeret said matter-of-factly, not taking his eyes off Karn as he spoke.

But then Karn straightened and stood. He looked down at Geth, Glissa, and Tezzeret. "Why do you torture me so?"

"You are changing, Father," Glissa said. "We are not torturing you. We have made this change ourselves already."

"Speak for yourself, oddity," Tezzeret said.

"But who am I?" Karn said.

"You are the Father of Machines," Geth said.

"I have known that name before, from a dream," Karn said. "But he was not me."

Tezzeret yawned. "He's you all right. Just ask either of these two."

"Who is this?" Karn said lucidly—pushing his chin at Tezzeret.

"That is Tezzeret, Father," Glissa said. "He has been sent to help us."

"Help how?"

"Help us finish our work here, I don't know," Glissa said, suddenly frustrated.

Karn looked from one to the other of them. "You are all three mad. I am leaving this place." He began walking toward the wall. Glissa did nothing to stop him.

Karn reached the nearest wall and tapped twice on it. Nothing happened. He tapped twice on it again. Still nothing happened. He turned back. "What have you done with my portals?"

"They are no longer yours," Glissa said. "They are ours, and we are you."

"Oh," Karn said, as casually as if she had told him the temperature of the air. But in the next moment the brightness seemed to drain out of Karn's eyes, and he slipped down the wall until his feet were bent under him. The fine droplets of oil appeared all over his body again.

"His body, or his mind, will not fully accept what we give," Glissa said.

"He is not one of us," Geth said.

Glissa turned on him. "He is as much Phyrexian as I am. Let nobody say otherwise. We need Karn if we are ever to fully integrate Mirrodin."

"How did you become so wise to the plan?" Tezzeret demanded.

"You already know more than your mandate dictates," Glissa said. "Now know this: you will infect this flesh creature and find the rebel settlement. Kill everything and bring their bodies back so we can utilize them. Bring the fully infected flesh creature to me personally. I like flesh. I find it interesting. I have my own collection, you know."

"Is that so?" Tezzeret said. "It disgusts me. Flesh is weakness."

"Yes!" Geth said, raising his one good claw.

"Silence, fool," Glissa said to Geth, who put his arm down. "Flesh has its uses." She turned back to Tezzeret.

"Now, you will travel on your little quest with my own guards. Do you understand?"

Tezzeret regarded her coolly.

"Do you understand?" Glissa repeated.

"Yes."

"Excellent. Now then," Glissa walked over to where Karn lay crumpled on the floor, panting. She took hold of his arm with her hand and the hooked part of her scythe hand. "Come, Father, why not sit comfortably atop your throne."

But she could not budge the silver golem. "You have taken my portals." He pulled his arm free and leveled a blow against the wall, denting it deeply.

Tezzeret tried to imagine what a blow like that would do to Glissa, or Geth for that matter. Tezzeret knew what he would do if Karn tried it with him: he'd throttle the life out of the mad bastard, no matter how much he respected his craftsmanship. Or at least he'd try. The truth was that Tezzeret loved what Karn was. Karn, the creator of planes and organizer of metals. To see such a magnificent artificer brought to that kind of subjugation was a blemish on what it meant to bend metal.

"Leave him be," Tezzeret said. "There squats the creator of Mirrodin," Tezzeret said, suddenly serious. "Neither of you have sung metals to form, have given everything you are to be great. You do not have the right to be in the same room with him."

"But you do?" Glissa said.

"I have stolen, killed, and scraped for the ability to create etherium. Nobody ever gave me an ounce of value. I took it and now I am one of very few to control this great metal that is essence."

"Are you finished, philosopher?" Glissa said.

"You promised me I would have a force of my own," Tezzeret said through unsmiling lips.

"I did, didn't I?" Glissa said. "But who trusts the word of a Phyrexian? Honor is a social construct. We do not follow constructs. We follow hunger. Anyway, who are we kidding? You want more than a force, you want an army. You have been building an army. We know this. We have been watching."

A force of ten Phyrexians slinked through the far door. They were each one worked through with patina-covered copper, with gray muscle herniating out between the gaps in the jagged structure. Their eyes were black and dripping.

"You can steal, kill, and scrape your way to the settlement with my minions. "You will find these harder to control than your blue ones," Glissa promised. "Now go."

Geth made to follow Tezzeret.

"No, Geth," Glissa said. "You stay. We will discuss what to do with enemies of the oil."

Geth grinned as Tezzeret passed.

"Symptoms of our cage!" Karn bellowed.

As Tezzeret left the chamber, he heard Karn's silver fingertips scraping the metal floor.

CHAPTER
7

The middle hole dropped them, as though in free fall. They had found the holes lined up one after the other and as each smelled as dank and foul as another, they chose the middle one. Much of the time Venser felt like he was traveling upside down. Some of the turns were so abrupt that his elbows slammed into the side of the strangely flexible tube. Other times the tube traveled straight. At one point the tube traveled straight for so long they actually stopped moving and had to crawl until they began to slide.

The speed picked up quickly and continued that way for so long that Venser seriously considered teleporting away. Yet still the speed increased, the turns coming one after the other without warning. Venser could hear Koth muttering as they skidded through the tunnel. Before long, even the usually quiet Elspeth began to bellow and bang her heels on the tube. Finally the chute dumped them in an unceremonious heap on the smooth floor of another vast room, gasping and blinking and stunned in the light.

Unlike any other room Venser had seen under Mirrodin, the room was bright. Very bright. It was as if its own sun had risen and sat directly overhead. They struggled to their feet and wandered, blinded, holding each other's sleeves like children, until Venser bumped into a wall and they all put their backs to its coolness and slid down onto the floor.

"Can you see?" Koth said.

"No," Venser said at last. When he opened his eyes the light hurt deep in his head. Still, he had hoped Elspeth would respond so he could gauge just how disturbed the tube had made her. From the sound of her cries as they slid, Venser wanted to know if she had come unhinged.

"Hold up your hand," Koth said. "Peer through the cracks between your fingers."

Venser brought up his filthy hand and rested it on his brow. Through the space between his middle and first fingers he was able to see without the sharp pain.

The ball of light was still blazing in the ceiling. The floor continued to vibrate. Sometimes the vibrations were more and sometimes less. But the light that burned down on them was as constant as any machine.

"My job in their prison," Elspeth said in a voice made rough by her prolonged bawl in the tube, "was to cut down the bodies the Phyrexians left behind. They liked to play and experiment and do other things. They would drive spikes through the space between the heel and tendon and hang their victims upside down. It was a prison."

"Yes," Venser said. "You told us that."

"No, I mean for Phyrexians," Elspeth said. "They took our parts for themselves. They are nothing more than perverse machines that want to masquerade as flesh and blood creatures, so they dress in our muscles, skin, and viscera."

"They imprison their own?" Koth said after a time.

"Yes. The imprisoned ones experimented on us to keep quiet. At night they were mostly locked in their own cages by other Phyrexians."

"That is fascinating," Venser said. "And how did they treat prisoners of their own kind, the Phyrexians?"

"With deference, almost kindness, if that is possible," Elspeth said. "If one of the prisoners was especially wild, some of the guards would collect around the door and sing to him."

"Sing?"

"Well," Elspeth said, "it did not sound like our singing. It was terrifying to hear."

"So you were a distraction?" Koth said.

"Yes. A distraction."

"And how are you here standing before us?" Koth said.

"Have some respect," Venser said.

But Elspeth put a gloved hand on Koth's shoulder. "Perhaps they did not prefer children? I do not know why. I ask myself that question quite often."

Koth nodded before turning and gazing between his fingers at the scene. Venser waited to hear if Elspeth said anything more about her time in the Phyrexian prison. When she didn't continue, Venser had a look at their surroundings—a truly vast space with flat floor and the light beating down. Venser could make out neither form nor the far-off shapes of doors. "I can't see anything out there," he said.

"Me neither," Koth said. "But I will tell you one thing. Without water we'll be hard pressed to last long in this room."

"Do you feel that vibration?" Elspeth said.

"Yes."

"That sound concerns me. It stops and starts."

"Let us see," Venser said.

With their hands resting on their brows, they walked forward in no particular direction. There were no landmarks so one direction was as good as any other. As they walked, their footfalls echoed away in the absolute stillness, punctuated by the sudden vibrations.

"Do you suppose those are the echoes from our feet returning to us?" Elspeth said. Once again, the quavering edge to her voice alarmed Venser.

"I thought of that," Venser said, "but no. Those vibrations are something else. They are not regular enough to be our footfalls."

They continued their march. The blinding light above their heads never moved, so it was difficult to tell how long they had been walking, but it would have been half of the day's movement of a normal sun. Finally the heat became so much that they stopped on the flat plain. Elspeth, who had the only water flask, shared what drops she had, but it was not enough. They walked again.

When Koth stopped grumbling, Venser started to worry. The ground was still flat and hot and the edges of the room were not within view.

It was Koth, still mute in the heat, who first tripped and fell slowly to his knees. He kneeled like that in the blazing heat with his hand over his eyes until Elspeth offered her hand and pulled the large vulshok to his feet. He stood wobbling for some seconds before taking a step and then another and they were on their slow way again.

"Nothing is changing," Koth said.

"Indeed," Elspeth said.

"I wouldn't say that exactly, geomancer," Venser said. He had stopped and was staring intently between his fingers in a certain direction.

"Do you detect something?" Elspeth asked.

"I am unsure. There is a dot."

"A moving dot?" Koth said.

Venser said nothing as he watched. Soon the dot became larger between Venser's fingers.

"It is moving," he said. "Toward us."

Koth leaned forward and sat down hard. "I will not move until it nears."

"What if it is Phyrexian?" Elspeth said.

"That is almost certainly what it is," Venser said. "And we are at our weakest."

Venser squinted at the moving dot. There was a snapping sound and in an instant the artificer was gone. Elspeth and Koth watched. The dot stopped. There was a tremendous screeching sound and then a *bang* and a *clank*. Then nothing. The dot did not move and Venser did not appear. They waited in the brightness until their heads were pounding, and then they started to walk to the dot. It took a long time to reach it. As they walked, the dot slowly got larger, until it was something larger than a galley.

It was a huge Phyrexian and its body was covered in dull pocked iron. It walked on six stubby legs with its belly raking the ground. The metal back was covered with spikes and holes. A tiny head of mostly chipped teeth popping out of a small mouth thrust out of the front. Pipes connected the side and back of the head to its massive body. Venser was not there.

The Phyrexian appeared to be asleep. Its eyes were closed and it lay on its stomach with all six of its stubby legs stretched out straight to the side.

There was another *bang* and a *crash* and a panel on the side of the Phyrexian popped open. Venser's head appeared.

"I believe this was a crusher," he said, struggling to get his body out of the round hole he'd opened.

"Yes," Koth said.

"It will function no more," Venser said. He threw down a wet wad of material, which splattered and clanged on the ground. It was covered in oil.

Venser tried to climb down the side of the large creature, but his oily hands lost their purchase and he began to slide. Elspeth caught him with a smile on her face.

"See," he said. "That's all it takes to loosen the mood around here."

They put their hands back over their eyes and looked at the beast.

"What is it doing in this room?" Koth said.

Venser shrugged. "Existing," Venser said. "Perhaps it could not leave the room before the Phyrexians took it over and it still cannot."

But Elspeth was not looking at the creature. She was looking back in the direction they had come from.

"I think yon creature is a friend to this one," she said. "It is advancing on us."

Koth turned. "Is there room inside this one?"

"No," Venser said. "Not for all of us and not for one of your size I would wager."

The far-off dot advanced. It moved slower than the other dot had. As it slowly neared they could make out strings. As it came still closer, they saw that the strings were actually chains.

If the first Phyrexian crusher had been large, the one approaching was very, very large. Venser took a step back and almost turned and ran. The creature lumbered forward on huge, crooked legs. It was easily as large as a small city and it dragged its inhabitants on chains behind it.

Some were alive, Venser saw, and walking slowly with the chains clipped around their necks. They were mostly humans, and in various states of phyresis. All were armed with swords.

"Moriok," Koth said. "Shadow-aligned humans."

Many were motionless bodies being dragged behind. Some were no more than rotted corpses. Venser noticed with not a little bit of unease that many of them were missing their legs. The moving city was made of dull, jagged metal, pocked and wound with sinew and with a single head the size of a dragon propped on top of its amazing bulk. The head, though small, looked all around from deep set eyes. Beside the small eyes, the rest of the space on the head was dominated by a huge mouth of sharp teeth, dripping with bright red blood. Many clawed hands on thin arms hung over its side.

It lumbered to a stop before the companions, and a huge rooster tail of steam shot up into the air. What flesh the being once had was long ago turned to black and metallic Phyrexian armor.

One of the giant's thin arms reached down and gave a chain a tug. The moriok attached to it struggled to stand, and when he could not, the Phyrexian lifted him by the chain as though a marionette. It dangled the struggling human into its open mouth. When the moriok's legs were kicking the creature's sharp teeth, the mouth closed with a *snap*. The moriok was without legs the next moment, screaming and flailing its arms as the blood and organs fell. The Phyrexian dropped the chain and chewed slowly as it regarded the companions.

"What's the plan?" Koth whispered.

Venser shrugged. "The head?" he said.

"Can we gain entrance to his body?" Elspeth said.

Nobody replied. Steam shot out its back as the crusher slowly began its charge. It put its arms out and choked a cry. Creaking and whining as it started to move, the moriok stood straighter and pulled swords. Venser closed his eyes and took quick stock of his reserves of mana. Not good. He reached out with his mind to catch a fluttering tether. Once he caught one he yanked it straight and felt the cool flow of energy emptying into his skull. Elspeth drew her sword, and Koth closed his eyes and mouth and held his breath. A moment later his body and face were as red as the melted rock Venser had seen in the Oxidda Chain. The geomancer stepped into the path of the lumbering Phyrexian, whose legs were moving it, crablike, at a fairly brisk clip toward them with the moriok advancing before it.

The first moriok swung its sword at Koth. The blade of the sword caught on the vulshok's suddenly red skin and melted before the moriok's eyes. Koth reached out and burned his hand into the man's chest and the moriok fell away screaming. Koth walked closer to the Phyrexian. The great beast did not stop, but merely swatted Koth to the side with one of his pitted arms. Koth flew far to the right.

Elspeth advanced and her sword flashed and blurred as she attacked at every angle imaginable. In no time a large area of the Phyrexian was covered with deep hacks. But the juggernaut let out a horrible chuckle that sounded like someone was being drowned, before attempting to bring one large claw down on Elspeth. The white knight stepped to the side to avoid the attack. She brought her sword across and caught the Phyrexian in the wrist, hacking its claw almost off. Three other arms swept down on Elspeth, knocking her away.

The Phyrexian raised one of its clawed hands and held it above Elspeth. But Koth was there when the hand fell. He pushed, and slowly his hot skin began melting through the hand. How will that help Elspeth? Venser found himself wondering. The hand will simply fall around Koth and crush her.

Venser breathed deeply through his nose and felt his will collecting in his throbbing brain and extending out and away.

He found the Phyrexian's brain, such as it was, and followed it back until he was fairly certain he was in the motor function area, though it was hard to be sure as the being had once been a crusher. To be sure, Venser sent a reverse-impulse request through the brain. The Phyrexian crusher lurched backward, a bewildered look on its tiny face. The hand pulled away with the rest of the body.

"Well," Koth said between breaths. "That could have gone better."

The Phyrexian stopped moving backward and began advancing again. Some of the moriok dropped their swords and simply plodded next to the crusher. A couple just sat down and let the huge machine drag them. The crusher creaked as it approached.

"I do not know how to strike such a thing," Elspeth said, inspecting the edge of her sword before carefully sheathing it.

Venser could see his compatriots were tired. How long had it been since they slept more than an hour?

Their water input amounted to what pools they could find collected in rust-metal divots, dripped down from the surface. Their dry tack was virtually inedible. Venser himself could lie down right there on the hot floor and sleep for three days. What he did not think he could fight right then was a massive crushing machine that traveled with its meals shackled to it.

A cry caught Venser's ear. He turned. Behind them stood an array of Phyrexians of various shapes and sizes, but all with bodies of twisted metal and stiffened veins. There were at least one hundred of them with their claws up and their frothing mouths opening and closing soundlessly. They collected around the crusher as the huge beast navigated itself forward.

"I don't suppose," Koth said, looking from the crusher to the new arrivals, "that you can teleport us all away? Even I would not mind a good teleport right now."

"No," Venser said. Even though he did not like to admit it, there was a certain feeling rising in his throat that was telling him to flee. He could. He could teleport out of the way and keep going, keep searching for Karn. He had not asked to come to the metal place. He would have come eventually, to be sure, but in his own time, and when he was properly provisioned and ready. His situation was madness. He cast his eyes around the vast cavern. Not one obstacle to hide behind for as far as he could see, which was not far when he had to peer between his fingers to see anything.

The crusher creaked and whined its dry joints as it began to move forward faster.

Venser took a quick breath and disappeared, only to snap into existence the next instant in front of the crusher. The Phyrexian was so surprised it stopped.

The chained moriok took one look at the swirls and waves of blue whirling around Venser's hands, and refused to move.

Venser swept a section of the Phyrexian's riveted plate out of the way. The metal, pliable to the artificer's mind, flowed in a graceful wave out of the path of his hand. Venser reached to his upper arms into the interior of the Phyrexian. He began rearranging. A moment later the crusher's arm impacted his side and Venser slid out over the smooth floor. He skittered to a stop at the foot of a huge Phyrexian with thick legs and a shelflike chest, skeletal arms and a head as large as its fist. Before Venser could stand, the Phyrexian seized his skull in the palm of one claw and lifted him off the ground. The creature's other hand was poised for a strike with two of its claw fingers extended to gouge into Venser's eye sockets.

Venser brushed the hand aside, but as the fingers and palm dripped back into the wrist, the tips of other claws poked out of the wrist, and another hand grew before his eyes, literally. Soon there was another claw.

Then something exceedingly odd happened. All the metal on the Phyrexian began to arc upward, as though it were dripping upside down. The dark metal of it began to dance and wind, much to the creature's amazement. Its exposed sinews and muscles looked strangely naked as its whole body began to tumble down without the metal's support. The metal of the creature's structure danced higher and higher in the air. The meat parts of the Phyrexian fell with a wet thump to the metal floor. But nobody was watching that. All eyes were on the metal, arcing up and down and side to side in graceful loops and peaks.

The metal turned colors as well—first red, then jet black, and then a bright, shimmering gold. Venser heard Koth's sharp intake of breath when the metal went a glassy blue. It pulled together into a square shape and fell with a hard thump on the ground next to the crumpled Phyrexian the metal had come from, who looked at it with eyeballs bare and wobbly.

Then somebody was clapping. Venser turned to see a line of Phyrexians different than any he'd seen up to that point. They were twisted and small of head, with teeth coming out everywhere, and their metal parts were shiny. Their hands had small devices and long, sharp tools of chrome attached to them. And standing at the center of them was a human, or most of a human. A bright light shone at his right shoulder. Venser felt his breath catch in his throat as he recognized the metal floating in strips around that radiant shoulder. The strips extended in a fluid motion down an arm that ended in a long-fingered hand. An arm that glowed as much as the shoulder. A metal arm unlike any Venser had ever seen. And as Venser stared, his jaw slack, the being continued to clap.

CHAPTER
8

W ell now," the being said, in a voice that, like his arm, seemed to modulate itself slightly. "I did not expect to find you all the way over here, with these clankers, down here in the muck and the filth. By all rights they should have been scrapped long ago."

It took a moment for Venser to find his tongue. "Where is here?"

The human chuckled. "Indeed," he said.

But the crusher and the dark Phyrexians did not see the humor in the situation. The crusher screeched as it adjusted its weight. Its tiny head looked back and forth from the being with the glowing arm to the Phyrexians that stood just behind him. The crusher's Phyrexians and moriok glanced uncertainly at the pile of flesh that had been one of their own.

The new arrival looked over the dark Phyrexians. He shook his head. "It's sometimes ridiculous what

115

this Phyrexian taint produces. Their forms are not pleasant, not that I mind the form of a thing. I know they have no control over how they turn out, but so many of their designs have such *flaws*." He gestured at the menagerie. If Venser did not know better he might have thought they were laughing. If he had not known that Phyrexians lacked the sentience for humor, even such simple humor as ridicule.

"Flaws or not, there are plenty of them," Koth said.

The being moved its strange eyes, blue as water, to Koth. He looked him over from foot to spiked hair. "You work with ore, vulshok, no?"

Koth nodded. "I have that honor."

"You have that honor," the being repeated.

The Phyrexian crusher lurched forward suddenly. The sound was so loud that Venser felt like moving the hand he had over his eyes to his ear. The being with the moving metal arm turned to the crusher. "I did tell you," he said.

He sniffed and raised both of his arms. After a series of motions with his hands, the Phyrexian's arms and legs were gone—the metal that had once been its legs and arms floated in a ball before the Phyrexian's face. The creature with the glowing arm turned back to Koth. The ball rearranged itself into a throne of sorts and came to rest on the metal floor. Two blue chrome Phyrexians rushed forward and moved the large seat behind the being. Without looking he sat down. The crusher looked on soundlessly.

"Do you work for your ore?" the being said to Koth.

"Our mother provides us with her blood."

"Your mother?"

Koth nodded.

Venser shifted his weight. To say the vulshok was impressed with the being was a great overstatement.

Venser could tell by his friend's expression that Koth thought the being nothing more than another Phyrexian.

"My mother is dead," the being said.

Koth seemed not to have heard this. "And what are you then?" Koth said.

"Unfortunately, there are still parts of me that are human," the human said. He extended his metal arm and moved it before his eyes. "I am Tezzeret. I have lived in filth and muck. I have lived in palaces. I prefer palaces."

"You are one of the ethersworn," Elspeth said. "I would know your flash anywhere."

The being almost smiled. "Ah, a good knight of Bant. What foolishness. This is a little homecoming of a sort."

"So you are one of these ethersworn?" Venser said.

"No. All hands are raised against me, except those that work for me."

"How do you bear no blemish of the Phyrexian taint?" Elspeth said. "You clearly bed with these abominations. Do they possess etherium?"

Tezzeret's eyes stayed on Elspeth. The white warrior stared back. Venser could tell without a doubt what Elspeth thought about the being—enemy.

Tezzeret seemed to read Elspeth's mind. "I am not your enemy. I am not Phyrexian. I have come to help you, actually."

"Phyrexian's are not our only enemies," Elspeth said.

Tezzeret nodded. He looked back at his chrome Phyrexians. Following an unseen command, his chrome troops leaped on the dark Phyrexians and began savagely tearing at them with their claws. There were more dark Phyrexians, but they were no match for the smaller troops, who moved faster and struck with arms that morphed from claws to needles and then to bludgeons in the blink of an eye. One of the shiny Phyrexian's claws shot out of its wrists and flew through the air attached with a chain. Venser watched as that Phyrexian's claw knocked another Phyrexian's head clean off its shoulders. The tortured snarls and rattle of the Phyrexians fighting reminded Venser of gnarl beasts, but with armor on. It was over when the last black Phyrexian lowered its spear-shaped head and charged at a chrome beast, which stood still and let the spear pierce its chest. Then it began tearing chunks of sinew and metal out of the other's back and neck. Soon there was nothing left of the dark Phyrexian except for its head impaled in the other's chrome chest.

"You have something," Tezzeret said to the chrome Phyrexian with the head through its chest. "Just here." He made a sweeping motion, as though gesturing to a stain on a shirt after a meal. The chrome Phyrexian cocked its head at Tezzeret, the bladed head jutting out of its chest. Tezzeret turned back to the compatriots and shook his head.

"You can't do anything with them," he said. "That one will need work. Now then, did that gain your trust?" Tezzeret looked from one to the other of them. "No," he said. "I can see it did not. What about you, artificer? Do you trust me some now?"

"I wish you would simply tell us what you want us to do," Venser said.

Tezzeret paused a moment. "Well, at least there is a glimmer of life somewhere down here. What makes you think you can help me?"

"Otherwise you would not be here showing off to us."

"I simply want to give you a gift."

118   "Don't think so," Koth said.

ROBERT B. WINTERMUTE

"Nonetheless," Tezzeret said. "You must come with me and my assistants to get this gift—I cannot hold it any longer."

Elspeth went to Venser's side. Her metal brow plate dinged into his helmet as she leaned as close as possible. "This feels foul," she said.

"Where do you want us to go?" Venser said.

Tezzeret made a fist with his metal hand, and watched the ripple that action caused in the metal of his arm. An isolated piece broke off and floated above the shoulder. "We will go deeper," Tezzeret said. "Much deeper."

"We can go deeper?" Koth said.

"Oh yes. You are still in the caverns here. We will go *into* the Phyrexians."

An involuntary shudder passed through Elspeth. She frowned.

"And if we refuse to go with you?" Venser said.

"Then I will simply leave you," Tezzeret said. "Your metal guide may or may not be following you still. Have you forgotten about the silver creature? Who do you think sent it?"

Venser stared at Tezzeret.

"And you will neither find your way out nor what you seek, whatever that is," Venser said, "without my help. And there are more clunkers in this cavern, and the light gets brighter. I can shut it off."

"Can you?" Koth said.

"Yes."

"Do that and I'll follow you to the Testicles of Nyrad," Koth said.

Tezzeret closed his eyes. A moment later the light simply shut off. He smiled, showing an array of brown, chipped teeth that were as dull as his arm was luminous. If I had an arm such as that I would want a pair of teeth to match, Venser thought. But the blinding light was off, and Venser could not help but smile himself.

"A simple request," Tezzeret said. "Do I have your trust now?"

"Absolutely not," Venser said.

But Koth was so happy he jumped in the air. Venser watched him. "But apparently we are traveling with you," Venser said.

"You will not regret it. What I have to show you is nothing short of miraculous."

"I have a question," Elspeth said. "What was the purpose of this light?"

Venser turned to Tezzeret. He wanted to know the answer to that as well. The metal-armed human smiled again and looked all around him at the wreckage of the Phyrexians.

"Phyrexians are about experimentation," he said. "If you like this then you will love the lower levels." And with that he began walking. The chrome Phyrexians followed, grunting as they passed the companions.

As they walked, the heavy darkness of that deep place settled in around them. From the echoes of their footfalls Venser began to suspect there was a wall ahead of them. And after some time the chrome Phyrexians began to glow slightly. Koth's body glowed as well. The far wall became apparent.

Venser could have teleported there in a second, but he wanted to save his strength. Plus, Tezzeret had not seen him use his special ability. It was a secret. It might prove useful sometime soon to have that secret.

As they walked, Venser heard water dripping somewhere far off. The echoed whine of corroded metal against metal set his teeth on edge. Aside from that, they heard only the clank of the Phyrexians ahead of them.

Some time later the metal floor bulged and they were moving up a low embankment.

Venser's head had been pounding since the bright light. The twitch was upon him, and starting to pull his chin to the right. He already had to squeeze both of his hands together to keep them from shaking. Why not, he thought. He reached into the special inner pocket against his chest and drew out the flat bottle. The tiny cork popped out easily. Venser brought the bottle to his chapped lips and drank a sip of the tingly, spicy fluid that he knew would someday bear him away. It burned his nose before he swallowed, but he liked the burn. Not much left, he noticed. No matter. This was it, the last bottle. If he had a bottle for each time he'd said that.

He slipped the bottle back into his pocket, feeling the mana course through the recesses of his brain, looping and jetting the tight curves.

"What is it?" A voice said.

Tezzeret must have been walking next to him for some time. Venser wondered if perhaps this one could teleport. Have to keep an eye on that. But the fluid he had just drunk made him too sharp to fluster, and he looked casually over at Tezzeret.

"Nothing. A trifle."

"A trifle?" Tezzeret said. "I see."

The two walked side by side for a time, Venser's head racing.

"See, to me that smells like extract of anneuropsis." Venser said nothing.

"I've been known to keep a bottle handy. It kills weaker metal dancers you know. Strictly people who needed killing. People of no real consequence."

Venser looked at the human walking next to him. With the anneuropsis in his brain and the other's glowing shoulder, Tezzeret appeared a dark visage indeed.

"Where did you steal so much etherium?" Venser said.

"I did not steal, artificer," Tezzeret said with more vehemence than Venser had expected. A sore point, Venser thought. Keep that for later.

Tezzeret flexed his arm, the light from it reflecting in his eyes. "This was hard won. This is my will to power, an escape from weakness and filth."

"So, what would a powerful being like you be doing here with the scourge?" Venser said.

Tezzeret straightened a bit. "I have masters like any man. I have jobs to do."

Venser nodded. That was the truest thing the human had said that day.

"What are you here to accomplish?"

"I will not tell you that, of course."

Venser said nothing.

"You are all very tired," Tezzeret said. "We will stop to sleep as soon as we gain entry into the interways. They will take us over and down deep under the furnace layer, where the contagion is having less luck incorporating the mindset of its denizens."

After more walking they arrived at a wall of metal. It was absolutely smooth and extended up into darkness. The chrome Phyrexians stood dripping fluids as Tezzeret stepped forward and made a sweeping motion with his arm. An opening appeared in the wall. The metal Tezzeret had removed hung against the wall, quivering in the glowing blue light from the chrome Phyrexians. They went first, jerking and convulsing through the hole and into the darkness on the other side.

Later, after a series of other doors leading into passages that smelled more or less like rotted meat, Tezzeret raised his hand, halting the group. They were in a room small enough that Venser could actually see the far and the near wall at the same time. It had the advantage of being low, with a ceiling that extended only a few feet above his helmet. Some of the Phyrexians had to crouch. One with the long legs of a spider was dragged by its comrades.

Tezzeret turned to the party. "This is the place for sleep."

Venser fell onto the metal floor and was asleep in moments. He dreamed of night watches. He dreamed that it was his watch. Suddenly Phyrexians made of flesh appeared all around him with blood dripping from their eyes. One seized him around the neck.

He woke to Elspeth shaking him.

"What is it?"

"Our guide is gone," she said.

Venser sat up. "Where?" He looked around in the pale glow from Koth, who sat leaning against the far wall, watching him with an unreadable expression. Venser stood. "Did anyone see him leave?"

Nobody said anything.

"We're really in it now," Koth said. "You've got us down here and now even I don't have a clue where we are."

Like he ever knew where we were, Venser thought. But he did not speak.

The tone in the vulshok's voice became more caustic. "None of this would have happened if I had been leading," Koth said.

"No," Venser said. "We would be squatting in some hole on the surface watching people die as they fought the invasion."

"It's an honest way to die," Koth said.

"I don't know if there is such a thing."

Koth was silent a moment. "Well, I don't trust this one leading us, do you, Elspeth?" Koth turned to Elspeth, who was standing a bit back, gazing into her sword's shiny surface. At the mention of her name she sheathed her sword.

"I do not . . ." she said, "trust friends of mine enemy."

Venser heard the creak of metal and raised his hand to stop their speaking. Moments later there was another creak and a grind and the blue Phyrexians appeared in a line in the darkness. Some of the Phyrexians glanced at one another and then back at Venser. Tezzeret was behind them.

"We have done a bit of scouting," Tezzeret said.

"Or trap planning," Koth muttered under his breath.

If Tezzeret heard Koth, he did not acknowledge it. He simply turned and began walking. The blue Phyrexians split and actually bowed as the companions passed between them. Koth and Elspeth looked at each other in confusion.

They walked through another hidden door, and through one that was already opened. As they moved, Venser became suddenly sure that they were moving downward, though never did they descend stair or tunnel. Then they came to a strange wall where Tezzeret stopped and waited for the group to catch up. Venser stood staring at the wall, if one could call it a wall. He realized it was more of a body.

Fibers were stretched over protrusions and bound off to other bulges, creating a taut sweep that reminded Venser strongly of muscles without the covering of skin. This impression was heightened

ROBERT B. WINTERMUTE

when he touched it and the wall trembled. Tezzeret turned and glanced at him.

"Did you touch it?"

"I did," Venser said.

"It feels interesting, yes?"

"What is it?"

"A Phyrexian."

Venser nodded. The others were approaching out of the darkness, but he had something to ask. "You mentioned before that the taint was having trouble with the furnace layer, whatever that is."

"That is true," Tezzeret said, brushing an unseen something off his sleeve.

"What did you mean?"

Tezzeret looked at him strangely, with a small smile curling the corner of his mouth. "They are gaining sentience somehow, all of these creatures, you know. It is a limited sentience, but they are beginning to understand that they exist and can die. This seems to have changed some. We . . . I am unsure if this change is only found in the denizens of that red layer, or if there has somehow been another dissident mindset injected into the group. It is hard to say."

"How are you privy to this kind of information?"

"I am involved with certain aspects of the centrality of this infestation."

"So why are you helping us?" Venser said. "Couldn't you drop yourself into tremendous trouble?"

"That is one possibility."

Venser glanced at the wall. An eye as large as his whole body was opened next to him. The cornea and slit iris were black, and it was staring directly at him. Venser took a step back. "Where is the mouth?" he said after a moment.

"We will be moving through it shortly," Tezzeret said.

Elspeth and Koth followed the chrome Phyrexians. Tezzeret pulled his breastplate down, revealing his bare chest. A glass vial hung by a thick lanyard around his neck.

"Would you take it?" Tezzeret asked Venser. "I cannot touch it."

"But it is touching your . . ." Elspeth started.

"My flesh, I know," Tezzeret said, as Venser looped the lanyard over Tezzeret's head. "But my etherium arm."

Venser held the vial up to the glow of the Phyrexians. "What is it?"

Tezzeret took the vial and opened it with his flesh arm. He dabbed his finger on it and touched his forehead with the dab. Then he handed it to Venser, who did the same. Elspeth followed. Koth smelled it and curled his nose.

"This smells like rot," he said.

"It is the essence of Phyrexian," Tezzeret said. "But do not worry. It is not infectious in itself."

Koth dabbed his forehead.

"Well, now we can take the next step," he tapped the muscles of the wall and suddenly a line creased and the muscle spread to reveal innards: long, twisting metal pipes and strange, small organs hanging like wet fruit. Out of the hanging muck on the wall, a mouth yawned wide. The many teeth crowded in the mouth were chipped and filed down, from the passing of many bodies, Venser assumed. He could see that they had been sharp enough once though.

"Why is the mouth under the skin?" Koth said.

Tezzeret stepped back and smiled his small smile. "Well then, who will be first?"

No one moved.

"Only making a joke," Tezzeret said. He stepped forward to the mouth, which was pulled open so wide that what passed for lips were stretched and cracked.

Tezzeret looked back over his shoulder. "Whatever you do, keep your arms in."

He stepped into the mouth, which closed around him and swallowed. Then it opened again. Venser looked at Elspeth, who shook her head. Venser stepped forward and after a pause, stepped into the mouth. It closed on him and he felt the muscles tighten around him. In the next second he was thrown forward and began to slide.

Venser slid, keeping his hands as close to his sides as possible. He was sometimes upside down and sometimes feetfirst. But always he moved, and fast. The throat banked and shot farther and farther down. The word *stomach* occurred to Venser and he remembered dissecting the dead Phyrexians he had managed to lay his hands on in Dominaria. They were precious because most, if not all, were burned after the great invasion. But he had found one and bought it off the black market. It had been preserved in a foul liquid, but that did not matter. He had worked on the specimen for days. When he had reached the stomach, he had been so shocked that he had dropped the charm he'd had to use to move through the half-flesh body and its metallic viscera.

The stomach itself had teeth. Somehow it too had teeth as if it might someday get out of its body prison and go hunting for itself.

Venser considered such thoughts as he shot through the intestinal track.

And then he popped out and went sliding along a floor. Tezzeret was standing, scooping slime off his cheeks. Venser tried to stand, but slid. He was covered with slime. He turned and looked at the puckered hole they came out of. As he watched, Elspeth and Koth popped out. He helped Elspeth to her feet. She stood, wet and dripping with oil and metallic viscera. Venser watched as Tezzeret walked to a part of the flesh wall. As before, he touched it and flesh yawned to reveal the wet innards, which in turn spread to reveal a mouth yawning wide. Tezzeret stepped into that other mouth, and the process repeated.

They shot down that throat, and then another. Each time Venser felt sicker and sicker. Every time the mouth seemed to get larger and larger. Once, he forgot to keep his arms at his sides. His wrist caught on something metal, and he yanked to a stop in the tube. He pulled and pulled, with the throat muscles closing in on him and squeezing, and finally his wrist came free. After what seemed like a hundred more throats and rooms, Venser stood and then sat back down on the metal floor.

"You are tired?" Tezzeret said.

"Yes," Venser said.

"That is good, because we have come to what I wanted to show you."

Venser looked around at the room. It appeared to be like all the others.

Tezzeret must have seen the doubt on Venser's face. He walked to the far side of the small room and put both his hands on the wall. Two eyes as large as his head appeared and blinked. Tezzeret spoke a series of words. A seam appeared in the muscle and then in the conduit guts beneath. The seam slid open to reveal a room on the other side.

CHAPTER 9

Elspeth popped out behind as Venser tried to get a good look into the room. He could not see anything save brightness. The room was well lit. Not bright like the room where they had met Tezzeret, but well lit. Koth popped out of the previous opening. Venser turned to Tezzeret. The metal-armed human was drumming the fingers of his metal arm on a wall. Waiting for his Phyrexians before entering the room, Venser guessed. Elspeth appeared beside Venser, still dripping and stinking. Her eyes wrenched down into suspicious slits. Her weapon was unsheathed in her white-knuckled fist.

"What is it?" Venser said.

Elspeth did not speak at first. Venser had to repeat his question.

"The smell," she said. "Do you smell it?"

Venser did not want to tell her how much she stunk, how much they all stunk. "I think we all have a particular stench about us now," he said.

Elspeth's head jerked curtly, her eyes never leaving the doorway into the well-lit room. "Not that smell. The other."

Venser took a good breath. His nose was usually fairly good, but he could not smell anything except the slight stink of rotting meat. He looked at Elspeth and shook his head. Her hands were shaking. Her lips were drawn into a tight, white line.

"I smell their tools," she said. "Their blades."

When the last of his chrome Phyrexians were dripping in the corner, Tezzeret stepped to the bright room. "This way," he said.

Venser suddenly became very aware of the Phyrexians behind him. He stopped walking. They stopped walking. Would it be possible to turn and leave, or would they not let him go?

Tezzeret was the first to enter the room. Venser followed, then Elspeth, and last Koth, cursing as he tried to ladle the slime off his arms.

Inside the room, lights were focused on haphazardly arranged tables. There were cages of metal ribs lining the room. Phyrexians of various sizes were moving between the tables.

They were chrome-type Phyrexians like Tezzeret's. One had a chrome breast and head, and unnaturally high shoulders. Each of its huge claws was festooned with blades and needles, and both of these claws were inside the cracked-open chest of a human lying on a table. The human was jerking and writhing as the surgeon pulled parts out and looked at them. A huge Phyrexian with a tiny skeletal head and patched-together arms as long as its legs held the humans down. As they watched in stunned silence, the blade-handed surgeon took out the human's liver and dropped it unceremoniously on the table with a *splat.* Another Phyrexian, with strips of discolored iron wrapped around its body, poked at the liver with its sharpened finger lances, while its other hand, shaped like scissors, snipped bits off.

Elspeth screamed.

It was a sound like none Venser had ever heard—a primal, rage-filled shriek. She ran forward and cut the first Phyrexian she met, leaving two hewn parts to slip to the floor. Her sword moved like a blur and two more Phyrexians fell. Elspeth's face was a grim mask and her blows were harder and less focused than normal—more wild hacking than anything else. She bellowed in a language Venser couldn't identify as she butchered every Phyrexian in the room.

Some of the chrome Phyrexians behind Venser twitched, but Tezzeret looked at them once and they stopped moving.

When Elspeth reached the nearest surgery, the large orderly Phyrexian raised his meaty arms from the patient and had them severed neatly at the forearm. The next flurried cut came fast on the heels of the first, and the Phyrexian's body slid apart in seven places. The surgeon pulled a syringed claw from the muck in the human's body but was cut down in place, still with one claw in the human's thorax. The Phyrexian doctor that had sliced up the liver looked from Elspeth to its chrome brethren at the doorway. The frantic knight's sword swept down with an overhead strike that split its head and shoulders from each other.

Elspeth turned and hacked at the side of the next Phyrexians, tears running down her cheeks, and strings of drool coming from the corners of her mouth.

There were perhaps twelve Phyrexians when they entered, but they were soon dispatched. Elspeth sunk to the bloody, reeking floor, still holding her sword, and began to cry in wrenching sobs. Venser walked toward her. Unexpectedly, the person who had been on the table sat up. With no orderly, the human tried to stand, its stomach open. It fell on the floor. As Venser passed the cages, the beings within began to moan. They reached from between the rib bars and clutched at his clothes with weak, white fingers.

Venser reached Elspeth and bent down and put his hand on her shoulder. She jerked away. He glanced at her sword before speaking.

"What is this place?" Venser said. He walked back toward Tezzeret. Koth was standing off to the side with eyes wider than Venser had ever seen. The Vulshok's vents at his ribs were wide and red. Venser could almost see the steam coming out of his ears.

"This is an experimentation chamber," Tezzeret said calmly, looking at his fingernails. Clearly the sight of all the carnage did not bother him in the least.

"And this does not affect you?" Venser said.

"This arm," Tezzeret said. "Is made of etherium, as you know. I had to collect it painstakingly over time, from bodies sometimes. I found them anywhere I could. I pulled them dead out of gutters after bar fights."

Venser stared at the beast standing before him.

"From filth and weak flesh," Tezzeret said, "to this purity." He flexed his shining arm. "Phyrexians strive to have flesh, to be of flesh. They fail to see that flesh is what makes them dirty and weak."

Elspeth's sobs continued. Suddenly Venser was very tired and he felt as though he might be sick. Sick from what Tezzeret was telling him. Sick from what he had just seen. No, there was a level he would not pass. You could offer him four etherium limbs and he would not take them if the metal had to be extracted from bodies. "Why did you bring us here?" Venser said wearily.

Tezzeret raised his etherium arm and pointed. "For her."

Tezzeret's finger pointed to a cage on the far wall. Koth was closer, and he moved toward it, stepping carefully over the lumped bodies of the Phyrexians. It took Venser longer to reach the cage. Koth was already peering in by the time he arrived. Venser looked at the cage's lock, which resembled nothing so much as a human heart of pocked metal. The artificer whispered words of power, moving mana to his hands from his head, and put his fingers into the lock's suddenly pliable metal. He moved his fingers around until the door swung open. Inside, a figure lay on the floor. Koth walked into the cage. Soon he came out with the female human. She was dressed in leather, an unusual material to use for clothes on Mirrodin, Venser knew. Must be from another plane, he thought. Aside from that she appeared a normal human, except she needed a good scrubbing.

Venser turned to Tezzeret.

"Do you notice anything about her?" Tezzeret said.

Elspeth stopped crying. She looked at the human.

"No," Venser said. "A human from somewhere else."

"Is she from somewhere else?"

"She's not Mirran," Koth said.

"No?" Tezzeret said.

"She's got no metal," Koth said, looking at the human with barely hidden disgust.

"Ahhh," Tezzeret said.

"What is your name?" Venser said.

The woman did not answer. She opened her mouth but no sound came out.

"Do you have a name?" Koth said.

"Leave her be," Elspeth said thickly. "Can you not see she is shocked to be free? Unlock the other cages. Let the wretches out."

"I would not do that," Tezzeret said.

"Why?" Venser said.

"They are mostly Phyrexian. They would strive to kill you. This place studies Phyrexian transformation."

"But she has no phyresis," Koth said, staring at the woman. "Not any that I can see."

Tezzeret nodded. His little smile reappeared. "Exactly."

Venser looked back at the woman. All flesh and no infection, he thought. As he watched, she teetered and then sat down abruptly.

Tezzeret gestured to the woman. "They have been looking at this fleshling for some time. She does not succumb to the oil that spreads their infection. That is why she is not mangled. They pour the oil on her. They inject it under her skin. Still she defies infection. Nobody knows why."

"She is the key to fighting their vile spread," Elspeth said.

Tezzeret nodded.

"And how are you not infected?" Koth said.

"I have certain other advantages," Tezzeret said. "Leading among these is my facility with etherium."

"But look at her," Koth said. "What I see here is something made to slow us down. This thing cannot travel with us."

The fleshling's head was weaving.

"Is that blood?" Elspeth said.

They rushed over to where the fleshling was sitting. Blood was running freely around her on the metal floor. Venser walked around her looking for the wound. The leather rags she was wearing were sodden on her back. He carefully pulled the leather back, and saw a yawning incision barely held together with crude, pocked staples.

"I am inclined to agree with Koth," Venser said. "How can we move quickly with such a wounded one?"

"Have you seen nothing, artificer?" Tezzeret challenged. "This one is not infected by the plague. That does not interest you?"

"What interests me is your motivation for giving us this being."

Tezzeret smiled. "And what a gift."

Elspeth hurried around behind the fleshling. Just then a shiver went through the muscle of the room's flesh wall. At the far end of the room a single eye snapped open and the golden iris dilated as it took in the light. It pivoted in its socket and focused on the companions. Then it snapped shut.

"This is not as good as it could be," Tezzeret said. He pointed to the door they had come in. Four of his chrome Phyrexians scrabbled to the doorway and hunched, waiting.

A part of the wall near the eye shook and a crease appeared, and then two tight lips opened to reveal sharp teeth. The teeth parted and the mouth, as large as Venser, opened wide. A shriek came from the mouth.

Tezzeret turned to Venser. "You have moments. That is an alarm."

Venser looked back at the fleshling. He knew Elspeth wanted to take the thing, and that Koth did not. His would be the deciding vote.

"She is the only being I have ever met to have this natural ability," Tezzeret said.

Venser knew he was right. Imagine the planes and people they could help if they could find out *why* she was immune. Imagine if Karn was infected and the fleshling could somehow bring him back to himself.

"She travels with us," Venser said.

Koth stomped his foot.

"She has a long cut on her back," Elspeth said, looking up from the fleshing. "I will try to at least close it so we can move."

"Flee, I would say," Tezzeret said. "Separately these creatures can be dealt with. But in the numbers that are rushing toward our location currently . . ." Tezzeret shrugged.

From the cavern on the other side of the doorway a muffled clatter broke the silence, then another.

Koth ran to the doorway. Venser went with him. Elspeth kneeled behind the fleshling, chanting. A milky glow radiated around the two. The chrome Phyrexians looked nervously over their shoulders at Elspeth, of all people. They fear the white warrior, Venser thought. But he had no time to ponder the question. A deep growling roar sounded on the other side of the doorway.

"I'll go have a quick look," Venser said. He closed his eyes. The mana moved into his ears and through his eye sockets and nose, sucking into his brain. In his mind's eye he saw the location in the cavern. He imagined he was hopping and when the *pop* occurred in his ears he opened his eyes. He was standing in a far corner of the cavern. He could see the glowing doorway and the blue Phyrexians staring out. He looked to the right before snapping back into the doorway.

"There are many," he said. "And some huge Phyrexian I have not seen before, with a white shell for a head and shoulders. It has many arms and a steely body and legs."

Tezzeret was behind him. "A bastion," he said.

"Is that good or bad?" Koth said.

"It is not good," Tezzeret said. "It was once white. Those are the worst ones: the ones that were crusaders. If there is one, then there will be more."

"I cannot close this wound," Elspeth yelled from the other side of the room. The shriek continued, just high enough to stick in Venser's ears and keep him from thinking quickly. "Keep trying," he said. "Can we jump down the screaming mouth?" he said to Tezzeret.

"I don't know," Tezzeret said. "You might be able to. Watch the teeth."

"You are leaving?"

"Oh, yes," Tezzeret said. "I wanted only to give you this creature."

More clatters sounded from the room. They sounded closer than before.

"But why?"

"I have my reasons for wanting the Phyrexian invasion to have to work hard. To perhaps encounter significant resistance."

"Have you seen Karn?" Venser said. "We need to find Karn."

Tezzeret nodded slowly, apparently thinking about the question Venser had just asked him. "Yes," he said finally. "I have seen the silver golem."

Venser waited. "Where is he?"

"He is in his throne room, of course," Tezzeret said.

"Where?" Venser said.

"Deeper still. At the heart of this metal clockworks." 137

At that moment there was a tremendous rattle in the cavern outside the experimentation room. The Phyrexians at the doorway rushed out, followed by Koth. Venser and Tezzeret were last.

The room outside the doorway was filled with Phyrexians of all shapes and sizes. Three creatures with white porcelain crusts for heads towered over the rest, four arms hanging at their sides. Tezzeret's chrome Phyrexians were already tearing into some of the closest creatures. Koth was glowing red and mucking up to his elbows in the thorax of another beast that, as they watched, fell back, a gaping red hole in its chest.

Venser blinked and appeared on the shoulders of one of the bastions. He pulled mana to him and when it was prickling his fingertips, he spread the back of the creature's porcelain shell and reached in. He was never sure what he was touching, what metal parts, in the Phyrexians, but he dissolved whatever it was. Eventually the creature took a staggered step forward, and then fell limp.

Venser blinked away and back to the doorway before he hit the ground. Tezzeret had not moved.

"Impressive," he said.

"But we cannot fight that army," Venser said. "We need a way out."

Tezzeret sighed, and walked back into the experimentation room. The mouth in the far wall continued screaming. It was all Venser could do to not clap his hands over his ears. Elspeth was still kneeling and chanting, with her hands on the fleshling. The sound of the fray outside the doorway was a loud rumble.

Tezzeret touched the wall, and another mouth opened. The mouth had no teeth. Venser, strangely, found himself feeling uneasy at the prospect of being swallowed by a toothless mouth.

"I'm not altogether sure where this one goes," Tezzeret said. "But in general the ones without teeth go upward. The larger the teeth the deeper the way goes. At least I've found that mostly to be true. Go to the furnace layer. That is over and up. The heat will tell you."

"Thank you," Venser said.

"No," Tezzeret said. "You have helped me more than you know. I would not have helped you otherwise."

A shriek from outside the doorway drew their attention.

"I will not remain around here to meet that," Tezzeret said.

With that, Tezzeret touched the wall and an extremely long-toothed mouth opened wide. He turned and winked at Venser before stepping in. Venser couldn't help but wonder if Tezzeret was at that moment traveling to Karn's throne room. He almost asked if he could accompany him. But the moment passed and Tezzeret was gone. After a couple of seconds the mouth closed.

Elspeth stirred. "I cannot fully heal this wound," she said. "It is too deep. I do not know if something vital was removed. The best I can do is close it so we can travel."

"So she can move?"

"Not by herself. We will have to assist her."

He nodded. "Well, that would be our mouth," he said, pointing at the toothless maw.

Venser walked across the room and looked out at the cavern. More Phyrexians had arrived. Tezzeret's chromes were still fighting hard, but their numbers were halved. As Venser watched, one of them received the huge ball arm from a huge Phyrexian on the top of its head. The head crushed down and the Phyrexian stopped moving and crumpled. Koth was as red as an ember, taking great, heaping handfuls of metal out of a Phyrexian three times his size. The metal went from molten to slag the moment it left the vulshok's hand and fell clanking to the metal floor.

When the Phyrexian fell, Venser yelled and beckoned Koth, who followed. The heat that he gave off as he approached made Venser step back.

"We're going now," Venser said.

"What? With all this fun to be had?" Koth said.

But he followed. Elspeth helped the fleshling to her feet. With her arm over Elspeth's shoulders, the white warrior led her to the mouth Venser had pointed out. The fleshling did not look good to Venser's eyes. She was pale and drawn. Her hair was dirty and infested with something that matted the locks. Bugs, he could not stand bugs—especially the ones that lived on the human body. But Mirrodin would not have bugs. Mirrodin would have something like bugs, but infinitely worse. A small shiver ran down Venser's spine as he stepped up to the toothless mouth, waiting.

Koth noticed the shiver, apparently, and interpreted it as disgust of the mouth. "Don't like the look of this one myself," he said.

Venser glanced at Koth before he understood. "Oh, yes, the etherium-arm creature said the ones without teeth lead upward."

"Don't know if I trust that one."

"I know I do not," Venser said, smiling.

Koth nodded. The walls buckled somehow and a sound even more terrible than the screaming mouth rent the air. A sound like shells crushed under foot.

Or skulls. The whine and snap of metal breaking came from the next room, and then the clank of many feet rushing over metal.

"We go now," Venser said. Just as he spoke the mouth began to close. Koth stepped forward and seized the lips and with some effort wrenched them wider. Elspeth and the fleshling stepped into the mouth.

"This will hurt," Elspeth was telling the fleshling as they disappeared into the maw.

"You go," Koth said, when Venser gestured for the vulshok to go.

"Go ahead."

Just as a bleeding Phyrexian stuck its small head into the doorway leading to the cavern—

Venser jumped headfirst into the oral cavity.

The sensation was different with the toothless mouth. It was tighter and slower. Many times Venser felt his breath would not hold out as the throat carried him upward in the way a snake might move its prey down the length of it. He found he could breathe better if he brought his arm up and held the bend of it over his eyes, creating a small air pocket. It was not comfortable, nobody would ever say that, but at least he did not feel like he was drowning. At one point he stopped. For that terrible time Venser was sure the Phyrexian whose mouth they were in knew a way to force regurgitation. But that did not happen and eventually he started moving again. The turns were few and Venser was glad for that, as they squeezed his body even more. After what seemed like forever, he was spit out and lay panting on the floor. Elspeth and the fleshling were leaning against the wall. But the wall was strange and bending, and neither Elspeth nor the fleshling looked comfortable.

The room was small, almost tiny. If Venser had ever imagined what it would be like to be inside a stomach, that would have been what he imagined. It was roughly circular and soft all over. The hole they had all been spit from opened again and pushed out Koth, who lay panting in the goo that covered them all.

"It's like being born again," the vulshok said, when he had his breath. Venser could not help but chuckle. Elspeth smiled. The fleshling blinked.

Venser touched the wall. Nothing happened. There were no other doors, just the tiny room. It seemed to get smaller after Venser touched the wall. He went to another side and touched the wall again. A mouth opened. A mouth with teeth.

"Try the other wall," Koth said.

Venser did, and a toothless mouth creased into existence.

"How is it there are mouths now when there were round, lidded doorways before?" Elspeth said. "When we started this trip."

Venser shrugged. "I think we are deeper than we were when we started. It seems we travel inside Phyrexians after we pass some point. That would be my guess."

But the mouth that had carried them out opened. From down its gullet, they heard the struggling cries of many Phyrexians.

"They are coming up after us," Koth said.

The next mouth appeared the same as the last they had used, and Elspeth went first. Koth followed and then Venser.

The trip was much the same as before, only longer. The mouth dropped them in a small fleshy room with a doorway into another vast cavern, the walls of which were covered in pipes and tubes.

The temperature was noticeably hotter. A glow emanated from far away across the cavern, and they walked that way. The fleshling walked between Elspeth and Koth, with her arms over both of their shoulders. Venser would not get too near the unwashed human.

They walked until Elspeth called a halt. The glow in the room only lit the lower portions, but upper reaches were dark. It was into that darkness that Elspeth pointed.

"What is that?" Elspeth said.

Venser squinted into the darkness. High up in the shadows a small form moved. It appeared to be flapping, but was very small and far away. As his eyes became accustomed to peering into the darkness, another form flapped itself into focus. Still another small thing was flying lower and the artificer made out its general form. It was very small, about as long as the last digit of his thumb. It had fleshy, beige membranes that it flapped, trailing bits of itself behind. Its body was round and oval shaped.

Next to Venser, Koth stared up at the same form. "It can't be," he said.

"What?" Elspeth said, looking at the vulshok.

"It's impossible."

"Do speak, vulshok," Venser said, staring at Koth.

"That," Koth said, "is a blinkmoth, unless I am a fool."

"I will not comment on whether or not you are a fool," Venser said, looking back at the strangely saggy little form flying at the edge of the darkness above. He had heard of the elusive creatures, of course, from Karn. He even happened to know that the drink he took to stave off the palsy contained some of their potent distillate.

They were farmed to near extinction long ago, Karn had told him. He had also told him how sad it made him that the only native life-form on Mirrodin had been used so poorly. But looking upon the rare creatures all he could think was how ugly they looked.

"How many are there up there?" Elspeth said.

Koth was beyond words, staring up at the moths.

"Four perhaps," Venser said. "Should we see? I think we can risk some light." Without waiting for an answer, Venser snapped a blue wisp into existence. He flung it up. The strand traveled up and up, and up some more. The ceiling was exceedingly high, but soon the wisp stopped. Venser concentrated on it and it began to glow brightly.

"Blazing ore!" Koth hissed.

The entire upper portion of the cavern was thick with the moths, flapping and bumping into one another. Koth looked around the room.

"Was this a farm?" he said. "I did not know they existed underground. They are never found in numbers such as this anymore. Never." He looked back to the blinkmoths.

"They are the only natives to this place and were made by Karn's hand," Venser said. "Therefore, they are living manifestations of his creative essence."

"Well, they do not fill me with awe," Elspeth said. She squinted at the other side of the huge space. "They are rather runty little things, in fact." She kept squinting.

"They were supposed to be gone long ago," Koth said. "Gone to vedalken harvest."

"They live, all right," Elspeth said. "It is us I worry about. I see shapes advancing on us."

Koth's eyes instantly turned to where Elspeth was staring. Many dark shapes no larger than the blinkmoths were loping toward them across the wide room.

ROBERT B. WINTERMUTE

"They are Phyrexians," Venser said, still watching the blinkmoths. The more he watched them the more he wanted some of his potion. The more his chin began to shake.

"How do you know?" It was Koth who spoke.

"I can feel their metal feet vibrating the floor."

The others were quiet as they felt for the vibrations. The floor trembled under their feet.

"There are very many of them," Koth said.

They were advancing from all sides, and in large numbers. The Phyrexians surged toward the island of blue light cast by Venser's wisps.

Koth was already as red as an ember. He cracked his neck and stretched his arms behind his back in preparation. Elspeth's sword was out. She held it loosely at her side watching the howling hoard advance on them. Venser was fighting hard to resist the desire rising in his chest to pull the tiny cork out of his flask and drain the few drops remaining down his throat. The three Planeswalkers had formed a triangle around the fleshling, who stood watching the advancing Phyrexians with a look of resolute detachment.

"How many are their numbers?" Koth asked.

"Plenty for all," Elspeth hissed.

Then they were close, the Phyrexians, and Elspeth raised her sword and began running. She crashed into the first line of the enemy at a brisk trot— cutting three down with strikes too fast to see. The Phyrexians in her area trampled one another as they struggled to form a dense clump around her while she moved about her grim work, chopping each and every one of them down. In the red-tinged light, with Venser's blue wisps overhead, her sword blazed a bright white, and many of the Phyrexians fell back, screaming.

Koth had grown long columns of loosely held rock out of his wrists which he used as whips. With these he was able to crush lines upon lines of Phyrexians.

But still more of the gabbling, dripping abominations pushed forward.

Venser fell back to stand next to the fleshling. When seven Phyrexians got too near, Venser blew out a cloud that caused their metal substructures to turn to the consistency of warm lead, and they fell apart into messes of writhing skin and sinew.

The pile of Phyrexian dead around Elspeth got higher and higher until Venser could not easily see the white warrior. But he could see her bright blade, and unless he was very wrong, it was not swinging as fast as it had been. Koth too was letting his rock whips rest on the floor as he huffed.

Venser watched a force of perhaps twenty Phyrexians break away from the group awaiting Elspeth's attention and circle around to him and the fleshling. Venser looked past them. He noticed that the darker, far away parts of the huge room were without Phyrexians. He could teleport them there and stage attacks from that relative safety.

With the fleshling's hand in his, Venser closed his eyes. He mouthed the words of power and felt the pull, then pop that told him he had left. But something was wrong. When he opened his eyes, both he and the fleshling were floating momentarily high above the ground, in the flock of blinkmoths. Far below, Venser saw Elspeth and Koth battling the Phyrexians in two pools of light. A blinkmoth flew into his check and another against his leg. The fleshling was convulsing and jerking on the end of his arm and Venser himself felt a tremendous fluttering all through his body like he would vomit three hundred times at once.

Then they began to fall.

He closed his eyes, but found it difficult to find the words that had come so easily before they appeared in the group of blinkmoths. As they picked up speed Venser set his mind on the floor, imaging what it looked like.

They were plummeting downward.

Venser took a last breath. He had only moments, he knew. He forced the words out of his mouth and with a sudden *pop* they appeared sprawled and dizzy on the hot floor.

Off to their side, Elspeth's sword flashed and the Phyrexians screamed in the rosy light. Koth's rock whips boomed on the floor. But Venser knew he could not stand. He lay with all of his limbs trembling so that he could not trust them to move where he told them. His heels banged on the floor rhythmically and his neck was jerking his chin back and forth. A blinkmoth crawled down his neck.

The fleshling was standing above him in the dimness, her eyes glowing a slight blue as she looked down at the artificer. Even in his state, Venser knew that the fleshling's eyes were not glowing before he had teleported with her. His trembling continued until suddenly it stopped. He lay gasping and exhausted until the last tremors finally left. It had never been that bad, even after that first teleport that caused the whole mess.

Still the fleshling stared down at Venser with her blue eyes glowing impassively. "I can feel the blinkmoths inside me," the fleshling said. "I can feel them flying in my skull."

There was a certain calmness to her that put Venser in mind of Karn. She was telling him there were moths in her skull as calmly as she might that she preferred cloudy skies to sunny.

"I feel . . . different," she said.

"I also do," Venser said. It was true. He felt much worse than he had before. Plus, his right hand would not totally stop shaking. Even if he concentrated, it would not stop. Concentration always stopped it in the past.

Venser managed to push himself up off the floor. His head spun and he sat down hard. Still the fleshling watched him. "Help me up," Venser said.

She bent and took Venser's hand and helped him to his feet. He felt awful, like his brain was still half-materialized in his head. He knew that each teleport made his condition worse, but it was a drastic worsening of symptoms.

"You are wounded?" the fleshling said, cocking her head to the side as she waited for the answer.

"Yes. Are you?"

"No," the fleshling said. "I feel every pore in my body."

"And what do they feel like?"

"They feel like they are dancing."

Unfortunately, Venser realized exactly what she was describing. He had felt it after he started drinking his potion. He had not felt that strong a reaction since he started depending on it.

Something screamed and they turned in time to see Elspeth hammer her blade down on the head of a large Phyrexian. As they watched, the creature's two parts peeled apart to the chest, and it fell back, kicking. It was the last of the beasts, and Elspeth put her sword tip down and leaned heavily on it, gasping for air, her shoulders stooped.

Koth was lying on his back with his arms and legs splayed, huffing. The bodies of the fallen enemy lay in stinking piles all around. The far-away glowing side of the cavern flickered.

Venser stood unsteadily.

"We must walk," the fleshling said. "We must." She turned and began walking toward the glow. Elspeth nodded and began stumbling after the fleshling, unbelievably dragging her sword behind her. Venser followed. Koth stood up from the floor and ambled after them.

They slept where they fell, each taking turns on watch. When Venser woke he went looking for water pools left from the dripping of the upper levels. He found some shallow pools to drink from. The others woke and Venser showed them the pools and then they all walked on, clanking steps on the metal floor.

Venser's hand was still shaking, and he kept it out of sight from the others. The fleshling's eyes were still glowing, and Elspeth and Koth, Venser noticed, did not move too close to her.

Time meant nothing in the dim cave, lit from the far-off glow. Without a sun or a moon it was impossible to keep track of time. But to Venser it seemed as though they walked for hours, perhaps days. Twice they stopped their march to sleep. Once they found a small pool rippling with warm, stagnant water which they fell on. The fleshling could not bend her back well. She drank out of Venser's helmet. As she was drinking Venser could not help but imagine what water out of his filthy helmet would taste like. He would never find out, that much he could guarantee.

By what might have been day four—or perhaps only ten hours—the glow had become noticeably brighter. They could easily see the expressions on one another's faces. Koth's face was smiling. There was the particular stench of sulfur in the air.

"I know raw metal when I smell it," Koth said.

He was correct. They kept walking and found a river of rosy material flowing along a wall of pipes, which were sweating in the sweltering heat. The flow of molten material ran along the side of the wall for a time before making an abrupt turn left and passing through a hole.

"Do we follow the river?" Elspeth whispered to Venser.

"What did you say?" Koth said.

"I only inquired if he thinks we should follow the lava."

"That is not lava," Koth said. "That's ore."

"Why is it here?" Venser said.

Koth shrugged and looked back at the river, smiling. After watching it move for a time the vulshok turned back.

"I will lead us from here," he said, casually. "I will bring us up to the surface."

"What is the furnace layer?" Venser said.

"Must be the area under the Red Lacunae, under Kuldotha."

"Can you take us there?" Venser said.

"Maybe. If I choose."

"Well, choose to take us there," Venser said. "Lead the way. That Tezzeret said the Phyrexians in the furnace layer are different than the others."

Koth grunted and looked away, the smile still large on his face.

They walked on with Koth strutting at the lead. For a time they followed as close to the river as the heat would allow. But when it disappeared they walked along the wall. Koth looked closely at the wall as they walked. Every so often he would stop and touch the wall. Venser, on the other hand, kept his eyes on the floor. In the light from the molten ore he could clearly see a part of the wall coming up with many scuffs, some of them deep, leading to a section of the wall.

When they reached that part of the wall, Koth continued walking. Venser stopped. He carefully shrugged out from under the fleshling's arm. He went to the part of the wall that the scuffs seemed to move to. The pipes were mostly rigid there. But after some feeling around and moving some of the more pliable conduit aside, he must have touched a trigger because a doorway opened. Koth walked back.

"Excellent," he said. But he did not look pleased, Venser thought. The smile he had earlier turned into a frown. "I would have found that eventually."

They gazed into the doorway. Inside was a largish, brightly lit room with no apparent ceiling. On the other side of the room were a set of metal stairs against the wall. They extended up and up until they were lost to the light in the room.

But the room was not empty. Two large Phyrexians were standing against the wall. The dark iron of their long claws was corroded, as were the plates on their backs and shoulders. But their helmets were off and thrown to the side. Their tiny white heads, which looked like stitched-together bone, bobbed as they made guttural sounds to each other. Other pieces of their metal coverings were cast aside in the swelter of the room. Venser could see their chests and necks, where tattered metal met chafed flesh.

They watched a writhing lump of something on the floor. It seemed a partially phyrexianized elf. It still had the ears of an elf, but plates of bloody, patinated copper pushed out of its skin and wove in with a darker metal to make a musclelike sheathing. The transformation was far from complete, and the elf convulsed on the floor, staring with eyes as black as oil at the dark ceiling.

But the Phyrexians seemed utterly absorbed in the process. As Venser watched, one of them lumbered up and pulled one of its claws across the elf's bare neck.

The blood that flowed out was mostly black. By the time the Phyrexian had moved back to its original spot, more of the copper and dark metal sheathing had wound itself up the elf's arm and to the slice, covering it.

Venser felt a shiver of disgust move up his spine at the sight of the elf's flesh turning to metal. But anger replaced that feeling. The fleshling shifted her weight to his shoulder as Elspeth detached herself. She stepped into the room and drew her sword quietly from its sheath. The Phyrexians did not notice her at first, and by the time they did Elspeth had gained the middle ground and was upon them. Venser had seen her many times use her sword ability to strike from every angle at once. Elspeth took exactly two swipes with the glittering blade. The first separated the Phyrexian's neck and arm from its body and sent it caterwauling away, and the second was a downward strike that split the other's head and shoulder from the neck offering up a virtual geyser of black, frothy material from the cut.

The smell of the material that poured from the thrashing Phyrexians' bodies put Venser in mind of the acrid reek of a crushed bug.

Elspeth moved to the elf next. The wretch watched her approach with black ichor clouding her eyes. With a flick of her wrist, the white warrior knocked the elf's head away.

Elspeth stared down at the headless body jerking around on the floor. She turned and went back to the fleshling, who put her arm over Elspeth's shoulder.

CHAPTER
10

Venser made it light when he blew out a puff of wispy shapes that danced and flickered blue before their eyes. In the ghostly light Koth looked at Elspeth and Venser and spat. They were reeking and sweating, with a crazed look about them.

The smell was nearly unbearable. Koth began breathing through his mouth.

The artificer stood and followed Koth, and the blue will-o'-the-wisp followed him. "It is getting warmer. We are on the right path, obviously."

Small metal creatures, no larger than humming-birds, suddenly appeared around a fallen Phyrexian, eating the meat on it. There were hundreds of them. Venser squatted down to watch them work. There was no sign of phyresis in these small metal creatures. They were neither sharp looking, nor possessing of tense, asymmetrical bodies laden with teeth.

153

"So this is how cleanup occurs on Mirrodin," Venser said. "I knew the ecosystem had to clean itself somehow."

"Breakdown artifacts," Koth said. "They devour whatever is small enough to be devoured. I have never seen so many in one place."

"Are these found on the surface?"

"Fewer and fewer lately."

"I wonder why?" Venser said. "And why they have no taint of phyresis on them?"

Koth shrugged. He looked closely at Venser. The artificer did not look well. His helmet was off and his sunken cheeks and pale skin unnerved Koth, who thought flesh looked disgusting enough even in the best case.

Elspeth stepped up next to Koth. She gazed around the huge room. So large was the room that Venser's wisp did not even reach to its edges—shadows formed and disappeared among the intestinelike pipe work that made up the walls.

"You think that the little silver demon went this way?" Koth said.

"I have to think not," Venser said.

"It could be following us," Elspeth ventured. "It did before."

"You mean Tezzeret sent it to keep an eye on us before," Koth said.

"That could be," Venser said.

"Do you smell that?" Koth said. He held his nose between two thick fingers.

They looked down at the Phyrexians. "All that smell cannot be coming from them," Elspeth said.

"They must have been guarding something to have been standing there," Venser said.

"Don't think I want to find it," Koth said.

But Venser was already at the wall, pushing and probing as he looked for the door that must surely be there. After a *snap*, a small door opened and a terrible stink wafted out.

"Why would we go into that place?" Koth said.

"Because they were guarding it," Elspeth said, drawing her blade and glancing at the dead Phyrexians.

"Exactly," Venser said. "And this may be the correct way, for all we know."

Holding their noses, they entered.

Unaccountably, they were walking through festering meat that reached a depth of mid-calf in places. The smell was absolutely disgusting, and Venser found himself breathing tiny breaths through his mouth. All words came out with a nasal numbness. Still Venser felt the gore pushing up from his stomach.

"This way," he said, pointing into the blackness ahead. Far ahead Elspeth thought she could see a faint light. When she pointed it out to Venser, he snapped his fingers and the blue wisps disappeared. There was a glow in the huge room—a white glow that sifted up through the darkness of the far corner.

"We should advance on this carefully," Venser whispered. "There might be many rooms like this one, and if we start a fight now, it might raise an alarm or follow us all the way to the furnace level."

"The alarm we must assume has already been raised," Elspeth said.

"Maybe," Venser said.

Koth stopped walking, or at least Venser could not hear his footfalls squishing next to him anymore.

"Wait." Koth said. "How far are we going?"

"We are finding Karn."

"And let me guess, you know where he sits?"

"I have ideas where my friend and ally would choose to sit, yes."

"And where would that be?" Koth said from directly behind, his voice raised a decibel.

"I think Karn would favor a room deep in the middle of his creation. A nerve center position," Venser said.

"I am needed on the surface," Koth said. "That's where I'm going. My people need me. My people are fighting a foe . . ."

Elspeth and Venser stopped walking.

"How will you leave?" Venser said.

"How will you ascend?" Elspeth said.

Koth was silent for a moment. "I will jump."

Venser put up his hand. "Quiet," he said. "We are nearing the glow."

But Koth was not quiet. "You know, you are not the leader of this group. I am. I organized this expedition. I talked Lady Elspeth here into coming. I did all of that. I direct this little nightmare."

Venser shook his head in the darkness. "This is larger than you and yours," he said. "This could concern more planes than a few. We must contain the spread."

"That is all fine and good," Koth said. "But don't try to yank my culpers. You are here for Karn. I don't think you care a bit for this plane. You made some pledge to this golem and you mean to keep that promise."

When Venser said nothing, Koth continued. "I've never met an artificer with a sense of duty, but there are wonders under all suns, we vulshok say. Why not be honest and tell us both that you are here for personal gain?"

"Why would you think that," Venser challenged, "when you brought me here?"

Elspeth was quiet. Venser could not be sure if she was on the edge of gagging in the fester, or if Koth's words had struck a chord and she was reevaluating his motivations. But he could not ask her at that moment, for they neared the lighted area.

At that side of the room the piles of meat were quite old, and the breakdown artifacts covered them from top to bottom. Their iridescent backs rippled and clicked in the dim light as the party neared. But the small machines were not what they looked at. A single glow orb hung in the air. Behind the orb, set back in the overgrown walls of conduit and ridges, like the spinal run of some unfamiliar creature, stood a round doorway. There was no handle that Venser could see. A long table stood in front of the doorway, mired halfway up its legs in the sloppy fester. On the table stood many dented metal bowls of differing sizes. A large bowl sat at the end of the others. It was of a very dark metal. As Venser watched, tiny motes of yellow, like fireflies, spun around its edges in seemingly perpetual orbit.

"Darksteel," Koth hissed beside him.

Venser squinted at the bowl. Darksteel, yes. He knew of it from his studies in metallurgy. A virtually indestructible metal found only on Mirrodin. Extremely difficult to work and very rare and expensive to buy. The bowl had something in it. From where he was crouched, Venser could not see what it was. The smaller bowls contained other, bloody things.

The sound of movement from behind made them freeze. Out of the corner of his eye Venser watched as a small form moved around a mound of meat. It walked with its head cast downward, but its jagged profile was unmistakable. The rows of crooked teeth filling a thin jaw completed the picture. It had eyes—glittering black things, four of them, but they were very small and appeared to not be of much use, as it passed within an arm's reach before moving toward the table. Once at the table the small Phyrexian placed what was in its hand in the first bowl. It was muttering something as it did so, in a tongue that made Elspeth's lip curl.

The first bowl turned a deeper purple and the creature scooped the fist-sized object into the next bowl, muttering again. The next bowl became suddenly bright silver. The little creature picked up the heart. Carefully the Phyrexian raised its right hand and out of its first finger a long, thin blade slid. The cut that the small creature made was thin and deep. The blood came from the heart and the Phyrexian held it over the third bowl. When the blood hit the bowl it sizzled and popped. The blade disappeared as quickly as it had appeared, and the creature took the heart in both its hands. It hinged the two sides open and closed at the cut line, like a mouth in a bloody little pantomime. That went on until the Phyrexian, apparently satisfied, dropped the heart unceremoniously in the second to last bowl.

Koth glanced at Elspeth, and then back to the strange creature. Venser watched as the Phyrexian opened another one of its fingers and sprayed a fluid into the second to last bowl. It let the cut heart sit in the fluid for a long time. Long enough that Venser found his eyelids falling. Then, with sudden and blinding speed it seized the heart and, as though the thing were struggling, it stuffed it into the darksteel bowl.

A moment later the Phyrexian turned and walked back out to the meat piles to find another heart. When the Phyrexian was gone the artificer crept from behind his heap of meat and to the round door. It did not open. He pushed on the door's soft sides and waved his hand before it, but still it did not open. The darksteel bowl was behind him. Venser tried not to gaze in, but he saw what was inside it anyway—many other hearts all sliced.

When he turned back to the door, the small Phyrexian was there. It stood very still, with its long, black face cocked at an angle like a bird eyeing something shiny. Venser also stood absolutely still. He tried to breathe mana into himself, but found, to his horror, that he did not have what he needed for a jump. The jump he had made with the fleshling had all but drained him to the last. To make matters worse, his heart was beating fast in his chest. Then it was beating faster still. The small Phyrexian jerked its head completely sideways so the hole in the side of its head that served as an ear was aimed at Venser's chest. It was with a certain concern that Venser noticed that the creature's hand was tapping out the beat of his speeding heart on its emaciated metal thigh. The artificer's heart was practically hammering on his chest.

Venser turned to run, and the Phyrexian raised its hand. The artificer stopped in his tracks. He closed his eyes and felt the grip of the creature's mana on his heart, which raced and skipped along in his chest. He had one chance. He reached out with the mana he had left, and formed a link with the beast. For one horrid moment he saw into the thing's mind—a murky place of blood and constant screaming and hunger and no light. Venser turned that part of his brain down. Then he began to drop the mental walls he kept constantly around his mind to protect from telepathic attack. If he did it correctly, the link he had with the creature's mind would allow the mana directed against him to move through and back to the sender, as if in a circuit. Sometimes it even worked. Once, when attacked by a mind-mage trying to steal one of his creations, Venser had tried to form the link and pass the thief's attack back to him, only to suffer a minor stroke when the attacker blocked his own mind.

So, if the sender threw up its own wall fast enough, then the full charge turned around and came thundering back.

Venser dropped his last mind barricade, and a moment later the Phyrexian stood upright and began jerking wildly. Venser made his hold tighter and tighter, until the thing sunk to its knobby knees in the stench and began to shriek.

The sound was so loud Venser almost lost his concentration. It echoed off the walls and down the cavernous room. Venser tightened his mind, and then tightened it again. A moment later the Phyrexian had black fluid running from its eyes and the holes of its ears pitched forward and did not rise again.

But the scream had not gone unanswered. From the far side of the room Venser heard a cry and the tromping of many feet running. He was almost too fatigued to move, but move he did. Koth and Elspeth were already at the door by the time he arrived. Koth punched the lidded doorway, to no effect.

"Stand away," Elspeth said. She drew her sword and thrust it deep into the rubbery flesh and drew downward, pulling a neat cut from top to bottom. Fluid spurted out and the cut yawned wide.

"You first," Elspeth said, stepping back for Koth.

The vulshok gazed uncertainly into the gash. Then he stepped through and his leg disappeared suddenly. The choking call was echoed behind them and Venser jumped through the gash. He felt himself carried along a tube in the dark, winding and turning and then tumbling downward, and suddenly stopping.

"Do these foes travel in this manner all the time," Elspeth said, picking herself off the ground. Cut hearts were strewn everywhere at the base of the eye, which irised closed behind them. Venser's foot slipped on one of the organs as he tried to stand.

Koth was already away from the hole. The room was as large as the last, and just as dark, but Koth was glowing all over his body. He turned. "Look at this," he said.

Venser walked over to where the vulshok was squatting. The glow emanating from the front of his body cut a rosy swath through the darkness. In the light, large chunks of rock cast severe shadows.

"Are those rocks?" Venser said.

Koth nodded. "These are rocks. I was a Planeswalker before I saw my first rock. "They are not known on Mirrodin."

"How are they here, in this deep place?" Elspeth said.

Koth shook his head.

Venser approached one of the rocks. It was really more of a boulder. It stood taller than Venser, and if he was to trust the jagged edges, then it was blasted or torn out of a mountain in some way.

"This is stanite," Venser said.

"What does that mean?" Koth said.

"It is a common rock, found on many planes."

"Very strong," Elspeth said.

"I can't think what the enemy needs this for."

Venser looked closely at the rock. "How long have you been away from Mirrodin?"

"About a season," Koth said.

"And the Phyrexians were here when you left?"

"Well, they weren't on the surface, I'll tell you that," Koth said, pushing his knuckles into the palm of his hand.

Venser looked back to the rock. "That is interesting."

"Why?" Elspeth said.

"Only that these rocks have been here for years," Venser said.

"How do you know?"

Venser put out his finger and pulled it across the top of one of the boulders. His finger left a deep trail on it. "Dust," Venser said.

"I do not think the Phyrexians pulled these here," Elspeth said.

But Koth was not paying attention to the boulders anymore. His eyes were back on the portal, which remained open. "Why have they not come after us?" he said.

Venser turned. "It could be that there are many splits in the tubing, and they don't know which one we took."

"Why did we take this one?"

"I have no idea," Venser admitted. "I had hoped you would be able to tell us."

"These openings and tubes are not Mirrodin technology."

CHAPTER
11

They moved between the boulders until they found a set of badly corroded stairs. The stairs went up and up, swaying and creaking as the four climbed them. Venser walked up them first as a test. If he fell or encountered anything unforeseen, he could teleport back down, or he could have counted on being able to do that before his trip with the fleshling. He abruptly wondered if he would ever teleport dependably again. But he did not encounter anything except stairs that did not stop.

Eventually he walked back down and they all started to walk up the open stairs. They climbed so high that they left the light below. Soon they could see the entire larger cavern, and then more caverns beneath them, all glowing in the pulsing light from the rivers of molten metal.

The stairs were wide, but not quite wide enough for Elspeth and the fleshling to walk abreast. Koth walked two steps below and made sure that the flesh-ling did not teeter backward.

Venser stayed ahead, with his blue wisps lighting the way before them. Twice they heard a tremendous roar vibrate the wall that the stairs were affixed to. The second time the walls and the steps vibrated and Venser thought for one tight second that they would all tumble. But the tremor passed quickly, and they encountered no true opposition, save the stairs themselves.

The air was so hot that Venser's throat tightened every time he took a breath. The air had taken on a particular smoky taste. Koth on the steps below breathed deeply and exhaled loudly.

"Ore," he said. "Lots of ore."

The stairs ended abruptly at a landing. A platform of hot metal. Venser could feel the heat through his boots. A doorway with a metal door, not an eye, not a mouth, no metal-and-flesh conduit, stood at the top of the landing. It was clad and shining. Venser tugged one of his mana tethers and felt the cool tingle as the power emptied into his cranium. He sniffed and whispered his spell of wrought, but the door remained solid and unmoving. Cursing under his breath Venser spoke other words, and even traced a sigil that sat glowing on the door. Then he seized the air in front of the door and twisted. The sweat popped out on his forehead as he turned the air. He clenched his teeth and kept turning. Eventually he was able to reach into the metal of the door and scooped the lock out. The door swung open.

The cavern on the other side of the door was filled with a red glow. It was a large room, Venser could tell—he could see no walls. He stepped into the room, followed by the others.

A movement drew his eye too late, and a huge Phyrexian moved into his field of view from the right. It was large and skeletal in appearance, and glowing. What looked like bone, however, proved to be glowing metal, and its thin arms trailed behind it as it stumbled along. The heat emanating from it made Venser's cheek tingle. The Phyrexian stopped and turned to them, examining them with its small head. Venser fell back and readied himself. But the Phyrexian turned away and continued walking. Soon it was gone, lost to the glow and fire.

Venser turned to look at the others.

"What was that?" Koth said.

And then Venser remembered that Tezzeret had mentioned that the Phyrexians in the furnace layer were different.

"The Phyrexians here are different," Venser said. "The metal-armed one told me that."

Koth shook his head, watching the form of the glowing skeleton move away.

"What is happening here in this place?" Elspeth said.

"I think those are forges," Koth said, not able to keep the amazement out of his voice. The vista showed massive buildinglike structures dotting the cavern. The buildings contained the cherry glow of ore, and there were rivers of ore connecting one building to the next. Each building had a veinlike tube attached to its top. Each tube extended upward into darkness.

Forms moved back and forth between the buildings, carrying globs of molten metal. Some of them were large, insectlike forms, picking their way over the rough, slag-littered ground with precise legs. But huge creatures with two legs and arms moved among the buildings as well. They dragged the motionless forms of other Phyrexians behind them toward the ore pools.

"Where is our destination in this place?" Elspeth said.

"I do not know," Venser said. The terrain was dotted with piles of slag. The glow of molten metal lit the distance, and insectlike Phyrexians moved in silhouette in front of it.

They started to walk. The way was more difficult than the steps, if that was possible. There were no trails, as the Phyrexians seemed to be large enough to mince between the slag piles and canals of ore. But twice Venser almost fell, tripping on hardened slag obscured on the shadowy ground.

Slowly they made their way to one of the buildings. As they got closer, it was clear to them all that it was no ordinary building . . . more of a Phyrexian on its stomach with a large open maw of teeth. One of the vein canals attached to its head. The bright white glow of molten metal shone from its mouth.

"The ore is coming in through that cord attached to its head," Koth said, shaking his head.

And it was. They could see the molten ore through breaks in the tube.

"But what is it doing?" Venser yelled above the blowing of the Phyrexian furnace.

"It is melting down Phyrexians for reuse."

The voice that had spoken was deep. They turned to see an elephantine humanoid standing on its rear legs, with an immense club slung casually over its shoulder. As they watched, six more forms appeared out of the flickering shadow: three humans, an elf, and a lionlike being walking on two legs. Each was armed, but none had their weapons up and at the ready.

"This is where the metal of the beasts are melted," the elephantine said. "It is a shameful place, but not a dangerous one."

"Have you ever watched sausage being made?" one of the humans offered.

Nobody said anything, and the elephantine human-oid glanced back at the human who had spoken.

"Well, it's not something you forget seeing," the human said. "It's disgusting. Like this."

They eat sausage on Mirrodin? Venser thought. He turned to look at his group. Koth was eyeing the strangers warily. Venser turned back. The humans were vulshok, he could tell by their spiky, metal hair. Why isn't Koth greeting them? Venser wondered.

"Where does your way take you?" the elephantine said.

"That is our own business," Koth said.

The elephantine one squinted to see Koth, who stood back a bit. "Ah, yes, a vulshok," he said.

"Loxodon," Koth said. "Why are you here?"

"We are looking for friends to resist what is happening on the surface," the loxodon said, scratching its trunk with its club. "Are you friends?"

"We are not enemies," Elspeth said. "And this one I have is wounded. She needs to lie down."

"Our assignment is to bring friends," the loxodon repeated.

"I am Venser and this is Lady Elspeth and Koth," Venser said. The loxodon's eyes stayed on the fleshling for a moment before looking back at Venser. "We are friends."

"Maalan they call me," the loxodon said, curling his trunk. "Follow me, friend."

They walked between the Phyrexians that were attached to the ground, receiving the molten ore of 167 reprocessed Phyrexians. The heat was overwhelming. Soon they were all drenched in sweat. Venser's head was pounding.

"Do you have water?" Venser asked the loxodon.

"Yes," Maalan said. "For friends."

"We already said we were friends," Koth said.

The loxodon took a canteen from a lanyard over his shoulder. Venser, Elspeth, and Koth took turns with it. Koth gulped more of the iron tasting water than the others, Venser noticed.

Maalan led them between the ore reprocessors. Many times large, wasplike creatures larger than themselves stopped to regard them. The creatures seemed to move ore from one processor to the other with willowy scoops sprouting from their thoraxes. The wasp Phyrexians seemed to look through the group. At one point the loxodon shooed a group that was blocking their path.

"Why don't they attack?" Koth said.

The loxodon regarded him coolly. "As near as we can tell, they do not regard us as a threat, son of Kamath."

Koth shrugged. "Every other Phyrexian does."

"That is true," Maalan said, and walked ahead.

The room seemed larger than any they had been in yet. It went on and on. All along what must have been the edge, Venser could see more of the wasp Phyrexians and other, stranger forms moving. The ore streamed down along the veins into the tops of the reprocessors.

"Where are the new Phyrexians created from this ore?" Venser said.

"That does not happen here," the loxodon said. "And not in that way."

"How does it happen?"

"I do not know that, friend. If I knew that I would tell you, I promise you that."

Venser watched Maalan walk next to him. What he really wanted to know was how the loxodon knew Koth's father's name. He wanted to know why Koth said nothing when the loxodon addressed him with his father's name.

Venser fell back from the group. When the others were some steps ahead, he put his hand under his armor and took out his vial. He held it up to the glow. His heart jumped into his throat when he saw how little was left. Less than a finger in height of the precious fluid glowed in the bottom of the bottle. He carefully removed the cork and took a tiny sip, feeling the energy impart itself into the contours of his mouth and make its way to his brain—causing it to glow, or so he always thought.

He looked at how much of the fluid remained before putting it back into the special pocket he had stitched in the cloth under his armor. There were other times he'd drained a bottle. But that was before he had depended on the distillation so much. And those times were bad. If he ran out down there, in that place, there would be great problems for him. And after his teleport with the fleshling, even his potion did not put his head right. He knew the day would come, but he had doubted it would be so soon. The teleport into the flock of blinkmoths must have exacerbated something. It had made him worse, just as it seems to have affected the fleshling in another way altogether.

He had run out of his potion other times. Once he had been unable to leave his bed for two days. Another time had found him at the mercy of psimortifiers, in their "exploration chambers." He had prevailed in each circumstance, but only through luck.

And all for what? Venser thought as he patted the bottle where it lay under his armor. For a fluid that really did nothing for him? It actually did less than nothing even before the teleport. It gave him a mana boost at first, and then depleted him later. Venser suspected that it depleted him more than it boosted. The boost was slight, and did not last for very long. But it felt like a large boost. It felt good.

He remembered the day he had started to need the potion on a daily basis. He and another artificer had traveled far afield in Dominaria looking for Phyrexian artifacts. There were still many battlefields where the forces of the scourge and Dominaria had clashed, but Venser had long since learned that such battlefields did not yield what he searched for.

Sure, one could find fragments and severed parts, but what Venser looked for was fully intact Phyrexians or the ships and vehicles they traveled in. He'd even found largely intact pieces once or twice, but he'd never seen anything like what he saw that fateful day.

He had been deep in the most remote wastes on a multi-day expedition. On the last day, the younger artificer he'd been traveling with had found a strange pile of black stones. At least they had felt like stones. They were hard and of the deepest color. Afus, the junior artificer, had found them piled perfectly into the shape of a tiny pyramid.

Against his better judgment, Venser had taken them, taken them all. He had known it was not wise to come into contact with objects of power that were unidentified. And they were powerful. Venser had felt the mana seething in them. They were worth coin anyhow. That was how he had rationalized taking them. They were worth gold.

And then he had made the worst mistake of all. He had teleported with them. Afus was traveling overland, but that was not how Venser chose to travel. He had learned early after developing his ability to teleport that it was not wise to travel with anything powerful that you did not want to become in some way enmeshed with. Inevitably whatever you traveled with ended up part of you after the mana put you and it back together. The black stones immediately affected him, causing the palsy. It was incurable and fatal. Afus, even though he had never teleported with the stones, had died shortly after finding them. His body had lain for a day in his studio before Venser had gotten up the courage to open him up and take a look inside. What he'd found still haunted his deepest nightmares: The young artificer's organs and lungs had become shriveled and transparent, as if they were ceasing to be.

Venser had no doubt that his organs would end up looking the same way. He just had not thought it would begin while he was on Mirrodin. The blink-moths had somehow accelerated the effect.

He had later figured out that the substance was in all likelihood some of the material residue left when Yawgmoth had been vaporized after the explosion that ended the Phyrexian invasion on Dominaria.

"You coming?" Koth said.

Venser blinked out of his ruminations. He had fallen far back from the rest of the group.

"Yes," Venser said, and started walking faster.

Koth walked ahead.

"Koth," Venser said. "Why did Maalan address you as 'son of Kamath'?"

The vulshok slowed his step. "Because my sire is Kamath."

"Yes, but how did he know?"

"I am known here."

Venser remembered the expression the loxodon had on his face when he addressed Koth. He was known all right, but not honored. For some reason Venser remembered Koth's mother. Koth's people could not have understood when he disappeared. They could not have known that he had left to find help for Mirrodin. To them, Venser thought, they would have seen a coward's motive.

They walked in silence. Eventually the wall of the cavern became apparent. The crew leading them trailed ahead in a ragged line that made its way to a particular part of the wall. As they neared it, Venser could see where someone had cut a jagged hole out in the metal wall with concentrated fire. It was through that hole that they walked, ducking their heads slightly.

Behind the wall were gridworks and supports, but no Phyrexian conduit guts. A ladder extended upward, and they climbed.

Many times they found other cutout doors leading to other hot, metal rooms connected with ladders. Venser lost count as to how many. But eventually they came to a smaller room that smelled of roasted meat, singed fat, and unwashed humans. Coal fires burned near ragged shelters scattered here and there. Some shelters were made of the thorax shells of large Phyrexians. Others were metallic skins stretched over a framework of the other parts of a Phyrexian. As they approached, every occupant of the small camp came out to stare as Venser, Koth, Elspeth, and the fleshling passed.

Venser heard whispers and some hisses as Koth passed. Eventually the loxodon stopped in front of a shelter made of only the rounded pieces of Phyrexians' belly armor that was raised off the ground slightly. An elf stuck his head out of the round hole in the side of the structure, and turned his milky white eye to them.

"Ah, yes," said Ezuri. "I recall these machine lovers. Wherever did you find them?"

The loxodon spoke up. "They were in furnace room minor wandering around."

Ezuri nodded slowly. To Venser it looked as though the elf had added a little weight onto his frame. The creases around his eyes were also not quite as deep as he remembered.

"You have prospered, Ezuri," Venser said.

The elf turned and looked him up and down. "You have not, artificer," he said. "I take it you have not found the one you seek. What was his name, Kurt, Kam?"

"Karn."

"Karn, just so," Ezuri said. In a moment the elf hopped out of the hole of his structure and stood before them in a robe of shimmering material that draped to his ankles.

"We have not found the golem, no," Venser said. He opened his mouth to tell the elf about Tezzeret telling them where Karn can be found, and to tell him about the fleshling, but something in the way Ezuri was staring at him made Venser close his mouth.

Ezuri's eyes moved over the rest of the companions, until it stopped on the fleshling leaning on Elspeth's shoulder.

"You are new. Who are you?"

The fleshling said nothing

"Speak up," Ezuri said.

"Melira," the fleshling said softly.

Melira? Venser thought.

"The disgusting flesh of an outlander?" Ezuri said. "Yet you have the mark of a Greenshank sylvok to my eyes."

Venser said nothing. Nothing at all.

Ezuri's eye did not leave the fleshling.

"Are you still prevailing against the forces of Phyrexia?" Elspeth said.

That made Ezuri's eye move off the fleshling and rest on Elspeth. "Why, hello, white lady."

"So, you have vanquished the Phyrexians from the surface?" Elspeth said, repeating her original question, which she could tell was a sore spot for the elf.

"We are making headway," Ezuri said casually.

Venser stepped forward before any more words could be spoken on the subject. "Ezuri," he said. "Could we stay here for a time, until we have rested?"

Ezuri glanced at Koth before curling his lip. The vulshok pretended not to notice. "All enemies of Phyrexia are welcome here," Ezuri said. "But I warn you that you may be asked to help our efforts."

"Thank you, Ezuri," Venser said.

The elf nodded. "Leaving will be your trick. But you are welcome to stay."

"Leaving will be our trick," Elspeth said.

Ezuri's eye drifted back to the fleshling before he turned and climbed back into his shelter.

The loxodon led them to another part of the settlement. He stopped at a small shelter—nothing more than a Phyrexian crusher's back panel leaned against the metal wall.

"This was a friend's place," the loxodon said. "Gone to shadow now. He had to be put away."

Elspeth wasted no time leading the fleshling into the shelter, and helping her lie down on her stomach.

"Water is found over there," the loxodon said,

gesturing to an indentation in the metal where water dripped. "The latrines are over there."

Venser walked over to the water pool and took a long drink. He filled up his canteen, aware that all of the eyes of the small settlement were on him. Three children appeared at the water pool. They watched Venser from a safe distance, but eventually came closer. He smiled at them and they trailed him as he walked back to the shelter. He noticed that some of the children had dark stains blotching their metal parts. Some even had the stain on their skin parts. One girl who walked with the other children behind Venser, giggling as she copied his walk with long loping steps, had more than a dark stain on her arm. Her stain had worn away skin, and appeared to be spreading up her arm.

The children followed him all the way back to the camp. Koth stood to shoo them away, but Venser frowned. "Leave them be," he said.

Koth glared at the children before sitting down next to Venser. The little girl stuck her tongue out at Koth, and then the children began to run after one another.

"You see the dark patches," Venser said.

"Phyresis," Koth said.

"Many show the sign," Venser said.

"Yes," Koth said. "It'll take them all."

Venser suddenly understood the loxodon's cryptic words from earlier when he described the occupants of their current shelter as "gone to shadow."

From inside, Venser heard Elspeth chanting. He stood and went into the shelter, which was open on two sides. He placed his full canteen next to Elspeth and then returned to sit next to Koth.

The children, having seen where Venser went, skirted around and poked their heads into the other entrance of the shelter. They stood and watched 175

Elspeth chant. After a time, all the children ran away but the girl with the large blotch on her arm. She inched closer and closer until she was sitting at the head of the fleshling.

Venser could not see what was happening in the shelter, but he heard Elspeth stop chanting. There was talking in the shelter.

"Why are you shunned here by these people," Venser said.

Koth said nothing at first. "For caring about Mirrodin," he said. "I disappeared, and my own tribe spoke against me. Their words echoed. Now my name draws harsh words."

"And you think you can gain their trust back by leading them against the Phyrexians?"

Koth nodded. "I know I can."

Venser heard the little girl's voice rise, as though she were telling a story.

"If I can show them that I am still a vulshok," Koth continued. "A Mirran that did not leave his mother and family to the nim and Phyrexians."

Venser forced away the images of Koth's mother in her hut. The terrible way her body jerked, controlled like a puppet by a Phyrexian. "There are other ways, you know," Venser said. "To show that you are not a coward."

The vulshok's eyes flashed at the word coward. "What would an artificer know about it?" Koth said, suddenly defensive.

"Nothing," Venser said.

They sat staring at each other. Suddenly the little girl in the shelter screamed.

CHAPTER
12

Venser was up and to the entrance of the shelter in an instant. He met the girl as she virtually exploded out of the right side of the lean-to. One of the largest smiles Venser had ever seen was spread across her face. She stopped and held up her arms. The dark blotches were gone. The place where the phyresis had corrupted her flesh was nothing more than a pink patch.

Venser shook his head.

From behind, Venser felt Koth shove him out of the way. "What is all this now?"

When the vulshok saw the girl's arms, he drew back as though she were infected worse than before. "What madness is this?"

Venser went into the small shelter. Even in the low light, he could see Elspeth staring down at the flesh-ling, who was lying on her stomach, with her cheek resting on her forearm. Elspeth looked up at him as he entered. The expression on the white warrior's face was impossible for Venser to read: a combination of absolute wonder and shock.

"What just happened?" Venser said.

"I'm still not completely sure," Elspeth whispered, her eyes still on the fleshling. Venser looked too. She was lying with her head turned. Her blue eyes were wet, and she regarded them calmly from the ground.

"She began to glow," Elspeth said.

"Glow?"

"The girl was telling us about her parents dying, and the flesh Mirran began to glow from her eyes."

"The fleshling?" Venser said. He felt strange calling the woman 'the fleshling' but he would have felt stranger calling her Melira, for some reason.

"This human woman," Elspeth said, gesturing to the fleshling, "began to glow from the eyes. Her eyes filled the room with light. It was bright for a time and then the girl screamed."

"And the little girl was healed?"

"The phyresis disappeared. Before our eyes."

"It can't be," Venser said. Nobody had ever been able to cure phyresis, and many great healers had tried, and on many different planes. It was the most virulent contagion known to any plane anywhere, and it was spreading. If it was true, then the fleshling could stop the spread. And suddenly Venser began to understand why Tezzeret had insisted that they take the fleshling with them. He understood Tezzeret calling her 'a gift.'

But he doubted very much that she was able to cure when he gave her to them. And Elspeth had mentioned her eyes glowing. Hadn't her eyes started glowing after their last teleport? Then it struck him. The blinkmoths. It must have been the blinkmoths

ROBERT B. WINTERMUTE

that imparted in her the capacity to share her natural ability with others. He did not know that for sure, but it stood to reason.

Later that day, there was a line outside the small shelter. Every person in the settlement with the beginnings of phyresis was queued and waiting patiently, and some not so patiently. Some of the vulshok were shifting their weight from leg to leg and exhaling in exasperation.

Koth stood next to the tent, keeping a close eye on all that entered, lest one be an agent for the Phyrexians. To his general amazement, many of the people waiting in line smiled at him. Some even congratulated him on his return to Mirrodin. It was quite a different reception than he had gotten even hours before.

"They saw you and Elspeth leading the fleshling into camp," Venser said to Koth's bewildered expression. "You are the reason they are being cured."

Ezuri appeared early the next morning, though he showed no taint of phyresis. He stood in front of the shelter smiling beatifically, as though the cure was facilitated by him and him alone.

Venser stayed near the entrance of the shelter. He had quickly come to understand that the fleshling's cure had its drawbacks, especially to the fleshling.

It had happened the first time by accident. But every time after took tremendous amounts of concentration on her part. She was recuperating from the injury on her back, and yet spent all her waking hours focusing most of her energies on curing every stranger that walked in the door.

Ezuri had been the first to suggest that they find a way to bottle the fleshling's cure. Venser was sure that the elf wanted a bottle for himself from which

179

he could dispense doses at will. For the right price, of course.

Ezuri could not figure out a way to bottle the cure, and the fleshling, Venser knew, would never have consented even if he had.

"She will heal any who come to her," Venser had said to Ezuri. The elf had not liked it, as Venser knew he wouldn't, but what could he do?

The fleshling healed all who came to her, and ended her days exhausted.

The line's end was in sight when Ezuri walked to where Venser stood, almost knocking over a sylvok who did not move out of his way fast enough.

"Well," Ezuri said. "The new day has turned out to be a good day."

"Yes," Venser agreed.

"Will you stay here with us?"

"No," Venser said. "We will continue our search."

But Ezuri's eyes were not on Venser as he spoke. They had strayed to the darkened entrance of the shelter, and the fleshling within. "And that amazing creature? Will she stay?"

"She will be healed soon, Elspeth tells me. She can decide if she wants to join our search or stay here."

Ezuri looked shocked. "You would take her on this mad quest to find some golem?"

"Yes," Venser said simply. How could he explain to the elf the importance of Karn? Why would he want to?

"It's strange," Venser continued. "But I don't recall telling you he was a golem."

Ezuri smiled. "I have heard the name of Karn the silver golem. Who has not?"

"Almost nobody on Mirrodin knows this name," Venser said. "Have you maybe seen Karn, or heard a rumor about him?"

"I may have heard what one of my scouts reported to me," Ezuri said.

"Yes?"

"They heard a being aligned with the Phyrexians say, 'the golem cannot be trusted.' "

" 'The golem cannot be trusted'?"

"Yes."

"Who said these words?"

"I have no way of knowing that. My scouts were slain shortly thereafter."

"What magic allows you to hear what your scouts hear?"

Ezuri smiled. "That is for me to know."

The golem cannot be trusted, Venser thought. Interesting.

"So," Ezuri said. "It is settled. The flesh being will stay while you go on this fool's errand." The elf turned to walk away.

"Wait," Venser said. "It is settled that the fleshling will decide to stay or come."

"Just so," Ezuri said. "I misspoke."

Venser looked back to the entrance of the shelter. Inside a loxodon sat quietly waiting for the fleshling to wake. As Venser waited, his mind went back to what the elf had said. *The golem cannot be trusted*, he thought. That is good, he decided.

Some days later Ezuri called a settlement meeting. Venser and the others arrived and sat cross-legged on the hard, hot metal floor. At the center stood Ezuri, cleaning the bits out from under his fingernails with the tip of a slim, curved dagger.

The fleshling was sitting next to Elspeth. With Elspeth's ministrations, the flesh of the incision site had grown back together and she was able to sit without pain. But she lacked certain organs, the white warrior had told Venser. Those could not be healed back into place. Venser found himself wondering what the Phyrexians had done with the organs they took out of the fleshling. Then he remembered the room of organs they had encountered on their trip toward the center. The small Phyrexians who had assayed them.

He thought of the carnage, of the pointless butchery, of the mountains of rotting meat and organs. Would he really go back into that?

No, it would be different the next time. If he could get a guide from the settlement, someone who knew the doors and passages, then maybe they could make a more direct route. But would Ezuri allow such a thing? Venser doubted it unless there was some arrangement that benefited him in some way.

He would see soon enough. Ezuri raised his hands and the chattering of the small crowd died away. The elf smiled his widest smile.

"We have here good water, and the news from the front has almost always been good."

There was a general grumble from the crowd.

Venser almost chuckled himself at the joke. Oh, he thought suddenly. He was being serious.

Ezuri's smile widened more. "Yet, we have never received quite so good-a-news as that which limped into camp five days ago. Her name is Melira and many of you have visited her and received her special ministrations. She was brought here by one of our own, Koth, son of Kamath, who has returned to Mirrodin to help us all."

The grumbles from the crowd turned to excited chattering. Ezuri raised his hands, palms down.

"But now our guests have decided to leave us," Ezuri continued.

ROBERT B. WINTERMUTE

Have they, Venser thought. Nobody had discussed leaving with Ezuri.

Elspeth leaned in. "It seems our welcome has worn thin."

But before Venser could respond, Ezuri was again talking, as he seemed almost always to be doing.

"But on the part of the settlement," the elf said, "I would like to extend an invitation to Melira. Please stay with us. We have a good life here, as life is going on Mirrodin at present. You can help others outside the settlement with your gift."

The fleshling looked around, bewildered at all the eyes on her. Venser remembered that she barely slept at night, and when she did she woke up screaming. She and Elspeth spent hours talking in hushed tones. He prepared himself to speak, but Koth stood up first.

"Yes," Koth said. "We hope she stays to help all of Mirrodin. With her, we may yet have hope of driving the infestation away."

The crowd was silent. There were no hisses, but neither were there any excited whispers.

But Ezuri spoke again. "Where do you travel now, companions?"

Koth opened his mouth, but Venser spoke first. "We travel to the center of Mirrodin. To find the one who can perhaps drive the scourge from your home."

A chorus of gasps went around the crowd.

Ezuri shook his head.

"It will be dangerous and deadly," Venser said. "The path, as you know, is hard and fraught with enemies." He glanced at Elspeth, who nodded. "But we have the white warrior to lead our way."

The crowd whispered excitedly.

"Yet still," Venser yelled. "We need a guide who knows the secret ways."

"Will the vulshok travel with you?" a member of the crowd yelled.

Venser turned to Koth, who stood.

"I think we should fight the Phyrexians on the surface," Koth said. "We can drive them away by force."

Many in the crowd clapped at Koth's comment. A vulshok stood and pointed at Koth. "You are welcome here. We need people we can depend on."

Ezuri raised his hands. "I think we all want to know what Melira has decided," Ezuri said.

All eyes turned to the fleshling. She stood stiffly and addressed the crowd. "I will go to the center of Mirrodin."

More whispering, and then Ezuri spoke again. "Unfortunately, we are not planning to attack the surface at present, vulshok. You may either stay with us or travel with your companions."

"I will stay with my people," Koth said, raising his fist high.

A small cheer went up.

Ezuri smiled as he turned to Venser. "And it is our hope that you all do not travel to the deep bowel-ways under our feet. You hold blame for the Phyrexians on the surface right now. Who knows what you may disturb next."

Very nice, Venser thought. A nice bit of deflection. His policy of fighting the enemy on the surface is failing—but it is not his fault, it's ours. This one will go far in positions of leadership.

But Venser did not have time to dwell on Ezuri's machinations. A scream echoed from the right, followed by a chorus of growling cries. Venser turned in time to see a line of very large Phyrexians with clubs for appendages charging into the camp, swinging their pendulous arms and knocking rebels aside as they came. Between and behind them stood line upon line of other Phyrexians, each line larger than the one that preceded it. They were the kind with shiny chrome parts. Tezzeret, Venser thought. They were being attacked by the same kind of Phyrexians that Tezzeret kept around him.

And they were fast. Venser ducked a club before teleporting away. He materialized outside of the lean-to that held the fleshling. Elspeth had her sword out and was preparing to attack, when he snapped out of the thin air. She glanced at him and then back at the hoard of Phyrexians who had not noticed them yet. The rebel camp was in full retreat. As they ran, the Phyrexians knocked them down and trampled over them.

"I see no end of them," Elspeth said.

"The numbers are not in our favor," Venser said. "We must move to better placement."

Elspeth said nothing.

"We must move for the fleshling," Venser said, sensing Elspeth's hesitancy to do anything like retreat.

Koth staggered out of the melee and made his way toward them. A Phyrexian noticed his departure and followed. But Koth turned and lunged forward to take hold of the thing's rib cage and gave a sudden heave just as he heated the creature's metal. The front of the Phyrexian's rib cage came off. Koth took it and beat the thing around the head with it until it fell down and did not get up. Koth spit at it and stomped up to Elspeth. "Time to go, my lady," he said. "You should go now."

"You will really stay?"

"Yes," Koth said. "I have been somewhat welcomed again. I will seize the opportunity."

"Your reunion may be short lived," Venser said. "They are making quick work of your insurgency."

Koth said nothing.

"Ahhh, look what we have here."

They turned to see Ezuri with a small band of rebels.

"Here he is now," Ezuri said. "The one that led the meat puppets to us."

Koth turned to look at Venser. "He did nothing of the sort," Koth said. "His loyalty to Mirrodin . . ."

"Silence, traitor," Ezuri hissed. "I speak of you. You, who led the Phyrexians to us."

"What?" Koth said.

"You are a traitor and a coward," Ezuri said.

Koth turned redder than he was already. "You can call me a traitor, elf. You can call me a killer of innocent men and women. But you may never call me a coward!" Koth leaped at Ezuri, who stepped to the side and hit Koth squarely in the side of the head with the shaft of his bow as he passed. The blow was meant to sting and Koth was up in a moment.

"See," Ezuri said. "He aims to kill me even now."

The other Mirrans in Ezuri's group glared at Koth.

"You are banished from us," Ezuri said. "Let none acknowledge you, for we have a war to fight and no time for those such as you."

The squad of Mirrans turned their backs on Koth. Ezuri sneered before turning his back.

"Come, Koth," Venser said. "Let us be off while the Phyrexians are busy."

Koth looked from the rebels to Venser. His face was a clash of emotions. Venser felt quite bad for him.

"Now is the time," Elspeth said, her eyes on the Phyrexians who were starting to look around from the dead Mirrans they were hunched over.

Koth nodded dumbly.

They walked along the wall until the last sounds of the battle dimmed behind them. Koth said nothing. The fleshling was able to walk by herself with the aid of a staff. Elspeth led. Suddenly she drew her sword and held it forward. A shape stepped out of the pipes along the shadowy wall—a humanoid with a hood over his head and face.

"I will guide you," the shape said. "You said you wanted a guide."

"Your people have all been slaughtered," Elspeth stammered. "Why do you offer this?" It was a good question, Venser thought.

"You will need a guide if you venture to those depths. That is Glissa's domain, and Geth descends from his perch at the Vault very commonly. The creatures there are very fell indeed."

Venser was not familiar with the names, but the form in the shadow spoke with force and honesty. Venser trusted his voice.

"Who are those names?"

"Glissa was an elf. Geth is undead but not a vampire. Now they are leaders of this invasion and exist below the surface. They are holding your golem."

"How do you know all of this?" Venser said. "How do you know of Karn, the silver golem?"

"I was scouting the deepest areas even before the surface invasion."

"Yet the invasion took you all by surprise. Didn't you tell anybody about what you saw?"

"I did."

The implication of that shocked even Venser. "And still your leaders did not act?"

The figure in the shadows said nothing for a moment. "This invasion has given opportunities to certain people. Old leaders died in the onslaught.

Certain other leaders who had formerly been commanders of squads gained position by simply being alive."

"And now where are they?" Elspeth said.

"Leading, of course. Preserving their skin."

"I think we understand each other," Venser said.

"You seem to know much," Elspeth said.

Indeed, Venser thought. He knows more than any they have encountered so far. He knows more than he should. The others could have been lying, of course. It is possible that many others know of this Glissa and Geth holding Karn. Have those others remained mute for reasons of their own? On the other hand, a guide suddenly appears offering to take them to exactly where they want to go. He gives them information they have never heard before, and asks them to follow him into the deepest regions of Mirrodin. Everything about this being standing in the shadows set the hairs on Venser's arm standing.

"Danger," Elspeth was saying, "does not scare us."

Koth, standing back a bit, adjusted his stance.

Venser cut in, "How do you feel about Phyrexia?" It was a strange question, Venser knew. And the shadow sensed the trap immediately. Venser could tell by the care he took in choosing his words.

"I will die stopping this infestation."

"That's not exactly an answer to the question," Venser said. "More a statement of fact." Venser knew he was being nitpicky and small, but he wanted to be certain that they were not being led by a Phyrexian agent or, worse, by one of Ezuri's people.

"Why are you in the dark like that?" Koth said.

The figure stepped forward. Venser could easily see where the blotches had covered his body, and where his skin had been peeling away in the most advanced stage of phyresis he had seen in the settlement so far. But he had obviously received the cure from the fleshling, for the blotches were no longer black, but pinkish. The places where his skin had been peeling had shiny pink scars. Still, he was disturbing to see.

"I will not lie to you," the figure said. "I know what I know because I had an arrangement with Glissa in the depths."

"That was before you were healed by the fleshling?" Venser said.

"Yes," the human said.

"And you know our plan, I am sure?" Venser said. It was a test. If he acted ignorant, then that would tell Venser certain things.

"If I were you I would take Melira to Karn and try to heal him, if he is infected."

"Why would you take us back down if you are now healed?" Elspeth said. "You are free now."

"I have my own debts to repay," the human said.

Venser had already decided to go with the man, but he wanted to know where the human's allegiances lay. It was acceptable if he was a spy for the Phyrexians or Ezuri, as long as Venser knew it. A spy could be very useful, if properly utilized. But the uneasy feeling in Venser's stomach did not leave when the man had stepped out of the shadows. It did not leave even when the man bowed and stepped away to let Elspeth, Koth, and Venser talk.

"He is a spy," Koth said. "I am sure."

"How are you so sure?" Elspeth said. She has no trust in him anymore, Venser thought.

"It is too good," Koth said. "He gives us everything we want."

"I do not think so," Elspeth said.

"You trust him?" Koth said.

"Yes."

"But you are a fool," Koth said. "You trust too easily and see everything as good and bad."

True again, Venser thought.

"But why would he be the spy you say he is?" Elspeth said.

"It is hard to understand another's motivation," Venser said. "They may have his wife or child. They may have promised him certain things as reward for his efforts."

"Or they may have killed his parents," Koth said grimly.

"The point is, we do not know," Venser said.

"But we travel with him anyway? A potential enemy?" Elspeth said.

"He is only an enemy if he thinks we know he is an enemy," Venser said. "If he thinks he has fooled us, then he will inadvertently tell us everything we need to know."

"Assuming he is actually an agent of Phyrexia," Elspeth said.

"True."

"If he is not an agent, then your thinking will lead us to confusion and delay."

"I suppose that is true."

"Really," Koth interjected. "What other choices do we have?"

"Also true. But everything is true if you ponder it the right way."

That night they slept against the wall. The dim light in the room never went out, and when they woke it was to the eerie feeling that they had never rested at all.

The guide did not appear. They began to walk and after a time they found the guide. He was alone and sitting in a dark hollow chewing on something and spitting around his boots.

"Are we ready?" he said, standing. A plain-looking human, Venser thought. He had no sword but carried a strange geared bow, a canteen, and a small pack. His boots were newly made, Venser noticed. New boots could mean all sorts of things, most of them bad.

New boots or not, the guide took them along the wall for a while until they found a hole. It was cut out of the wall and as large as a human man. The guide ducked his head and walked through the darkened hole.

CHAPTER
13

They walked in darkness for a time. A choked call echoed through the vast cavern they were walking in. The guide was sometimes by their side and sometimes nowhere to be found.

"How do we hear the Phyrexian's calls but they do not find us?" Elspeth said.

No one answered.

"It is strange," Venser agreed.

"They do find us, or haven't you noticed?" Koth said.

"I have not seen any other passages or doors," Venser said, changing the subject. "But they must be here. Where is the guide?"

"I have not seen him in . . . ," Elspeth said.

It was hard to judge time and Elspeth let her words hang unfinished.

They walked back to the door they had just come through.

"Do you remember how many hearts were in the room with the small Phyrexian?" Elspeth asked.

"There were thirty-three," Venser said.

"What were they used for?" Koth pressed. He had perked up remarkably, Venser thought, after being cast out by his people again. What a strange being, Venser thought.

"Who is to say?" Venser grunted.

"What if something took them?" Koth proposed.

"Something might have. Maybe that small silver creature that led us for a time," Venser said.

"And now we have another guide," Elspeth said. "Who is also leading us unbidden."

"I too am suspicious," Venser said.

They searched the walls for another door. Covered with metal and flesh, the veinlike tubes that glistened and squished when they parted them to look for a door made Venser feel as if he were searching through the intestines of a huge creature. And he found nothing.

"Why would the silver creature lead us and then disappear?" asked Elspeth. She turned to Venser—dark, sticky oil covered her hands and arms. The more time he spent around the white warrior, the less he felt he knew about her, and the more nervous she made him. The way she shook when she fought Phyrexians put his hairs up. They were the enemy, there was no doubt of that, but that someone could harbor such a complete hatred of anything made him uneasy. What did you have to do to get on Elspeth's list of hated things, and what would you do if you did?

"Have you found something?" Koth said.

Venser turned back to his search. He looked and looked but it was Koth who finally found a small hole behind a bank of articulated columns of shiny metal, which swayed slightly to an unheard rhythm. The columns moved to the side when he pushed on them. The door that lay behind was perhaps the perfect size for a seven-year-old human child. Except its handle was smeared with blood and clots had formed in the drip line that stretched to the floor.

"It stretches," Koth said, reaching down and pulling the edge of the fleshy hole wider. "Even I can fit." The small door was merely a plug. They pulled it off and propped it against the ductwork.

"Do we go down this?" Elspeth said.

"Why not?" Koth demanded.

The guide stepped out of the shadows. Venser had the strong feeling that he had been watching them the whole time. But why would that be?

"We may travel that way," the guide said.

Koth nodded at him and then turned to Elspeth.

"We go this way," Venser said, with more force than he meant.

Elspeth nodded.

Koth looked away.

"Are we ready?" Venser repeated.

"Yes, I am ready," Koth said. "But I do not follow your orders."

"You don't follow my orders," Venser repeated. "Then will you take a *suggestion* and tell fair Elspeth and myself if you are ready to walk through this door and confront what may be there?"

"As I said, I am ready."

"All right, I will go first." Venser went through the door feetfirst. It was not a pleasant sensation pushing through the space, which seemed to close in on you from all sides, as if there was water on the other side. He could hear the echoed reverberations of movement all around him, and he could hear strange modulations of sound. For one moment he thought he heard the deep boom of Karn's voice crying out in rage. But he had never known his old mentor and friend to make sounds like those. They had to have been made by something else.

CHAPTER
14

The door Venser exited was massive—easily as large as seven humans standing feet on heads—and it stank of rotting flesh. Stinking or not, it was tiny in comparison to the space it opened into. They were on a ledge that looked over an absolutely massive cavern of metal. Colossal columns of metallic material stood at its center and long tendrils attached each to the other like rope to a pole. Sometimes many tendrils met at a huge chunk. The chunks were easily as large as rooms.

"What is that?" Venser said, his voice echoing away across the enormous space.

"Don't know," Koth said. "Don't have any idea."

"How large would you say this cavern is?" Venser said.

Elspeth shrugged. "Leagues," she said. "Perhaps larger."

"And yet these columns continue. Look there, that

197

column seems to have grown into the metal of the wall. I wonder if it keeps its shape under the metal? I wonder if the strands do?"

They all looked to the guide, who stood back a bit. He looked back at them.

"The center of Mirrodin is solid," Koth said. "We vulshok know this. It is the heart of our ore. We explore and use our geomancy to delve with sound through the core."

"This does not appear solid," Venser said.

"How can we ever know the truth of this situation?" Elspeth said. "We waste time surmising."

"This place is Phyrexian corruption," Koth said. Clearly disgusted, he turned away from the view.

But Venser did not turn away. "Very strange," he said. "Very strange."

"Where do we go?" Koth said.

"There. This trail before us leads that way . . . to where that strand is melted and its inner tube is exposed," the guide said, pointing.

"We walk *into* one of those strands? I think not," Koth said.

"It is through these that one moves around the core of Mirrodin."

"How do you know?" Elspeth said.

"I know," the guide said, his face expressionless.

"It makes sense," Venser said.

"How does that make sense?"

"Well," Venser said. "Do you see how the top of that column is dark and crumbling? It is clearly dead. Yet below it the metal is greenish and healthy."

Koth nodded slowly, as if he knew what he was about to hear would be as ridiculous as the artificer himself.

"It seems that whatever flows up along that column can't go up any longer. Up is plugged by that dark, dead-looking material. It must go sideways. Sideways is those tendrils. They are of different lengths. What if they are of different ages as well?"

Koth shook his head as he listened.

Venser did not seem to notice. He kept speaking. "What if those tendrils are caused by whatever is traveling up along the column? Perhaps when enough of those tendrils come together and connect with another column, they form a layer. A new layer under the crust."

Koth was narrowing his eyes as he gazed across the vast expanse before them. "A crazy idea, I'll give you that. I don't believe a word of it. And how would you explain that?" Koth pointed.

It took some time for Venser to spot what he was looking at. The vastness of the cavern was all made of metal of one sort or another. There were inclusions of dark ore and marbles of lighter metal. But as his eyes moved over the calico of colors, they stopped on a flash. He looked closer. The flash came from what appeared to be a golden bubble. It clung to the wall near the column half-melted into the metal wall.

"What is that?" Koth said, gloat in his voice.

"I don't know," Venser said. "But we can get to it to find out. If we travel to that tendril and walk through it we should come out near the column, very near that bubble. It appears to be older than the column, which has grown around it, as you can see."

"Yes," Koth said, reluctantly.

Venser stood up straight and looked right to left. "Yes, right."

Venser nodded. Koth looked down at his feet. There were many drips in the vast expanse. Some sounded closer than others. There was also the sound of movement . . . of rusted movement and metal banging into metal. But there were no Phyrexian cries.

The guide was already walking ahead. Elspeth walked along the precipice after the guide. The precipice continued until a small lip appeared and the path they were walking on began to sink as the lip rose. They walked until, had they been on the surface, the suns would have moved significantly in the sky. At that point they were walking in a half tube. A small trickle of water appeared running down the middle of the curved path.

"Where does the water come from?" Elspeth said.

Venser remembered the rain above, and the holes it ran down. At the time he wondered where the holes led. Now he knew. "The surface has holes and the rain runs into them."

Elspeth nodded and wiped her mouth..

"I could have told you *that*," Koth said.

"Noted," Elspeth said.

Koth pulled his cracked lips into a smile. "When do we begin walking down the tendril, artificer?" Koth said.

"Unless I'm wrong," Venser said, "we're on it right now."

The path had become wider as they walked. It was curved and as wide as ten men lying lengthwise. The lips at the edges were as high as Koth's chest. To the right was a solid wall that had a smooth surface of cooled ore. Far ahead their path seemed to disappear into a hole that extended half in the wall.

"We travel through the wall for a short time and come back out again," Venser said. "But we won't see that we are out of the wall, because the tube will be complete. From the point ahead, we will walk about a league. Then we should be at the golden bubble we saw."

Koth stared blankly at Venser, who moved his eyes to Elspeth.

"How will we know when we are near the bubble?" Elspeth asked.

Venser gestured grandly at Koth. "We have a geomancer, who is familiar with alloy and true metals. He will begin to taste the gold in the air."

Koth looked doubtfully at the artificer. "There is no smell in the dark of a tube."

"Of course there is," Venser said. "Let us have light and we'll have a look."

Venser raised his finger, and the glowing blue wisps crept from it and twirled into the air.

"Guess I'll be able to see the gold inclusions in the native metal," Koth grumbled.

They walked the rest of the distance in silence. They stopped where the path came together overhead and peered into the darkness.

"If I were Phyrexian I would lay a trap here," Elspeth said.

Their guide was squatting and staring ahead. He was very still for some time. Then he stood. "There is no Phyrexian there," he said.

Venser sent his wisps into the hole. Soon it was bright within. The tunnel was strangely uncluttered and smooth. Venser leaned close and could see the grow lines on the side of it. The lines reminded him of those he'd seen on shells near the ocean. "I don't know how long it took the tube to grow this distance, but I can't think it happened slowly."

"Why?" Elspeth said.

"Neither the old nor the new sections show any oxidation," Venser said. "But the very old parts, like just here, they show discoloration." The artificer walked a distance farther and pointed. "These happened a good time ago. Without knowing what type of metal this is, I cannot tell how long it takes to oxidize."

They entered the hole. Venser went first and Koth came second. Elspeth drew her sword and its glow cast light enough for all to walk. They walked until the air in the tube became oppressive and close. Venser could feel the heat in the tube collecting around his face. Sweat trailed down his neck and forehead. His sleeves were wet by the time he stopped.

"Koth," he said. "What do you smell?"

"Rust," Koth said. "And metal."

"Do you smell gold?"

"No," he said. "And you know I cannot sniff out metals like a dog, don't you?"

"How does gold smell?" Elspeth said.

"Sweet, sort of," Venser said. "Would you mind melting us an escape, Koth?"

The geomancer scrambled over to where Venser pointed. The roof of the small passage was low and twice already Koth had hit his head.

But he did not straighten as he placed his hands on the warm metal of the tube. Soon it began glowing and then it disappeared from around his hands. The dark void of the vast chamber was visible. Koth moved his hands to another part of the metal. Soon there was a rough opening.

"Not there," Koth said. He moved his hands down and did the same thing. The second hole revealed not the darkness of the cavern, but a bright shine. Koth cleared the edges so the hole was large enough for him to crawl through. The guide stood by the hole and waited as Elspeth and Venser crawled through.

The room they crawled into was large and made out of a golden metal. It shined, and by some power there was light enough to fill the entire room. Cracked orbs floated in the dusty air. At one side of the room was a very large throne of tiny gears and machine works. The walls were covered with crackling images that moved. Blurred moving images of the surface of Mirrodin. Some of the walls were dark. Most were dark. Another panel showed an absolutely vast horde of torn and twisted phyrexianized soldiers with huge metal claws and limbs of snaking metal intertwined with what appeared to be pulsing pink nerve clusters wound into tubes. There were hundreds of them, thousands, all marching across the bleak terrain.

"This must be part of the Panopticon," Venser said. "Destroyed at the green sun's ascent. I read about it."

"What did you just say?" Elspeth said.

"Memnarch, the Father of Machines, the annals on Dominaria say. He had an observation room. This might be where the Father of Machines looked through the eyes of his spies."

They heard a shuffling sound and spun on their heels. Three forms charged out from behind the throne. They were huffing, with black oil dripping in globs from their mouths and eyes. Their mouths were huge and tooth crammed and their eyes were tiny. Their bodies were covered with runes. In places, the runic metal was peeling away to show the duller metal underneath. Their claws were huge and of pocked, greenish metal. And they wasted not a moment in their attack. They scrambled forward, swinging their claws.

Koth jumped to evade the first troll's savage cross swing. He stepped in and seized the arm, which went red and fell from the Phyrexian's body. It all happened quickly, but not quickly enough. The other troll swung at Koth from the side and connected with his chest, sending him flailing, his chest cut wide. The blood came but Venser did not have time to watch before the foe was on him. A second later he blinked away and appeared behind the Phyrexians. Venser rushed forward with the words of power playing on his lips. He took a breath, and with his hands glowing he plunged them up to the elbow through the metal back of the nearest Phyrexian. The mechanized insides of the creature felt odd and alien to his fingers. But he found the metallic organs and conduits and twisted. He took a strong handful and yanked. The creature threw its arms up and then convulsed. It realized what was happening and turned, pulling Venser around like a rag doll. But before the creature could fully turn, it went limp and tumbled into its compatriot, knocking it over. Elspeth was there with her sword to end the Phyrexian's frenzied stirrings. All three lay dead a moment later.

"Those were trolls," Koth said, pushing his toe into one of the still bodies.

"Where did they come from?" Venser said.

"They were lying down behind the throne," Koth said. "I think they wait until prey becomes available."

Elspeth had a queer look on her face. Venser looked for a wound, a tear in her white robe, but saw nothing. "What is it?" he said.

"I may have discovered something," Elspeth said.

"Yes?"

"That beast did not notice me until I moved."

"What do you mean?" Koth said.

"I froze next to you both, and that Phyrexian did not attack me initially. When I drew my weapon I was attacked."

Venser thought back. He had not noticed that behavior. On Dominaria during the wars against the Phyrexians, they had moved quickly no matter what you did. But that was a different place. Mirrodin's Phyrexians were different than those he'd observed in other places. That was to be expected, because phyresis incorporated differently. Certain groups took to infection very easily, he suspected. It's the ones that didn't take to infection that they needed to find.

"So, you didn't move and the buggies didn't bother you?"

"Essentially, yes."

"This is possible," Venser said. "I suspect."

"I don't want to wait and have one of them tear out my innards because I didn't move."

"Well no," Elspeth said. "And I have not noticed it with the others we encountered."

"Wouldn't say you hung back much with those," Koth said.

"That is true."

Venser was staring at one of the panels on the wall, the one with all the moving Phyrexians. As he watched, they crammed together surging to move, seething.

"This room amazes me," Venser said simply. "I can imagine all of these panels showing a different view."

"Where are they going?" Elspeth said about the clustered Phyrexians on the screen.

"Maybe nowhere," Venser said.

"Why do they always move?"

"Phyresis affects the nervous system. It fuses all the natural jumps of the body, making the creature very fast, but unable to fully turn off the pulses. When the stimulus comes, the body of a Phyrexian is unable to dissipate it. The charge causes movement, always."

"Not good at ambushes, at least."

"I wouldn't say that. They can be quiet and they can go into a catatonic state," Venser said. "But these states are difficult to wake from, and they are groggy for a time."

Elspeth put her sword in its sheath. "Well, they are not so much to deal with here."

"We have mostly encountered small guard or workers," the guide called into the room. "Their strength is in numbers and speed. Do not feel your skills are greater than theirs. We want to avoid a direct fight, as we would be quickly overwhelmed and destroyed."

Elspeth looked doubtful. "I have fought these beasts before. I know how they work."

"Obviously not, if you just figured out that freezing causes them to not see you."

"And you knew this?"

"Yes," the guide said. "Their sight is bad. But most times it is not possible to freeze indefinitely."

"What did we find out coming into this golden room?" Koth interjected.

"That this is older than the columns and their tendrils," Venser said. "Can't you see that? It's clear."

"Clear to you," Koth said. "But far from clear."

"This room is intact from the inside," Venser said. "From the outside the tendril had grown around it. To me it means that the tendril is newer. Yes?"

Koth nodded. "Maybe. Or maybe the golden metal this room is made of has bitten deep into the tendril? It could be a special alloy."

Venser stared at Koth a couple of seconds before bobbing his head. "Yes. That is also possible."

"Thank you," Koth said.

"But I do not think it is the case," Venser said.

"Clearly, you don't."

Venser looked around the room. He sucked in his cheeks as he thought. "Right," he said at last. "Should we be on our way?" He did not wait for a response, but walked over to the hole Koth had made and crawled out into the tendril-tube.

The guide led them left and proceeded down the tube in a slightly hunched gait.

They moved through the tunnel until it became thicker. Soon it became high, and then higher still. Then the passage widened into another vast cavern. They made their way down, along the crumbly ore until a floor of sorts became apparent. It was riddled with boulders and dusts of many colors, and even a couple of partial skeletons in various degrees of decomposition. Leagues passed under their feet as they walked along the bottom of the cavern, and then even the bottom of the cavern fell away suddenly. A circular hole so wide across they could not see the other side was thrust up. The bottom was similarly cloaked in darkness. Koth picked up a chunk of slag from the floor of the cavern.

"Do not think of throwing that over the side," Elspeth warned.

Koth threw the chunk into the air and caught it easily. "Wouldn't think of it," he said.

In the blue light from Venser's wisp, the air looked ghostly and distorted. Venser put his hand out over the hole. "Do you feel anything?" he asked.

The others put their hands out.

"I feel the wind," Elspeth said.

"I feel heat," Koth said. "And something else."

Koth turned his hand over and then back.

"I feel mana, I think," Koth said. "My hand is tingling. My nose hairs are tickling."

"I feel that too," Venser said. He looked up. The hole continued upward for a short time before stopping in a mass of slag and blacked char. The slag that stopped the top of the huge chute appeared different than the dull metal of the surrounding cavern.

"Let me see that chunk of yours," Venser said, holding out his hand to Koth.

Koth placed the chunk of metal in Venser's gloved hand. The artificer held the piece out above his foot and dropped it. The chunk should have fallen and crushed his toe, but instead it fell only a short distance before slowing down to float like a feather.

"Well," Venser said. "That *is* strange, but it seems to be in our favor."

"How's that?" Koth said. He reached out and poked the rock, which spun sideways and then continued its lazy fall.

The guide watched all of this. "I do not know of this chute. If we go this way it is into the unknown."

Elspeth shifted her weight from one thick leg to the other.

"It will allow us to travel down the shaft," Venser said. "Otherwise it might have been a dangerous climb."

"My way has a climb," the guide said.

Elspeth stared at the guide as though he were mad. "A climb?" she said. "I am not in favor of that path then."

Koth coughed. "You want us to go down that sheer hole?"

"As you can see," Venser said. "We will float. It will be fast and safe."

Elspeth opened her mouth but waited a moment before speaking. "That is not the point," she said. "It is a hole."

"Yes," Koth said, pointing at Elspeth. "What she said."

"This is a stroke of luck," Venser said. "I think this shaft goes very deep. Almost to the mana core of this metal place. It's little more than a conduit."

"It is possible," the guide said.

"But a blocked conduit," Elspeth said, pointing upward at the slag plug.

"Exactly," Venser said. "It seems it once vented, but is now plugged. That is why the mana concentration is so great. Koth can feel it and so can I. It is so dense that the normal force of matter seems interrupted, I would guess."

"If we float down how do we know there are passages like this one branching off from the stem?" It was Elspeth who spoke.

"We don't," Venser said. "But it would stand to reason that . . ."

"This is foolishness," Koth said.

"I agree," said Elspeth. "We could fall forever."

"This branch is here," Venser said. "We saw others branching off from the column. There must be other branches."

"But we have no reason to believe that they are hollow," Koth said.

Venser took off his helmet. "Have you *ever* read the *Chronicles of Arrival*? It has some good thoughts on the uncertainness of life. One of its revelations is this: 'No one has promised us a tomorrow.' "

Koth pushed his chest out. "Are you accusing me of cravenness?"

"Not at all," Venser said. "I'm accusing you of bad logic . . . and that's worse."

"I'll give you logic," Koth said. A large flame leaped from his right fist. Venser was near the edge of the huge shaft. Koth reached out with his huge flaming hand and tried to seize Venser's shoulder. The artificer whispered a word and appeared with a sudden strobe of light behind Koth. With one finger Venser pushed the geomancer, who tripped forward and fell headfirst over the edge of the shaft. As he fell his whole body sputtered and burst into flame and the slits along his ribs yawned wide and red. But Koth did not fall far before his body seemed to stop in midair. Then he began to fall as slowly as a leaf falling from a tree in fall. His breeches bagged up as he executed a flip.

"This is amazing," Koth yelled.

Elspeth looked back along the tube they had just traveled. "Hush, dolt," she said.

Venser turned to her. "You are next, my lady," Venser said. He slipped his helmet back on and smiled at her. A strange sight, Elspeth thought. A man in a helmet smiling at her. Men in helmets were usually trying to kill her. "I do not think this is wise," she said, stepping to the edge. She undid the buckle holding her sword around her waist. Then she slipped the belt over her shoulder and fastened the buckle again. She stepped to the edge and then back again.

"I am not overly fond of heights," she said.

"I can't tell," Venser said.

Koth did another flip and giggled.

"I think the problem here will not be falling too fast," Venser said. "But rather too slowly. We have to get to Karn before the Phyrexians control the whole plane. It might be too late by that point."

Elspeth closed her eyes and stepped off . . . and floated. Venser followed her. Without a sound the guide followed.

Elspeth floated lazily downward, with her white tunic billowing around her. It felt wonderful and she did not ever want to stop. *If there are other columns will they also have this feature?*

"I don't know," Venser said.

Elspeth stared at Venser. "Did you just listen to the thoughts in my head?"

"Of course not," Venser said.

They floated slowly downward for very long. Soon they were tired of floating and lay motionless in the air. Venser watched as cavelike openings passed in the blue light of his wisps.

"How far will we go?" Koth said.

"Do you have a suggestion?"

Koth shrugged and floated away.

CHAPTER
15

Venser might have fallen asleep. Sometimes he heard strange sounds, and once even music, hypnotic and repeating. At another point it was screams—hundreds of beings screaming all at one time. Still they floated. Elspeth woke, fell asleep, and woke again. Cave openings passed in the blue shadows. At one, Koth insisted that they leave the shaft, and using his hands he brought himself close to the cave mouth. But after seeing something in the cave he became very quiet and did not mention leaving again.

It was hard to know how deep they were in Mirrodin. Venser had stopped caring. Eventually the guide floated up next to Venser and pointed. "It will have to be there," he said.

Koth paddled up beside him, as did Elspeth. A cave was passing, dark and small. No more than a tube hole.

"Why that one?"

"We are as deep as we should go," Venser said.

"I for one am ready to leave this place," Elspeth said. "It feels as death might. This is a sensation I am not overly interested in."

Koth grunted. "I agree with the white one."

"Yes," Venser said. "Death no, squeezing down this tube, yes."

Venser paddled to the hole. It took longer than he had thought it would, and by the time he was near his arms were tired. The side of the shaft moved past faster than he'd expected.

"Are you all ready?" Venser said. "The side here is moving fast. We'll have to not miss the hole or I don't know how you'll follow. Who wants to go first?"

"I will," Elspeth said. "I have no fear of this hole . . . as long as it leads me to more Phyrexians to slaughter." She stroked closer to the wall of the shaft, which really was moving past at a fairly quick clip. Koth stroked over so he was above Elspeth, and touching the wall as he slipped downward. Venser aligned behind them both.

Elspeth caught the hole's rim and amidst her clattering armor, she thrust into it as deep as her midsection. She struggled for a moment as the current of the shaft caught her legs and pulled them downward. Then she was wriggling through with only her feet extending out of the hole. Then her feet were gone.

Koth did not have quite so easy a time. He could not dive as deeply into the hole. And for a desperate couple of moments, he was grasping the inside of the tube while his waist and lower body dangled out and were pulled down. The geomancer heated his hands until his fingers sunk into the wall of the tube as though it were warm butter. With a good handhold, he was able to haul himself up and into the hole. The metal walls of the hole were still hot as Venser threaded into it. He burned the palm of his right hand and cursed under his breath as he scraped his right knee on one of the five rough divots Koth's fingers had made in the cooling metal.

The tube they found themselves in was very tight indeed. Koth had to fight a growing impulse to push outward. There was no light and any attempt at light, Venser knew, would only illuminate the area between each of them and not pass ahead. So they crawled. The tube seemed to stay fairly level and the crawling was not especially difficult. Then they started to slide a bit. At first nobody was sure if they were sliding down or up. Venser concluded that the tube was angling downward, but he could not really tell.

They turned a tight corner and Venser heard a *whoosh* and Koth was no longer crawling in front of him. Venser carefully crawled forward and felt a pull and then he was yanked by Koth's suction . . . traveling suddenly fast enough to feel the slight imperfections of the tube banging into his elbows and knees.

It continued, the downward slide, until suddenly they shot out of the slide and into the air. Venser knew only that there was darkness one moment and light the next, coupled with the feeling of falling. He was able to see the floor for one split second before the plummet. He breathed the mana stream extending from his head into him and a moment later he felt the familiar explosion in his skull and teleported, appearing in a squat on the level floor.

Koth, Elspeth, and the guide did not have as easy a time. The white warrior executed a flip and went skittering across the shiny floor on her rump. Koth tucked his shoulder and hit the ground with the tremendous clatter of metal on metal. He left a long scrape in the floor.

"That could have gone better," Koth said, testing the rotation of his shoulder in its joint as he stood.

The guide stood and bent his neck side to side.

Elspeth was sitting on the floor, legs splayed. She was staring at the room they had jettisoned into. Other tubes met in the room and at the far end others left in the same way. But in the middle was another huge room. The metal walls, roof, and floor were shiny. The light came in organic patches that clung in irregular shapes to the walls.

Off to the right a round, human-height door woven with bars was visible. There was movement in the room—reflections on the walls shifted and moved, as though something were inside the room moving fast, casting its reflection. Venser squinted, but saw nothing.

To the left, a huge square set of meat steps extended up in a series of turns that ended at a set of what look suspiciously like a wooden gallows. There were pieces of metal hammered together unevenly and at odd angles. A single chain hung unmoving from the edge of the hammered-together structure.

A warm wind stirred their sweat-soaked hair. Venser took off his helmet.

Venser had not at first realized just how large the room was. As he looked, its walls seemed to stretch far, far away. Yet another larger room. He could see lines of smoke in the distance as if a brush fire were burning. But what was there to burn down in these metallic bowels?

More movement along the walls near the door . . . Venser turned in time to see a circular crease appear in the wall. Another crease appeared down the middle of the circle. All the creases split open and from its epicenter stepped Phyrexians, one after another.

Something had been moving in the barred portal to the right of the newly formed hole, but when the Phyrexians stepped out, all movement ceased. Then whatever was in the barred room started thrashing and clicking, as if the room on the other side of the barred portal was full of giant insects all clicking together in a maddening frenzy.

What stepped out of the round portal was even more shocking. A line of ten thin beings stood before the door. Each of the beings stood in exactly the same way. Each looked at the party with its white, porcelain face cocked to the right. Eyes that were no more than dark holes bored into the face stared with neither lid nor iris. Their mouths were nothing more than expressionless notches. Their bodies were an exterior, shell-like white porcelain. But underneath the filth- and oil-smeared ceramic the creatures were composed of barbed, dim gristle.

They took a step forward in unison. Large barbed metal wings snapped out from their backs and spread wide. A moment later the Phyrexians took flight. They ascended high into the air. The chamber seemed to have no ceiling, and for a terrible moment, Elspeth lost sight of them.

It was Koth who found them in the dark air. "To the right, coming low," he bellowed.

They looked right and there were the ten skimming the floor with their sharp fingers spread wide, ready to rake the party from their boots.

Venser breathed deeply and in his cranium he imagined the mana moving the turns and curls of his brain, lighting the regions until it glowed from within. Then he imagined a blue smoke coming

217

from his nose as he repeated the rounded syllables of the incantation. His eyes pulsed blue. Their bodies doubled, and then doubled again, six of them stood in a rough line against the flying Phyrexians. Then their bodies copied again, and again.

Four Elspeths drew swords and fell into a wide stance. Four Koths began to grunt and growl the spells of incineration and blaze. Koth raised his hands and four huge balls of fire blasted from his fingertips at the Phyrexians. They dodged the balls, but Venser watched as the fire shot across the room and did not stop. The balls streaked for as long as Venser was watching. The enemy was almost upon them before he took his eyes off the fireballs.

Elspeth stepped into the Phyrexians and brought her sword's blade down in an overhead attack. As she did so, the steel flashed and blurred into a mass of flashing blades. But something was different. Instead of the sound of thousands of swishing swords Venser was used to hearing, he heard thousands of clanging sounds. Thousands of glancing blows. One of the Phyrexians did find its torso split, and with the same rapt expression on its plain face, it fell in two pieces.

Four Koths seized Phyrexian wrists and spun to the left, but only one actually cast its foe into the gallow-like structure made of meat, where it hit hard so that the pieces of metal at the top vibrated like a tuning fork and the creature did not move again.

Venser pulled more power from the folds of his cranium. He dodged to the left to avoid the pocked claws of a Phyrexian that had guessed which Venser was real. As he passed he touched the creature's leg. A blue charge traveled up the leg and into the barbed flesh. The charge circled and shot along all straight angles.

Finally it found the creature's skull. The Phyrexian's

eyes flashed blue and a moment later it went limp and fell in a heap of wrong angles.

The Phyrexians stopped and with their wings flapping furiously, they hovered and began raking with their claws. Koth's eyes went red and cuffs of metal popped out along his forearms. A Phyrexian claw glanced off his arms and he shoved his hands into the thing's barbed abdomen. His hands sunk into the metal and the geomancer pulled great hunks out. Oil fell out and the Phyrexian clawed at Koth, but the vulshok continued to yank bits out until he tore the creature out of the air and threw it down. The Phyrexian tried to rise but Koth fell on its chest with his knees and began banging its head savagely on the metal floor.

Another hovered above Koth, sweeping gashes in his back and hair. Koth turned and knocked the Phyrexian out of the air with a blazing fist.

Elspeth was beside herself. Venser had never seen such rage. She was screaming as she hacked at the nearest Phyrexian, leveling gashes out of its porcelain shell. The Phyrexian caught her sword, twisted, and wrenched it from Elspeth's grasp. It cast the sword aside and came at the white warrior's chest with its claws forward. Instead of falling back Elspeth lunged forward, catching the Phyrexian's claws in her hands. They grappled a few feet off the ground until Koth seized the Phyrexian's foot and dragged it down and began twisting its head on its neck. The head turned freely and seemed to have little effect on the Phyrexian, who continued to try to scrabble a path through Elspeth's hands to the white warrior's chest.

Koth began pulling up on the head. He heaved and twisted and eventually the head popped neatly off. The Phyrexian's body went limp and fell to the ground. Koth held the head up and looked at it.

He tapped the porcelain shell with the back of his knuckle. "It's like egg shell," he said.

Two of the other Phyrexians grabbed Koth's arms and swept him high into the air. The geomancer laughed as he flew high. Elspeth, in one smooth movement, reached down for the knife in her boot, raised up, and threw. The bright blade glittered in the air before finding its target: the right eye of the Phyrexian holding Koth's left arm.

Both the creatures stopped flying upward. The one with the knife sticking out of its eye turned and looked at its compatriot. They both cocked their heads as their wings flapped.

"You have something in your eye," Koth said.

The Phyrexian turned its strange gaze on the geomancer. Its wing beats slowed before stopping altogether, causing it to plummet.

As the beast fell it did not release its hold on Koth's arm . . . neither would the other Phyrexian, who strained against the combined weight, and then fell as well. Koth managed to turn as he fell so that the Phyrexians were between him and the metal floor. They hit first. By the time Koth hit, the Phyrexians were dead and offered enough resistance to break his fall. He bounced high off their bodies and came to rest near Venser, who helped him up.

Elspeth, meanwhile, had dispatched the two remaining Phyrexians with her blade, which she had retrieved.

Koth shook off Venser's arm. "That was fun," he said. "I'd like to try that again. Should we? Should we do that again?"

Venser shook his head. The geomancer was acting stranger and stranger. When was the last time any of them had eaten food or had more than a mouthful of water? They were each in their own way starting to show the strain of the trip. Venser knew that at some point he could, in likelihood, have to fight and restrain the much larger vulshok. Venser smiled. He'd fought larger and more powerful beings in his time. Koth would be easily dealt with.

Elspeth, on the other hand, showed absolutely no signs of stress, except when fighting. That made Venser all the more nervous. She had become blood-thirsty, but that could hardly be blamed. She'd mentioned her imprisonment at the hands of the enemy. A traumatic event like that could not help but leave scars. Yes, Venser would have to watch her for signs of stress. He would have to watch them both, and in the meantime it was up to him to think rationally. The mission could not be compromised. They must find Karn, and by any means at his disposal, Venser would make that happen . . . even if that meant dealing with every Phyrexian in that rat's nest under the surface. Even if that meant dealing with Koth and Elspeth. He would find Karn, oh yes.

"Mr. Artificer, sir," Koth waved his hand before Venser's eyes. "Are you there, sir?"

Venser blinked. "I am here, you dolt."

"There he is," Koth said. "I thought for a time that you'd have to be put out of your misery. That you were becoming like *them*." He pushed one of the still Phyrexians with his foot.

"I am not affected by the black oil," Venser said defensively.

"Oh, no?" Koth said. "Why not."

Venser stepped around the vulshok and went to stand next to Elspeth. Her eyes were narrowed and her lip was drawn in the corner into a snarl. She stared down at one of the dead Phyrexians.

In the barred window behind them the sound of thousands of clicking insects continued. The wide fire in the distance flickered and danced, giving off plumes of smoke that rose high in the absolutely vast room.

"Their claws are cold and cruel," Elspeth said. She was looking down at her hands as she spoke. She clenched one gloved hand. "Once they touch you it is hard to forget that feeling."

"Are you hurt?" Venser said.

Elspeth turned on him. For one quick moment Venser thought she would stab him with the knife she had just pulled out of the Phyrexian's eye. But the sneer quivered and disappeared. "I do not allow them to hurt me," Elspeth said.

The sudden stillness of the room was beginning to unnerve him. The huge space and many others on Mirrodin, he realized suddenly, reminded him of when he was a child running in the streets and he found the set of a theatrical play. He and the other children he was with could never afford to attend such a play, but they found the set. The set builders had just left the premises and the back door was open. He and his friends wandered in and stood in the hush of the room with its small castle with an open side. There was also a tree built of wood planks. It was for appearance of course, and nobody was around. That's how the rooms felt to Venser there in the bowels of Mirrodin.

The clicking in the barred room started again. "Are they cruel?"

"I'm sorry?" Elspeth said.

"Are the Phyrexians cruel, by nature?"

Elspeth thought for a moment. "The prison I was in was little more than a factory. Conveyer belt ran from room to room. They like organs and flesh. They like to hold them and play with them. One of their loves is interchanging parts for other parts."

"I see."

"You do not," Elspeth said. "I was eight years old and I saw people ripped apart . . . slowly. The beasts are semisentient. They can play with you. They understand how to hurt and cause fear. They would force me to watch, only to see the look on my face."

"They are that aware?"

"Oh yes."

Koth had walked up to listen. "This has made you stronger. Now you are mighty."

Elspeth said nothing. She wiped the blade of her knife on the leather of her underjerkin before slipping it back into the scabbard in her boot. Then she looked over at the round portal next to the barred window. "Shall we look at that situation?" she said.

The guide had watched them, as he always did— unspeaking and very still. When they moved toward the door, he followed.

Unlike the other doors they had approached, the door opened to reveal a dimly lit room. There were three large holes in the metal floor that looked strangely fleshy, organic. They quivered slightly as the party stepped in the room. Another circular door opened into another, vast room. That other room was filled with large objects, hundreds of them. Each object was made up of an arm attached to a large cylindrical tank with a spine fused to it. There were literally hundreds, maybe thousands of the devices, and each arm was pushing down on something, keeping whatever was in the tank down.

Each tank had a small set of eyes near its top. The top of its tank was rimmed with sharp teeth, all pointing downward.

"What are those arms holding down?" Koth said, stating the question playing over each of their tongues.

Without warning a head sputtering black fluid popped out of the nearest cylinder. The arm attached to the device immediately moved its claw and shoved the head back down.

But not before Venser recognized an elf's ears.

"These must be propagation tanks," Venser said. "Breeding tanks."

"Phyrexians don't need to breed," Elspeth said.

Venser thought for a moment. "Perhaps they want to turn more beings to Phyrexians faster than normal," Elspeth said.

"I have never heard of such a thing," Venser said.

The guide was silent, watching.

"We should destroy them," Elspeth said.

"But how?" Koth said. "It would take countless hours. What we should do is move toward the surface and find others and then return."

"Koth is right," Venser said.

The vulshok turned with a shocked look on his face. "Did you just say *I* was correct?"

"Only in that we have to leave this place now," Venser said. "Not that we should travel to the surface."

"Oh," Koth said. "Well then, artificer, now that you've decided not to assist these poor beings," Koth's voice was rising as he talked. Venser had noticed that that was happening more and more frequently with the geomancer. The sweat had collected on his face, and the iron dust stuck to it. He looks like he's losing his mind, Venser thought.

"Which of the three holes will you take us down?" Koth said.

"We cannot help these creatures. Their fate is already decided. Destroying these tanks would only slow our path," the guide said.

The arm on the nearest tank flexed and its spines clicked as the tank readjusted its hold.

CHAPTER
16

The guide led them along pathways hewn in the metal walls and ways hidden to all eyes save his. There was a quietness about the sylvok that made Venser uneasy. When he spoke, it was with an accent that he had never heard before. That made sense, as Venser was not a Mirran, but when he watched Koth out of the corner of his eye as the guide talked, the vulshok's face pinched itself in confusion at his accent. The fleshling blinked when he spoke, but she did that when anyone spoke, so it was hard to glean anything from that.

But the guide was certainly from Mirrodin. His coppery legs, green with patina, gave that away. However, he bore none of the signs of infection they had seen in the camp, and he was not what Venser would ever have called shifty or evasive. He merely never spoke or made noise. He was as silent a creature as a romei buck.

Once, after they had spent hours descending a series of foot- and handholds in the honeycomb support structure between two walls, they encountered a brace of Phyrexians and the guide did something unusual. They had finally found the floor and, with legs wobbling from their climb, Venser and the others moved toward a hole cut in the wall. Light showed from the hole, telling Venser that it led to yet another vast cavernlike room. Koth arrived at the door first. He caught sight of a pack of Phyrexians struggling over something just outside the doorway.

Elspeth pushed to the front—ready to fall upon them and quickly make good of the thing. But the guide put a light hand on her arm and pulled her back. He held one finger up to his lips and squatted against the inside of the wall.

They waited that way for what seemed like days. When the troupe of the enemy moved away, Koth was snoring softly on the floor, and Venser was quickly on his way to sleep. But the guide was on his feet and tugging on Koth's sleeve.

The room was of medium size. They entered it by cutting into a Phyrexian's intestine tube and forcing open the eye at the bottom. Standing in the middle of the room was a beast that reminded Venser somewhat of a horse, but with shiny metal plates for skin, and a head of glinting metal. Still, its eyes had the same dim expression of boredom he'd always disliked in horses. They entered the room and heard the *tip tap* of small feet scampering away. The guide froze, his expression blank. He looked around quickly and his nostrils flared.

He may not have heard anything more, but there was plenty to see, Venser thought. The edges of the room were piled high with the neatly cut parts of Mirran creatures. What flesh they had on them was festering, and the air in the room was foul enough for the guide to pinch his noise. The horse in the middle of the room stood still, regarding them with pupilless eyes.

After the sound of the scampering feet, the room was absolutely silent except for what appeared to be a clock on the wall, ticking lightly. But Venser could not understand what it was timing. There was one hand, which was moving toward a red circle.

Elspeth moved forward, until she stopped near the creature at the center of the room. It did not move and Elspeth began to move around it.

The hand on the clock moved closer to the red circle.

What is the red circle? Venser thought suddenly.

The question had occurred to the guide also. He moved forward and motioned Elspeth back. She ignored him and looked intently instead at the shiny metal along the creature's back.

The fleshling, who was standing between Venser and Koth, watched the proceedings with as much of an impartial face as the guide. But her eyes jumped from the cut pieces, to the creature, and then back again.

The hand was four ticks from the red circle.

Suddenly the fleshling surged forward, ran to Elspeth, and shoved her hard away from the creature at the center of the room. Elspeth fell and so did the fleshling. The hand on the clock clicked to the red circle. At that moment there was a tremendous whooshing sound, and air blew in their faces as something large moved through the air nearby.

The Mirran horse fell to pieces before their eyes. Its parts clattered to the floor and Venser got a good look at just how deeply the metal that made up the creature's skin went until the meat and tendons took over. There was blood, but it pooled for only a moment before disappearing down drains that must have been hidden in the floor.

Elspeth looked up from the floor with wide eyes. The fleshling looked as though she might weep. But she did not weep, and the moment quickly passed. She was on her feet the second after that. Elspeth struggled against her armor and finally stood herself.

"What?" Koth said, staring at the bloodied pieces on the floor.

They all looked at the guide, whose eyes were moving from place to place along the wall of the room.

"Why is it here?" Koth asked. "What do they get from doing any of this?"

Venser would have shrugged if he hadn't disliked the shrug as an expression. He understood exactly what Koth was asking. What were the Phyrexians after down in the bowels of Mirrodin? He had seen many rooms, and exactly none of them made any sense. For instance, how could the Phyrexians melt down and recast their dead in the furnace? Were they not made by transformation via a contagion? What was accomplished by melting down the metal bodies of the dead? Didn't Phyrexians grow their own armor? But, clearly, there were no answers anywhere down there. Only confusion and more questions.

The guide moved slowly to where the pieces lay. He looked carefully at the pieces before standing again and looking around the room.

He certainly looked like a guide to Venser. He certainly appeared to be genuine, and not a spy. But what was to say that the forces standing against them had not found a way to recruit a real guide?

The guide located an eyeway in the corner. After he cut it open with a long knife, they all moved through and into the darkened room on the other side.

And into another room, where they found no Phyrexians. The guide moved them along the outer side of the room and then through another eyeway. Then there were more rooms of metal and more exits. Sometimes the exits joined into long tunnels. In one tunnel the guide suddenly stopped walking. He stopped and fell to his hands and knees and began looking closely at the floor of the tunnel, using his fingernails to find any seam. Eventually he found something, and pulled up a hinged panel of metal. They clambered down through the hole and descended a strange ladder of what appeared to be ribs. After that, the guide took them along another passage, and more after that.

"I don't understand," Koth said. "What do we accomplish by this running around down here? We have the fleshling. Why don't we go heal everybody on the surface?

"I am not sure there are survivors on the surface," Elspeth said, mirroring Venser's own thoughts.

"There are survivors," Koth said. "And they deserve our help, but we do not help them."

The guide raised his hand.

"Hush," Venser said to Koth.

Koth shot him an evil face in response to the chastisement.

Next they were in another passage that descended at an angle that required them to squat to move. At the bottom was a doorway, barely visible in the blue glow from Venser's wisps. The doorway was not an eyeway, or a rough-cut hole, but a simple entranceway with smooth sides. This kind of entranceway was uncommon enough. But as soon as they stopped, Venser heard it, the odd sound the guide ahead must have heard: a sort of skittering. At irregular intervals something heavy bounced along the ground. But at other times there was no sound but the whoosh of wind.

Wind down here? Venser wondered.

When the guide moved his hand forward, they advanced. Soon they were at the entrance, and Venser turned off his wisps, so they were once again in darkness. Silently they each felt their way into another vast room. Venser could tell by the echoes from his feet. Water dripped off to the right somewhere. The air was still and stagnant. Like almost every room they had moved through, it smelled vaguely of rotting meat. It was strange air in these underground rooms: it always felt to Venser as though some creature was crouching in it, with its twisted spine as tight as a spring, and ready to pounce.

But there was no attack, and soon Venser's eyes began adjusting as best they could to the almost total darkness. If there was any light in the room, Venser was not sure where it would have come from. But still his eyes found enough of what they needed to make out something: white blurs.

It was hard to say how far away the shapes were. A hand grasped his, and Venser felt what he thought must be the thick glove of Elspeth's sword hand. Understanding what was supposed to happen, Venser reached back and found Koth's strangely smooth palm and held it.

Hand in hand in the darkness they moved. At first Venser thought they were moving toward the blurring shapes, but then they turned and walked until they bumped into the wall. Then the guide, for Venser hoped it was the guide who was leading them, turned them left and they skirted the wall.

As they walked, Elspeth's hand squeezed tighter and tighter. A couple of times Venser had to disengage his hand and then find Elspeth's hand again, lest she crush his knuckles and fingers.

But traveling along the wall still took them near the blurred shapes. They became larger and larger until Venser recognized them for what they were. Elspeth's hand tightened dramatically, and then let go of his and went, Venser assumed, to the grip of her sword.

Venser could see why.

The white blurs were actually strange Phyrexian angels. All white, with what appeared to be a porcelain exoskeleton, covered with chips. Pink tendons wormed from one section of porcelain to another, apparently holding them together. They had tattered metal wings that flapped, keeping them aloft. Their heads were all porcelain, with black round holes for eyes, and a thin black line for a mouth.

And between them they were throwing something round and shaggy. They were throwing the round shape as fast as they could, in a joyless game that Venser could not begin to understand. In that vast room they stood playing catch. Venser thought back to the conversation they were having earlier. Why was any of this here?

One of the angels missed its catch, and the ball fell to the ground with a dull thump. It rolled over and Venser recognized it for what it was. He looked away from the tortured line of a mouth and a flattened nose.

The angels noticed them at that moment, and shot up into the darkness. Venser could see their blurs, and a moment later an angel shot out of the dark and raked a claw down his body armor, knocking him over with the force of the blow. The pain was sharp as he rose, but didn't feel critical enough to stay on the ground.

233

By the time he was up, Koth was grappling with one of the angels, who flapped its wings, pulling Koth with it into the air. Venser snapped his mana to his raised fingers, and furls of power radiated out and softened the metal of the angel's wings, so they drooped and the angel fell. The impact gave Koth the opportunity to wrap his hands around the angel's head and begin beating it against the floor.

Off to the side, Venser could see Elspeth and the second angel brawling. Surprisingly quick, the angel was able to dodge Elspeth's attacks. The white warrior began to move her own mana to her sword for a thousand-cuts-in-one strike. But the angel put up its hand and Elspeth's weapon dropped from her fingers.

She reached down for the sword, but the angel surged forward and palmed Elspeth's head in its claw. It turned, raised Elspeth off the ground, and threw her away into the darkness, leaving her sword glittering on the ground.

The angel looked down at the sword and cocked its head to the side. Venser began running for the sword. He did not think about what would happen if the Phyrexian had the weapon, he just ran. By the time he reached the place, the angel had bent over the sword and was reaching down with its claw. Venser kicked the sword and it went skittering away.

He'd been struck hard plenty of times in his life. He was raised in Urborg, after all, and his childhood had been far from perfect: his father had broken his nose when he was ten, and that blow had knocked him out for almost an hour. He'd fought in the insurrection there and been wounded in the abdomen with a spear that went through him, knocked him way back, and pinned him to a tree. That one had hurt.

But the blow that the Phyrexian lashed out with was worse.

Elspeth saw it from the shadows. She was on her knees feeling for her blade and happened to look up. Her own head pounded where the Phyrexian angel's metal claw had squeezed, but otherwise she was unhurt. She looked up in time to see the Phyrexian's strike: Venser cartwheeled limp through the air like a tossed doll, his helmet spinning off to the side.

He landed with an unsettling thud. Elspeth turned back to her search. She moved to where she thought Venser had kicked the sword. By the time she found it, the angel was tearing the armor off Venser's chest. It did not sense her approach, which was good because she was terrified to look it once more face-to-face. But still she could not strike an opponent's back. She tapped it on the shoulder with the tip of her sword, but it did not turn. Having fulfilled the Etiquette of the Field with the tap, she wasted no time with enchantments, but simply swiped the creature's head neatly off its shoulders, cutting the tops of its wings off in the process.

Yet it continued to move, to claw at Venser's unmoving form. Without eyes its movements were gross and imprecise. Such imprecision alone was enough to make Elspeth kill it again. She swung again and severed it at the waist, cutting off the bottoms of its wings, and in that way it fell.

She shoved the angel's torso off of Venser and kneeled over him. Off to the side his helmet sat with a tremendous dent the rough size of the angel's claw. Elspeth turned back to Venser. He was breathing, she was glad to see. She felt his head and found a large lump above his ear. Koth and the fleshling appeared. Then the guide.

"What's this now?" Koth said.

Elspeth ignored the knave. She put her hand on Venser's forehead. Down her arm trickled the mana she had in reserve. It moved into her hand and settled into Venser's forehead.

"This would not have happened if I were leading," Koth mumbled. "We wouldn't be down here with mutes and trackers, tearing angels apart."

"I am not mute," the fleshling said.

Elspeth concentrated more mana into Venser, trying to wake him from his slumber. *Please*, she thought.

Venser's eyes popped open. They looked around wildly, and then settled on Elspeth's face. He brought his hand to his face and wiped his hair out of his eyes. *His hair is long now,* she thought. *Hadn't it been short when Koth talked her into kidnapping him? How long have we been in the bowels of this place?*

Venser sat up and winced. The random slashes from the where the angel tore off his chest armor bled freely.

"They are not deep," Elspeth said, smiling. Something she had not done in days, maybe months. It felt strange to her face.

Koth scoffed and turned away. "We will all die down here," he said. "All of us. I'm leaving. I should never have come." He walked away into the darkness.

A strange look passed over Venser's face, and he could feel his limbs begin to tremble. Then his cheek began to twitch. He turned and quickly, but with trembling fingers, fumbled through the pieces of metal and leather that had been his chest armor. In the torn underclothes he found the small white bottle Elspeth had seen him clutching before. The relief was obvious on his face.

"What is that really?" Elspeth said.

"This?" Venser said. "Nothing, medicine."

Elspeth nodded. She'd never seen a medicine that glowed that color. Venser struggled to stand. With the scout's help he finally did. Elspeth watched his twitching legs support one step, then another and then Venser was walking, looking pale and sweaty in the close air.

He noticed the pained look on her face. "I am as good as dead, you know," he said.

"Really?"

"The sickness that is in me has no cure," he said. "It will take me one day, and it could be soon."

"Does the medicine help?"

"Not anymore. I lose some of myself with every teleport. For some reason I lost much more when the fleshling and I teleported into the flock of blinkmoths."

Elspeth nodded, clearly uneasy with the direction the conversation had taken.

"Where is the fleshling?" Venser said, happy to direct the conversation away from the bottle.

Elspeth looked around. "She was just here."

"So was Koth," Venser said.

"She left with the vulshok," the guide said from the shadows.

"Left?" Elspeth said.

The guide nodded.

Venser wondered if the man was perhaps a stuffed suit of skin, or he'd been kicked as a youth.

"Did you think that was strange?" Elspeth said.

The guide shook his head.

"Well, which way did they go?"

The guide pointed into the darkness.

CHAPTER
17

They pursued Koth and the fleshling through the vast room. Venser put his blue wisps before them so they could see. Far in the distance the guide said he could see a slight red glow, which they understood to be Koth's own light. Venser remarked at how someone as large as Koth could move so quickly.

"They are captured," Elspeth said.

"Has any Phyrexian tried to capture us yet?" Venser said.

"They captured you."

"Well, Koth is not captured. He has the fleshling."

"Where are they going?" Elspeth said, turning to the guide, her voice raised.

Even though his chest and head were administering a fair amount of pain to him, Venser still noticed how the disappearance of the fleshling had affected Elspeth's mood for the worse.

"I do not know," the guide said. "I know no door that way."

"That cannot be good," Venser said. "How could Koth know his way down here?"

"Because he's a spy," Elspeth said. "I don't know."

To Venser the room seemed to never end. They walked for a time and then they ran. Hours passed and perhaps days, but Elspeth would not let them stop. Even when the cuts on Venser's chest began to throb and his thinking was muddled by the blow to his head, even then Elspeth would not let them stop.

"Drink some of your magic potion," she snapped.

He did not. But he did pat the small bottle in his torn shirt. He would be having a sip soon enough.

Elspeth's temper shortened as the trail cooled. At one point, the guide stopped and looked back the way they had come, then forward again with a confused look on his face.

"What is it?" Elspeth said.

"It seems we are being followed," he said.

"But where are the fleshling and the other one?"

The guide looked ahead. "I do not see the light anymore."

"You have lost the trail?"

The guide stared ahead. He bent to a crouch and carefully removed the glove from his left hand, which was metal. He placed his fingertips on the metal floor.

"Yes, I feel the tramp of many feet from behind," the guide said. "And none from ahead."

"How many behind?" Venser said.

The guide was silent with his fingers to the metal. "Many," he said at last. "Very many are running, metal on metal."

"Like Phyrexians?" Venser said.

The guide said nothing.

Elspeth shook her head. All they needed right now. More Phyrexians.

"What is ahead of us?" Venser said to the guide.

"As I said earlier, I know of no doors ahead."

"And the wall?" Venser said. "Is just ahead, I suppose?"

The guide nodded.

"So we are flanked," Elspeth said.

"It seems so," the guide said.

"Then let's run and see if there is a new doorway in the wall," Venser said.

But Elspeth barely ran. She jogged along behind Venser and the guide, and when they reached the wall she stood staring behind. Venser and the guide began feeling for inconsistencies on the smooth wall, but found none. Elspeth continued staring back.

"I won't go back into their care," Elspeth said.

Venser and the guide had moved on to the floor, and found nothing. When Elspeth spoke, Venser stood and walked over to her. By then he could feel the tramp of metal feet and heavy machinery through his boots. Elspeth turned as Venser approached.

"I will not go back into their prisons again," Elspeth repeated.

"So you say," Venser said.

Elspeth looked down at his belt, where his dented helmet was strapped. "What will you do with it?"

"Mend it when I have more energy," he said.

The floor was starting to vibrate hard. The guide appeared out of the darkness. "They are a very large force," he said, breathless from running. "And they are looking for something."

"They are looking for the fleshling," Venser said. "At least she is away with Koth and not here." Venser looked over his shoulder, half expecting the fleshling and Koth to step out of the shadows at his pronouncement.

Elspeth drew her sword out of its scabbard. She felt better than she had in years, and her sword gleamed brighter than ever.

"This is a force we cannot hope to prevail against," the guide said.

"What other options do we have?" Venser said.

"You can jump away," Elspeth said.

"But I won't."

"But you should. Go. Attack them from the rear if that gives you the justification you need. As I remember, you were able to give me justifications for retreat earlier in this quest. I am giving you the same for teleporting."

Venser cocked his head at Elspeth. "Are those tears on your cheeks?"

"Heroes shed no tears," Elspeth said.

From beyond Venser's blue wisps came the calls of the enemy. As Elspeth watched, a horde broke into view. They were all shapes and sizes, legs and elbows jabbing out and eyes iridescent. Long-legged shanks and howling mouths filled with chipped and jagged teeth—all charged the small circle of blue light.

Elspeth, her teeth gritted and tears streaming down her face, charged. Her cry was so fierce and her form so terrible, that the first line of Phyrexians shied and fell back at her advance. Her sword was held above her head and it shined like the very essence of metal in the darkened room. When she struck, the sword's blade became a blur. Phyrexians fell around her, first three then more. Soon there was a pile of twisted, skeletal bodies around her. But still she did not stop.

Venser breathed four breaths, and with these he pulled every ounce of mana he could tether or muster from the world around. His ears became full with the ringing of its arrival, and soon his brainpan felt as though it would overflow. Phyrexians ran to him and Venser reached out and seized the first one's arm, bending its body so it fell, baying, to the floor. In the next moment he blinked away and appeared in the very middle of the horde, where he began tapping. Each tap sent a pulse through the metal exoskeleton. The pulse traveled the raceway of metal, picking up speed and amplifying itself. By the time it reached the brains of the creatures, it was powerful enough to cause a massive attack. The creatures fell seconds after he touched them.

There were piles of dead Phyrexians laid out over the shadowy circle of blue light. Few Phyrexians remained, and those left were being dealt with by Elspeth, who had begun slashing through them one at a time. For one mad second, Venser thought they might actually prevail.

Then more Phyrexians howled into sight. Many more of them, huge levelers, nattering micronaughts, and stinking long-legged beasts with hammered-together armor and black holes for eyes. A force three times again as large as the one they had decimated.

Venser blinked back to Elspeth's side. The white warrior glanced at him. Her face was sheathed in sweat as she went back to hoisting her sword and slashing it down. Venser's arms burned and his legs felt flimsy and useless.

The new force of Phyrexians fell on them. Venser was forced back. He looked over just in time to see a pack of large Phyrexians encircle Elspeth so that he could only see the tip of her sword doing its grim work. Then, the sword's tip, too, disappeared from sight.

This was when he could disappear, Venser knew. This was when he could blink into the darkness and away. He was sure that the guide was out in the darkness waiting. In all likelihood he could find him. But then what? He could not leave, as infected as he was with the Phyrexian oil. He turned back to the Phyrexians.

What had Elspeth said?

'Heroes shed no tears.'

The Phyrexians hurled themselves onto him, knocking him over. They were on him, smelling like the sewer and popping their joints as they raked their frenzied claws over him. He could not move under the weight of them.

"Hold."

The voice came loud and clear, and the Phyrexians froze. Venser felt a cold drip on his forehead. A huge Phyrexian was dripping black oil on him from its left eye socket.

"Pull them up," the voice said again.

Venser was yanked to his feet.

"Good to see you again and all that," Tezzeret said.

Venser opened his mouth to speak, but no words came. Elspeth, still struggling, was pulled into the circle.

"You?" she said.

Tezzeret yawned. "I know, it's me again. I'm looking for the flesh being."

"Is that why you attacked the rebels?" Venser said.

Tezzeret ignored him and looked at Elspeth, raising his eyebrows.

"She is not here," Elspeth said.

"I see that," Tezzeret said. "Where, oh, where did she run off to? A party somewhere?"

"She left us before you arrived," Elspeth said.

Tezzeret looked at Elspeth for a long time. Then he turned to Venser and stared at him. Venser could feel a tickle in the center of his brain, and he knew that Tezzeret was searching for truth. Venser blocked the intrusion, but Tezzeret clearly got enough.

"That is unfortunate," Tezzeret said. "We will have to keep looking. You both will be going back to Glissa for skinning." Tezzeret turned and began walking away. He gestured back at them as he walked. "I don't know why. You will have to ask her." The Phyrexians parted and he walked between them.

Venser and Elspeth were hoisted. With the screech of rusted metal on metal the Phyrexians began to run. They ran their prisoners across the room. When they reached the wall, hours later, the Phyrexians in the front stopped and began looking at the wall, feeling at it with their claws. The lead Phyrexians scraped at the metal, but no opening occurred, neither was there an eyeway in evidence. They waited for Tezzeret to come forward, but he did not.

When it was clear that Tezzeret was not with them anymore, Venser leaned over to Elspeth.

"Tezzeret must have guided them," Venser whispered to Elspeth. "They cannot find the portal without him."

And it seemed to be true. The Phyrexians stood at the wall for many hours. First it was one and then all of them poked, scraped, and struck the metal wall. No portal opened.

Elspeth and Venser were still held, but by only one Phyrexian each: a large, white bastion. The bastions were encrusted with what looked like porcelain, chipped to expose the dark metal underneath. Venser's was large, and held him with two of its four arms. It smelled like dead beetles. The 245 bastions did not move to try their hands at opening the portal.

Then Venser saw something strange indeed—a form standing back in the darkness. It took him a moment of staring to figure out that it was Koth. Behind Koth he could just make out another humanoid outline. The fleshling. Venser leaned over to Elspeth. "Look slowly behind," he whispered.

Elspeth nodded when she'd seen the vulshok.

The bastions that were holding them were three lengths away from the others, who had moved toward the wall to see if they could find the portal. Venser reached out with his mind into the dark recesses of the bastion that was holding him. As with every time he did that with a Phyrexian, he was shocked by the images he saw, the terror and violence, endless lines of headless, armless, legless torsos hung on hooks like so many hocks, a red-eyed face staring from a mud-daubed hut, stairs in a limitless room running up to an alter, where bodies were burning on a pyre. Strange visions leftover, no doubt, from the original being whose body the Phyrexian had grown from. Once he was connected with the vile mass in the bastion's skull, he channeled cooling mana. Soon what he had left of his mana filled the beast's skull with calmness. The calmness became lethargy and moved into stupefaction just before the creature's knees buckled. Koth was behind to seize the Phyrexian around the waist and ease it soundlessly to the ground. Elspeth had found her Phyrexian's chest and mouth, and was busy choking it, as it banged on her back.

Once Venser's Phyrexian was on the floor, Koth rushed to Elspeth and held two of the creature's arms so it could not strike. Venser held the other two.

Soon it too fell.

They walked away into the darkness with the sound of the Phyrexians banging on the wall echoing behind them. The fleshling was there, and after a time the guide appeared out of the darkness. Koth walked ahead.

"We will not talk about what I did," Koth said. "Ever."

Venser glanced back over his shoulder. He could not see the Phyrexians, but he could hear them tapping on the wall.

"We leave it where it lies." Koth said.

The guide pointed them to the right and they followed. Before long a choking cry of alarm went up, and they began running. They ran as hard as they could. When they reached the wall Venser let out a sigh of relief, knowing he could not have run for much longer.

The guide tapped once on the wall and nothing happened. The wall remained smooth and unlined. The scream increased in volume behind them.

"Try again," Elspeth said.

The guide tried again, nothing opened. "The portals might have been deactivated somehow."

Venser glanced back. That would explain the Phyrexian's inability to open the portal. He would have liked to have cast his wisps, but he had exactly no mana left after putting the Phyrexian to sleep. Nothing.

"Can I tear it open?" Koth said.

"It does not work that way with these portals," the guide said.

"And the Phyrexians would know which way we went," Elspeth said.

"I think they already know which way we went," Venser said.

He turned back to the wall.

"How do these work?" Venser said.

"Don't think now is the time to tinker, artificer," Koth growled.

"How do they?" Venser repeated.

The cries of the Phyrexians were close.

"Are they mechanical?" Venser said.

"Yes," the guide said.

Venser knew what he had to do. He knew what it would mean later, but if there was no later all their effort would have been wasted. He put his hand in his torn shirt and brought out the small bottle, which he uncorked, and emptied the remaining fluid into his mouth.

Venser felt the mana rush into his pores and surge up his brain stem. He shook some of the mana into his fingertips.

"Where should it be?" he asked.

The guide pointed.

Carefully he inserted his hands into the metal of the wall, which gave way like dough. He felt around for a couple of seconds.

"There is a mechanism here," he said. "I cannot tell how it works yet, but it does not want to open."

Koth flinched at the closeness of the Phyrexian's cries behind. "We knew that already," Koth said.

"They are mechanisms at this level," the guide said, "very old ones from before the Phyrexians. They open outward."

"Karn made this then," Venser said, and as he spoke, the portal's door swung out to reveal deeper darkness than they were currently standing in.

They each stepped carefully inside. Venser closed the door and put his hands back into the wall to lock it. Seemingly moments later they heard the first Phyrexians arrive and begin hammering on the wall.

"These walls are thick," the guide said.

"Who locked the portals?" Koth said.

Nobody said anything.

"Tezzeret, maybe," Venser said. "But I do not know why, exactly."

"Let us be off, lest they find a way through," Elspeth said.

CHAPTER
18

They walked in the near darkness until Venser felt the long fingers of exhaustion pushing into his joints. When the guide was sure they were far enough away from the portal, they stopped.

Koth took a deep breath and held it. Soon he began to glow, giving off both light and heat. The room they found themselves in was different than many they had seen in recent days. It had a more organic feel. The walls showed growth lines, as if the large metal walls and ceiling had grown like trees. The ceiling was sloped and no line was straight anywhere.

The organicity made Venser relax somehow. "Why is this room different?" Venser asked, his head still spinning with tiredness.

"This is one of the many passages and rooms that have been growing," the guide said, "creating themselves since the Phyrexians. None of the guides know why."

Venser stopped to look at the walls. "What is the green material?" he said, pinching the dark green strands hanging from the walls. "It's not metal."

The guide shrugged, but the fleshling approached the wall for a closer look.

"This is lamina," she said. "A growing material we revere in the Tangle. It is an effect of the True Sun," she said to the bewildered faces around her.

"Why is it down here?" Koth said.

"It is commonly found in these depths," the guide said.

A tremendous crash thundered through the room, followed by the creaking sound of bending metal.

"They have broken through," Koth said.

They began running. Venser was the last to stand. His legs had felt like boiled eggs before the Phyrexians had broken into that cavern, and he would have to run more. To top it off, his mind had started to drift to the empty bottle in his shirt. The *empty* bottle. He could already feel his arms and legs quake at the thought of the empty bottle. He'd tried living without sips once before, and that hadn't worked out too well, had it?

The clatter behind became the booming of many scrambling feet as the Phyrexians charged along the passage and then into the large room, which they found empty.

The guide led them along branchways, where the passages were growing sideways in long tubes. As they ran, they passed places where new passages shot through one another and they crumbled, leaving large rooms. Lamina, as the fleshling called it, hung randomly.

There were so many small passageways and crumbled walls with holes in them that the Phyrexians had trouble following their trail, though not for lack of trying. As they ran, Venser could hear the enemy crashing through walls and retching out their screams.

Venser stopped.

"Keep running," Elspeth said.

"I can't," he said. "Let me rest for a moment." His legs were so wobbly that he felt he would trip with each step. Tripping would not be advised just then. The growing metal of the passage they were running in was jagged and strangely colored.

"Why is it different colors?" Venser panted.

But the guide was watching behind them. He did not hear Venser.

"Now we go," the guide said.

They kept running. Sometimes the Phyrexians sounded far away. Sometimes they sounded as if they were in the same passage. They kept running. Eventually the walls took on different lines of color. Some of the rings were yellow and others were green. They looked like minerals and base metals. At one point Venser stopped running and touched a wetted finger to one of the rough lines. He put the finger in his mouth, then spat.

"Valatitium," Venser said. "This is found on other planes."

Koth stopped and looked at the line of yellow. "These are deposits," he said. "If the vulshok could delve this deep we could haul quite a lot of good minerals and metal."

"Keep running," the guide yelled.

But soon Venser could not run anymore. He stopped again. The Phyrexians had dropped back, farther than they had been. Still, their banging movements were clearly audible.

"We cannot stop," The guide said. "There are branches ahead that may afford us a way to lose our pursuers."

"I cannot run anymore," Venser said. His legs were so tired that he sat hard on the floor. He had run so hard that his lungs burned and a metallic taste was at the back of his throat. "I cannot."

"You must," the guide said.

But Venser's eyes were on the color bands in the wall. There was a new color he had not seen before. He inched closer to the wall and put a finger to it. A bit of the color crumbled easily at his touch. Venser turned to Koth.

"Do you know this mineral?" Venser said.

"We call it ker," Koth said.

"I know it as kaachmine," Venser said, his mind racing. He suddenly snapped his fingers. "We need to collect as much of it as we can." He took out the knife that lay in his boot and began chipping chunks of ker from the wall. It came off easily.

"We must go," the guide said.

"Stand away," Venser said.

As he worked, Koth glowed slightly. Venser noticed it and frowned. "Don't get hot around this material," Venser said.

"Let us run," Elspeth said.

"I have no more energy or mana," Venser said, as he crumbled some of the ker chunks into powder. "If this works, it will require neither of those."

By the time he had a good-sized pile, the Phyrexians were quite near, their thrashing made them sound like they were in the next passage.

Venser led Elspeth, the fleshling, and the guide down the passage. Koth stayed near the pile. When the rest of them were a good distance down the passage, Venser pushed each one of them into a depression in the wall, and then waved to Koth.

The vulshok tore a strip off his cloth shirt. He wound the strand of cloth up tight and placed one piece in the pile of ker, which reached to the height of his knee. He trailed the other end of the cloth away from the pile.

Then the Phyrexians appeared at the end of the passage. When Koth saw them he casually leaned over the end of the cloth. He made a motion, and sparks flew off the flint and steel in his hand. Soon he'd lit the end of the cloth, which flamed strangely well. As it burned, Koth backed up carefully, watching to see if it would go out. When it was obvious that the flame had caught and caught well on the fabric, Koth turned and sprinted faster than anyone had ever seen him run. The Phyrexians, seeing him running, bounded ahead.

"Down," Venser yelled.

There was a huge *pop* and a *whoosh* of air, and in the next moment Venser found himself facedown on the metal floor, far from where he had been standing. He shook his head as he sat up. A high ringing filled his skull. Nearby Elspeth was already on her feet and looking down at him. Her mouth was moving, but Venser could not hear any of her words.

Where the mound of ker had been, there was only the tangled mass of many parts of many more Phyrexians. Venser doubted if he could climb over the pile, it was so high. Some of the enemy had been torn asunder while others had their metal parts melted to the floor. All was still.

Elspeth put out her hand and helped Venser to his feet. The guide was mysteriously on his feet and unscathed. Elspeth had black powder burns on her arm and face. Venser could only imagine how he looked. If how he felt was any indication, then it was bad indeed. His head still hurt from the attack that had dented his helmet, as the ringing in his ears began to subside, he felt like lying down and sleeping for sixty rotations of a Dominaria sun.

But it wasn't to be. From beyond the heap of destroyed Phyrexians came a series of grunting gags that sounded very much alive.

Venser turned to Elspeth. He was the very essence of depleted. He had nothing left. Well, he had the knife he kept in his boot with which to fight off all attackers. So, really, he had nothing. Even Elspeth, who was always willing to slay Phyrexians, looked around helplessly.

"Did you hear that?" Venser could once again hear himself speak, though the echoing in his skull sounded strange. He could more feel his words' echo than properly hear them.

Elspeth was looking around. "Where is Koth?" she said.

They found him farther down the passage, lying on his side, groaning. A piece of twisted metal, which could have fit on a Phyrexian, had pierced the side of his abdomen.

Elspeth carefully took hold of the piece of metal and yanked it out. Koth grunted through gritted teeth. The piece was slathered with blood and Elspeth threw it clattering away. Koth relaxed and rolled over on his back. From behind them another Phyrexian call echoed.

"What will happen now?" Venser asked. "Perhaps the guide can fight off the Phyrexians and heal Koth?"

Elspeth did not laugh. She looked far too tired to laugh, Venser thought.

Instead she took a lanyard from around her neck. At the end of the lanyard was a small bottle. "You aren't the only one with a bottle," she said.

A Phyrexian call cut the air very close by. When Venser looked back, one of the enemy was standing atop the pile of its brethren. Venser held his breath as he waited for more of them to come streaming around that one. He kept waiting. He stood, and the Phyrexian on the pile—one of the ones swathed in layers of black, pitted metal and with a tiny, almost skeletal head bobbing on a thin neck—thought better of things and retreated, dragging its claws as it did.

"I saw only one," Venser reported. Nobody responded. Elspeth had just poured some of her elixir into Koth's mouth. The vulshok lay back and closed his eyes.

"Did you deliver him from misery?" Venser said, after a moment.

Elspeth's face took on a look of horror. "No, you imbecile. I am sworn never to do what you speak of. He is healing from the inside."

Koth opened his eyes. "I took her before," he said, looking at the fleshling, who regarded him with a blank expression. "I took her to go with me to the surface. I'm sorry."

"That is not something to worry about now," Elspeth said.

We'll worry about it later, Venser thought. Rest assured about that.

"I only wanted to help my people, who hate me," Koth said.

"Yes," Elspeth said. "We knew you were trying to help."

The single Phyrexian called again from behind. That time a second Phyrexian responded from somewhere farther away. Then they heard the faint screech of another.

Koth heard it too. His eyes popped open and he tried to sit up. Elspeth pushed him back down. "What I gave you is speeding your body's healing process, but it will still take a bit of time."

Venser waited for her to elaborate, or for someone to ask how long it would take, but the guide and the fleshling stared down at Koth as though he were some new and exotic creature they had never seen before. Nobody appeared to be about to ask any sort of question. One thing was for sure, Venser was not carrying the vulshok who had tried to steal what they were lucky enough to have. Venser looked over at the fleshling, who was still staring down at Koth. What was going on in that one's head, he wondered. He had yet to catch her with any expression showing itself on her smooth face. She almost never spoke. What was wrong with her? He had considered performing an exploration of her brain, but such an exploration took time and energy and he did not have much of either.

"How long until he can walk?" Venser said. On that note, he wondered how long he himself would be able to walk. One thing was for certain, if he sat down again he would fall asleep.

"A bit longer," Elspeth said.

"We do not seem to have that," Venser said. He waited for a Phyrexian call but there was, of course, none when he needed it to prove a point.

"We have to make that time for Koth," Elspeth said, standing with a groan. "Vital parts of him are knitting themselves together as I say this. We cannot move him."

A Phyrexian bawled somewhere far off. Sure, Venser thought. Now you make some noise.

Elspeth drew her sword. Venser had seen her sword look better. Its blade was chipped, and unless Venser was mistaken, it was slightly bent. It's no wonder with all the Phyrexians that had met its keen edge.

Elspeth lowered the blade and faced the pile of Phyrexians. "We'll know when Koth is ready to travel. He will awake and stand, if he survives."

"If he survives?"

"The potion I gave him can sometimes affect individuals adversely."

"Yet you . . ."

"His kidney was pierced," Elspeth said in a lower tone. "He would have perished without the elixir."

The guide slipped away into the passage ahead, to scout, Venser assumed.

"How did the Phyrexian force know where we were in the first place?" Venser asked.

"An interesting question," Elspeth said. "And one I have been pondering."

"What has your pondering led you to?"

"Nothing," Elspeth admitted.

More Phyrexians called from various parts of the passage, drawing toward them. Soon Venser could hear them clicking and gagging just on the other side of the slag pile of the dead. He could tell by the creaking that there was at least one very large Phyrexian. But there was something else too. Something with a voice. He could hear its smooth-toned orders.

"What do they wait for?" Venser said.

"There numbers are not great," the guide said, suddenly behind them again.

Venser waited. He slipped down into a cross-legged position and sat back against the wall. He closed his eyes for a moment, and when he opened them again Koth was sitting up. He did not look perfect, the potion's effect was not complete, clearly, but he was able to blink and look around.

And there was plenty to look and listen to. Whatever the Phyrexians' numbers when Koth was wounded, they had grown to much more. They were creaking on the other side of the pile in numbers sufficient to vibrate the walls and floor.

"They are just on the other side of the pile," Venser said.

"Yes," Elspeth said. "Nothing has changed."

"Except it seems there are about five hundred of them now."

"Their numbers have increased," Elspeth said.

A figure climbed the pile. A female Phyrexian who had clearly once been an elf. Her hair had twisted into thick cables, some of which were long and moved independently like snakes around her head. Her eyes were black with oil, and some of the oil dripped out of her sockets and down her cheeks. Her left hand was an immense scythe and the other was a claw most terrible in size and aspect. She held up the scythe and all noise from the Phyrexians ceased at once. "Give us the creature who is all flesh."

"Deal," Venser said.

Elspeth turned to glare at him.

"Only jesting," Venser said. "How could we give her to you? Maybe ask her opinion. Perhaps she'll be agreeable to your proposal. You can never tell."

"What do you want with her?" Elspeth said.

"Only that she is our property and you stole our property."

"Springheads have property?" Koth said.

Venser had not heard the phrase springheads used to refer to Phyrexians before. He liked it. But the female Phyrexian bristled at the words. She frowned and disappeared down the side of the pile. When she appeared again, it was with many Phyrexians in tow.

"Now," she said. "Say that again so they know who to slay first."

But Koth had closed his eyes.

"Who are you," Venser said suddenly.

"I am Glissa, the bringer of your death."

She lowered her scythe hand and the Phyrexians began moving forward.

CHAPTER
19

Koth did not open his eyes. Elspeth looked uneasily back at Venser. The guide was unarmed, as far as Venser had ever seen, and sure enough, when Venser looked, the guide was gone. The fleshling was standing back between Venser and Koth. She had no weapon.

Venser looked around him for something to swing. As depleted of mana as he was, there was nothing more he could do but fight hand-to-hand. A twisted piece from a Phyrexian skeleton would work. He was lucky enough to find one lying within reach, and he picked it up and turned back to Glissa. The Phyrexians at her control were almost at the bottom of the pile of dead Phyrexians. Venser counted thirty-four of various shapes and sizes. One had the metal legs of a spider, but with a tremendous thorax that glowed bright blue. Elspeth moved her sword from left to right hand.

Venser had seen her slay countless Phyrexians in a battle, but never when she was so tired and never in one fight, at one time. Plus, any single one of those Phyrexians seemed keen enough to bare them away. They gnashed their teeth and popped their limbs in and out of their sockets as they approached slowly, fanning out to the sides to prevent retreat.

As Venser watched, he knew in his heart that Elspeth would be unable to prevail. It seemed the same thought had just occurred to Elspeth, for she looked down at her battle-scarred sword and then back at Venser.

The Phyrexians were very close, and Venser remembered suddenly when he was a child and he went walking under the linnean trees near his home on Dominaria. He saw the dogs too late. There were sometimes packs of wild dogs in the forests, yet he went there anyway because there were also to be found the ruins of airships and other wrecks of wars long finished. He would collect wreckage and tinker with it. But the wild dogs were hungry and they were especially hungry that day. They stalked him for the better part of an hour. There was no way to know how long they had been watching him with their red eyes. Venser had many times thought that the wild dogs that lived near his house had been some of the bravest creatures that he had ever encountered. Men and women would have their sport killing them, and still the dogs did not flee or shy away. They remained a threat. Find me a beast half as brave here, Venser thought.

He had escaped the dogs by jumping away. It was one of the first times he had ever teleported, which was why he was remembering it. He suddenly yearned to jump away once again.

And so the dogs would have him, it seemed.

The Phyrexians were formed into a crescent around Elspeth, with the left flank facing Venser. Atop the pile Glissa stood watching.

Tezzeret stepped out of the shadows, to the right of the Phyrexians' left flank. When the nearest Phyrexian saw him, it shied back. "This was not the plan," Tezzeret said.

Glissa looked surprised to see him. The Phyrexian advancing on Elspeth stopped.

Behind Tezzeret a cadre of blue-glowing Phyrexians looked on. Tezzeret's Phyrexians were fewer in number, but they looked to Venser even crueler in aspect.

"Plan?" Glissa said.

"Yes," Tezzeret said. "You have your plan. I have my plan. You sent me to get the flesh creature. I had no intention of doing that. Why would I do that when it was I who gave them the creature in the first place?"

The expression on Glissa's face did not change perceptibly at the news. But when she spoke, there was a hitch in her voice that betrayed her unease. "Why would you give them such a creature?"

Tezzeret waved his glowing metal hand dismissively. "The creature is no concern of mine, neither is her innate ability. They will not be able to do significant damage with her. They lack the knowledge." Tezzeret smiled at Venser before turning back to Glissa. "No, I gave her to them to get you out here."

Glissa glanced away quickly.

"Oh," Tezzeret said sadly. "You know I have deactivated that portal you just looked to."

"What do you want?" Glissa said.

"Only your death," Tezzeret said. "Geth is already mine. With you gone I control every Phyrexian in this place."

"The Father of Machines controls his children," Glissa corrected.

"Can't you see that he will never be Phyrexian? It is an impossibility."

"How wrong you are," Glissa said. "And without me, you will not be able to control him."

"That may be true," Tezzeret admitted. "But what if someone else were to ascend that throne of his? This thought has just occurred to me, but what if it was someone like me? I have some metal to me after all."

Glissa did not speak for a moment. "Why would you want that?"

"What an army!" Tezzeret said. "I would be the master, after all. I could utilize such an army to great effect."

"The madness from your arm has greatly affected your brain." Glissa said.

Tezzeret's smile disappeared. "That," he said, "is uncalled for. You have hurt my feelings. You have never known a person more in touch with his facilities as me. Now, I have a choice for you."

"You can step away from Karn, and let me take your place, or—and this next choice is possibly the more favored by me, as I don't like to have an enemy lingering—you can die at my hand. Either way, I cannot endure anymore of my current situation. My master sent me here and now I will make of it everything that I can."

Glissa nodded, as if weighing the pros and cons of Tezzeret's plan.

Meanwhile, the Phyrexians from both sides waited. Some even sat down. Venser caught Elspeth's eye. He pushed out his chin toward the end of the passage they had been traveling down when Glissa's henchmen arrived. Elspeth winked.

Glissa spoke. "So you are here to kill me?"

"You were supposed to have died at their hands with the main force of your soldiers, I am only here to finish."

"That was a bad plan," Glissa said. "I'm sorry, but it is, and it shows your inability to read a situation correctly. That is a necessity in a leader. You must learn that, or you will make other more critical mistakes than this."

"Enough talking now," Tezzeret said, clearly not liking what Glissa was saying.

"I agree," Glissa said. She snapped her fingers and the pile of Phyrexians she was standing on began to wriggle and then to shake.

Venser stepped forward and tugged on Elspeth's tunic. He gestured her to follow, and they both took ten steps back, so they were not in the middle of what was about to become a battlefield.

The pile of mangled and melted metal lurched forward, Glissa standing atop it. Tezzeret stood still and then the pile suddenly unfolded arms and legs and stood crablike to fill the passage. It wasted no time in snapping a claw made of the spine and three legs of other Phyrexians around Tezzeret.

Glissa screamed in triumph, and smiled to show long teeth dyed green with lamina.

But Tezzeret started pushing his head into the creature's fist. He appeared to be squeezing together into a ball, until only his banded ropes of hair were visible. In a moment even that was gone. The Phyrexian giant opened his hand, and to everyone's surprise, nothing fell out.

Venser and Elspeth took ten more steps backward. It had worked before when the Phyrexians were searching for their portal. They had been able to sneak away then, why not again? The guide was somewhere in the shadows waiting for them. Elspeth tapped the fleshling on the shoulder as they stepped back. Glissa was busy staring at the giant's open hand and did not seem to notice their movements.

The fleshling squatted down and with Elspeth's help, they lifted Koth between them.

Two hands appeared on the giant's chest. One was metal and one was flesh, but both parted the metal chest as if it was a fallen autumn leaf. Tezzeret's head poked through the hole, his eyes glowing.

Glissa, standing on the giant's right shoulder, reached around its head and swung her scythe in a wide arc.

Tezzeret held up his etherium arm. The scythe appeared to pass through the arm. A moment later the top of Glissa's scythe hand fell away, a blue seam glowing on the metal where the scythe had struck the arm. But not before the metal of the giant's shoulder began to vine up around Tezzeret's leg. In a moment it was entwined up to his waist. Tezzeret pulled to free his legs, but to no avail. Glissa took hold and swung around the front of the giant's head and planted her feet squarely in Tezzeret's face, snapping his head back.

Then the Phyrexians who had come with Glissa and Tezzeret fell upon one another with the tremendous sound of metal crushing into metal. The ground became a melee of blurring arms and black oil spatter. A Phyrexian nearby punched another's teeth in, still another tore off an arm and cast it spinning aside.

When they were sure that all the Phyrexians and Glissa were busy, Venser, the fleshling, Koth, and Elspeth took ten more steps back. The shadows began to fall in around them, and they turned and ran.

The guide appeared as if from the darkness itself.

How was he able to do that? Venser wondered. Could the guide teleport? It seemed unlikely, but he resolved to keep more of an eye on the human.

The passage went on in the darkness. Venser ran into the darkness willingly, without thinking. The floor was smooth enough and he only tripped once, but was up and running again in a moment. The pitched battle behind slowly fell away, but the echoes continued. When the guide struck fire they all stopped running. He was standing next to a stretch of wall exactly like the other stretches of wall in the passage. Elspeth and the fleshling slowly eased Koth down and leaned him against the wall. Koth groaned and his eyes fluttered but did not open.

"We must be somewhat close to Karn now," Venser said.

"We are deep," the guide said, tapping on the wall. "Soon I will be as deep as I've ever been."

"What perchance happens then?" Elspeth said. "When you do not know where you are?"

The guide kept tapping on the wall. "You find what you search for."

"Those aren't the most heartening words I've heard today," Koth rasped from the floor.

"I have never actually been to the chamber you say Karn resides in," the guide said. "I knew of it, of course. I cannot think it will be too difficult to find if the Father of Machines resides therein."

Venser pursed his lips. Let us hope he is not difficult to find, he thought.

The guide stopped his tapping on a certain spot. He tapped six more times around the place.

"Let us hope that this portal is not locked, as some of the others were," Venser said.

But when the guide pushed, the circular section of metal swung outward and the hole became visible. The guide took the small lamp he'd lit and leaned into the hole. "It appears to be a chute," he said, his voice echoing.

"What good news," Koth moaned.

CHAPTER
20

To Venser it did not seem possible that they could go any deeper. But deeper still they went. The chute turned out to be not just a chute, but a chute that branched and reconnected and became as wide as a large pay road. Venser was glad to not encounter a toll master though, as that would surely have been a fell Phyrexian indeed. He could *feel* their depth somehow. Anything that deep would have been a type of creature he would rather avoid than engage, he suspected. A couple of times as they slid Venser felt his skin crinkle and when he looked into the darkness next to him he thought he saw something sliding next to him

But his paranoia could have been triggered by the knowledge that he would have no more fluid. His hand went to the empty pocket in his shirt, where the small bottle had been. He could feel the beginnings of his tremors. Most likely his body and brain were shutting themselves down. He was nearing his end. That much was clear.

He remembered as an apprentice being warned against anneuropsis extract. The other students called it moth juice or moth extract. Some used it despite their teacher's warnings. It had been, if Venser recalled correctly, a big help in study and retention.

And retention was important with the amount of information they had to metabolize on a daily basis. There were so many newly discovered metals and mana matrices, how could the teachers or anyone over the rank of distillate possibly understand the difficulties encountered memorizing it all.

That was the general justification for its use, anyhow. He knew it was a bad idea to use the fluid. On the other hand, his marks were excellent, and he kept sipping the bottles. He kept sipping it even after he left the high walls of the academy behind him and went into a life of invention and adventure, study, and planeswalking. He kept sipping it even after most of his friends from the academy had stopped.

But they never did what he did. They never went where he went and took the chances he took. They were stuck on Dominaria working for the collective, or eking out a living teaching. With how he lived, Venser *needed* what the moth extract seemed to deliver. Who cared if the fluid really did not do what he thought it did. The important thing was that it *felt* like it did.

His teachers had warned the students about how dependent an artificer could become on the juice. They had told him how it happened—they brought in a former potioner to talk about how he made the fluid. Venser did not remember all the ingredients that went into it. He knew most though. What he did remember completely was how it was made. And it disgusted him. It was left in ceramic jars in tar pits for a certain amount of time, if he remembered rightly, and then buried in a special kind of mud, things like that. If his memory served, it was even buried in the dung of different creatures, some of the dung came from obscure planes—the dung of a huge beast from Zendikar was used, as well as strange plants from that wilderness.

And as he slid to almost certain death, he wished more than anything he had ever wished that he had another bottle. Wished it so much that his palsy began to shudder down his synapses. Venser looked to the side. The glow from Koth's gills illuminated a circle around them as they slid at different speeds down the wide chute. Elspeth was carrying her sheathed sword in her hand. Koth was between her and the fleshling, looking remarkably comfortable as he slid on his back. His abdominal wound was wrapped in lengths of torn white linen Elspeth had packed for just that purpose.

The guide was nowhere to be seen, of course. But when the chute ended, he appeared again, leaning against the wall in the room the slide emptied into. The room seemed to be writhing, somehow. They had come once again into a room of guts and veins, with wet tubes threading through everything and walls that stunk and appeared to sweat or bleed. Koth looked around and sneered. Elspeth's nose twitched. The fleshling peered into the darker corners. But still the guide leaned against the wall. For one mad second, Venser remembered the terror of Koth's mother being puppeteered by a Phyrexian. Then the guide stood away from the wall.

"The way is over here, when you are recovered," he said.

Venser was pleased to see his mouth and lips working normally, as they had before. Koth's mother's movements were jerky, and her mouth's motions did not match the words being spoken, he remembered.

The chute had flung them into the middle of the pocked floor. Koth shrugged away Elspeth's proffered hand, and stood. He did not stand quite straight, but looked much improved from earlier.

Elspeth obviously agreed. She nodded at him. "You'll feel the wound for a day or two, but the enchantments have sped the healing and you will be able to fight shortly, do not worry."

Koth did not look overjoyed at the news.

"I know you have been anxious to fight again," Elspeth continued, pursing her lips.

It was hard with the white warrior, Venser reflected, who had almost no apparent humor about her, to tell when she was trying to be funny. This time was no exception, and Venser puffed out his chest and began walking.

"This way," the guide said. Koth turned about-face from his original direction and followed the guide.

The guide led them across the darkened room, which was veritably throbbing. The tubes and pipes were larger than Venser remembered seeing in other rooms, and he mentioned that to the guide, who shrugged. But to Venser it seemed that something was being pumped. The tubes, veins in actuality, expanded and contracted and there was a whooshing sound as well as a rhythmic booming, as though someone was striking a vast metal drum.

The guide approached what looked suspiciously like a real door, except its size was greater than what Venser would have expected in that deep place. Double a man's height and as wide as two more, the door showed, in metal relief, the gears and cogs that made up a machine. Hundreds of different colored metals made up the different inlays and parts of the door, which Venser thought mere decorations. But the guide turned the huge brass knob, and cogs in the door began turning. Soon all the works that made up the door began to turn and move and the door opened and creaked inward. The guide stepped aside like a doorman at a ball and ushered them inside.

Why all the mechanisms? Venser wondered. If it is a lock then why did it open so easily at the guide's touch?

He soon found out why. They followed the guide into the chamber, which like almost all the places in the depths of Mirrodin, was dimly lit. The room smelled strongly of metal falling to corrosion. The droning sound was softer there. The room and the sound reminded Venser of something, but he could not recall what.

A huge column stood at the far end of the room. Hundreds of tiny yellow mites sped around it in a circular orbit. Venser turned to ask the guide what the place was, but he found the guide staring stock-still at the top of the column. Venser waited a moment, but the guide didn't move. Elspeth had noticed it too. She reached out and took the guide's wrist. After a moment of feeling his wrist for the beat of his heart, Elspeth frowned. She checked once again that her finger was in the right place behind his thumb before pulling her hand away. The guide's arm fell.

"I feel nothing," she said.

Koth, who was walking with virtually no hunch by then, did not even look over. But the fleshling did. "He is a machine," the fleshling said softly. She looked at each of their faces. "Surely you knew that."

"A Phyrexian?" Koth said.

"No," Venser said, waving his hand before the guide's eyes. "He shows none of the tell-tale signs. This is an extremely deftly made mechanism that fooled us all. Even me."

"He seems to have brought us where he was supposed to," Elspeth said.

"It's dark everywhere," Koth said, as if in explanation of the deception. "We were running the whole time."

Elspeth gave Koth a dark glance. "Yes *we* were, weren't *we*?"

But Koth either didn't notice or did not acknowledge the jab. He walked over to the guide and brazenly knocked on his forehead. "Yep, he's metal," Koth said. He turned to Venser. "Well," Koth said. "Where are we now? Is this the goal of all your superior leading?"

"You have nerve," Elspeth said to Koth. "I'll give you that."

Koth gave Elspeth a wide smile. "I feel good for the first time in a day."

"What is on the walls?" Venser said. He had not noticed the walls because they were shrouded in shadow, but he moved closer for a look and was shocked at what he saw.

Koth moved closer to the wall. "They are bones, of course," Koth said. The bones were stuck to the wall in a certain pattern, four sideways then four vertically. The pattern covered all the walls, except where ribs and other bones were set in circles or triangles or other geometric patterns. Eventually the bones changed to machine shapes and more cogs.

Nobody said anything. There were enough bones for hundreds of humans to have used. And thick, black, rubbery tubes ran around the bones and through them. At some places the bones were obscured by curtains of smaller black tubes. The whole room pulsed.

Venser shook his head. "What is that sound?" Venser said, holding his head, which felt like it might explode. Was it starting? He thought desperately. The palsy's toll?

"I hear it also," Elspeth said.

"Feel it in my chest," Koth said.

The guide jerked once, and then stood still.

"That sound is my children running to this place. That sound is all of their feet."

The booming voice seemed to come from everywhere in the room at once. Venser stood up a bit straighter. "Karn?" Venser said.

The words seemed to hang in the air.

"I have not heard that name in eons," the voice said.

"It has not been that long, old friend," Venser said.

"Old friend? Do I know you? What is your name?"

"It is Venser of Urborg."

"Venser of Urborg," the voice repeated uncertainly.

"From not so long ago," Venser said.

"Yes," Karn said. "I sent somebody for you."

"I'm sorry?"

"I sent a guide to lead you to me, but I cannot remember why."

Venser looked to his side, where the guide was staring up at the top of the column with rapt fascination.

There was a terrific clatter as something began moving at the top of the column. Before their eyes, the column began coming apart. Venser stepped back. He noticed small, dark creatures that had been holding the sections of the column on their backs lowering the sections downward, hand to hand. Each of them was a duplicate of the small silver creature they had all followed down into the depths below the Vault of Whispers. Soon the last section of column was set vertically on the floor. A silver figure began climbing down a small ladder built into the metal of that section of column. The large figure was dwarfed beside the huge column it climbed down. It stopped midway down the ladder and launched into a series of violent convulsions before letting go of the rungs and falling the rest of the way to the metal floor.

CHAPTER
21

Venser rushed over. The silver golem was lying on the floor inside the dent it had created by falling. Venser noticed the other, similar dents in the floor.

The golem's eyes were silver slits and his wide jaw was thrust out. Karn reached out, took a handful of the metal floor as though it were dough, and pulled himself to his feet, where he stood looking down at Venser. Venser noticed with unease that the silver golem was smeared with black oil. What appeared to be droplets of the material dotted his silver body. Venser forced himself to smile. "We have been searching for you, old friend."

Karn frowned down at Venser. "You are here to destroy me, I know this."

Venser held up the palms of his hands. "That is not true."

"You want to," Karn shook his head once before continuing. "You want me to become a Phyrexian."

"We want just the opposite," Venser said.

"We want you to leave," Koth cut in.

Venser ignored the vulshok. "We do not want you to leave," Venser said. "We are here to heal the sickness you have."

"I am not sick," Karn said. "I should crush you for saying such."

"Then leave, why don't you," Koth said. "Go away, you are not wanted here."

Venser stepped closer to Karn. "Karn, it is I—your old student and friend."

But Karn's eyes popped open wide and his metallic nostrils flared. "You dare approach," he shoved Venser, who flew back skittering across the floor and into a wall.

"Now you really are going to leave," Koth said, "in pieces if possible."

Koth grabbed one of Karn's arms and yanked him off his feet. The silver golem looked bewildered as Koth took a step, pivoted, and threw Karn down and onto his back. He hopped onto Karn's chest and his hand went white-hot in a blink. Koth moved to plunge his hand into Karn's chest, but Elspeth held his arm back at the bicep. Koth struggled to free himself, but Elspeth had better purchase and was able to keep the arm back.

Karn's face had once again pinched itself into a malevolent expression. He brought his knee up and slammed Koth in the back, sending him over the golem's head and into wall, where the geomancer lay still.

With the fluidity of a snake, Karn hopped to his feet and stood facing Elspeth. "They are almost here," Karn said. "When they arrive I will let my children have their way with you," he said. His slit eyes moved to the fleshling, who was standing next to Elspeth. "They like skin you know."

"Stop."

Venser hobbled up to them. By its strange angle, Elspeth could tell Venser's left arm was broken. The dented helmet was still under his arm. He stepped to Karn's side. Karn raised his arm to strike when he saw Venser. But the artificer did not cringe.

"Remember our time together, Karn?" Venser said. "Do you remember exploring the Valley of Echoes? Where we found those scrolls and I could not read the writing, but you could somehow?"

The golem's face softened. He lowered his arm. "I do not remember that, but I should like to."

"You are Karn," Venser said.

". . . Father of Machines," Karn boomed. The echo vibrated the walls.

"No," Venser said, when the walls had stilled. "The creator of Mirrodin. You are powerful and kind."

Koth's crumpled form stirred.

"We are here to heal you from what is attacking you," Elspeth said.

Confusion spread across Karn's face, and then in a moment the expression changed again. "Or maybe you will help hold up my column." Karn reached out and clamped his large hands on Elspeth's head, one hand on each ear. She struggled, but the silver golem's grip was immovable. He closed his eyes. When he opened them again they were black and glowing.

"Tell me what you remember of your childhood," the fleshling said.

The fleshling's words were not loud, but the strangeness of their context stopped everybody.

Karn blinked and his eyes went back to silver. "What?" he said.

"Your childhood," the fleshling repeated. "Tell me about that."

"My childhood?" Karn said. "Did I have one? I cannot remember."

Venser glanced uneasily at the fleshling.

"When I was a boy," Venser volunteered. "We knew of this swamp . . ."

"Tell me about when you learned that all flesh dies," the fleshling interrupted.

Venser had seen the fleshling in the camp, when she had been healing the people who lived there. He remembered watching her whispering to them. Was *this* what she was asking them? Questions about their childhoods? Still, if it could help Karn. Venser thought back to when he was a child.

"It must have been when my father never returned."

The fleshling nodded. "Tell me about that."

"He went out one day into the swamps to work," Venser started. "And he simply never came back." To Venser's amazement and embarrassment, his voice suddenly broke as he spoke. He suddenly remembered vividly what that felt like, being that boy again and being alone.

"And you knew, someday you would also not come back?"

"Yes, I missed him and I did not want that to happen to him, or to me," Venser said. His father's disappearance had set in motion a series of events that changed him forever. He and his mother had had to stay with his aunt, and the man who lived with his aunt. He ran away not so very long after that.

He could feel them now, the tears. They were hot on his cheek but cooled quickly. Venser suddenly became very aware that everybody in the room was looking at him, and he wiped the tears away with the heel of his palm.

"We are not machines," the fleshling said. "The real secret the Phyrexians are trying to hide by keeping me in captivity is that flesh is stronger than metal. They are obsessed with flesh for this reason. They cannot copy the strength. This is a secret they do not want known."

Venser could see a change occurring in the fleshling's eyes. They began to glow strongly with a blue and then a green light. Very soon the air went thick with light and an intense *buzz* wormed into Venser's ears. The fleshling laid her gaze on Karn. The colored air between them began to bend and distort and her smooth brow furrowed in concentration.

Venser had seen it happen from far away, but being so close, he felt the power radiating from the fleshling's sweaty visage. Her chin began to quiver as he watched.

Karn yawned.

The fleshling blinked.

"What happens now?" Venser said.

"Do you feel different?" Elspeth said to Karn.

The silver golem's eyes narrowed as the black oil droplets popped out all over the metal of his body. "Why would I feel different?"

The tramping of millions of metal feet was starting to vibrate the room. Karn heard it too. He smiled. "They are almost here," he said. "And then you will have something."

Karn reached out and grabbed the fleshing by the scruff of her leather jerkin. "I will hold you for my children, as they are partial to flesh."

Venser exhaled. It was worse than he had imagined. Without Karn, he knew that Mirrodin was truly lost, no matter what Koth said. They couldn't leave, so they were also lost. They could not hope to prevail against the Phyrexians without Karn.

"His heart is too far gone to the contagion," the fleshling whispered.

"His heart?" Venser said. "How do you know it is his heart?"

"The heart is where it finishes. Usually they look like Phyrexians by the time the heart if converted," the fleshling said.

"And if his heart were clean?"

The fleshling frowned. "Then I suppose he would be healed. His body is healed now."

"That is so?" Venser said.

"Yes. Does he not look himself?"

He did look like himself, except for the black oil droplets. Venser looked out over the throne room. How many would die if he didn't act? How many more would suffer and die? Karn would eventually become fully Phyrexian, and then all the planes would know to fear metal. They would all fall.

Elspeth came to stand with Venser. "Do we have a plan?" Elspeth said to Venser. "Your face betrays that we do not."

"I have no plan. We're trapped in this room with Karn," Venser said, then to the fleshling, "But what if Karn had a new heart?"

"If the heart was uninfected then he would be healed." Karn had her by her jerkin. The silver golem was listening to the thunder of his minion's feet with a smile twisting his large face.

"Is *my* heart infected?" Venser said.

"No, none of us is near that stage," the fleshling said. She tugged against Karn's huge fist. He turned his gaze and stared intently at the skin on her neck.

Venser nodded. But I have other things wrong with me, he thought.

"Once the contagion reaches the heart it is too late," the fleshling said. "Nothing has reached our hearts."

Elspeth sighed. "Surely there is another way," she said.

"What would that way be?" Venser said. "Take somebody else's heart? Who? You?"

"Not you," Elspeth said.

The fleshling was looking from one to the other of them. "How would you do what you speak of?" she said.

Karn let go of the fleshling. The black oil droplets had disappeared, and his eyes were once again open and not slit. He sat down on the ground and watched the argument calmly.

Venser closed his eyes and took a deep breath. Yes, he could do it, he thought. He had built up just enough mana over the last hour to do such a tiny jump and teleport his heart into Karn's chest. But just enough, and he would have, obviously, just one chance.

"Lie down, Karn," Venser said.

Karn leaned back and eased himself to the shiny floor.

"Let us consider other possibilities," Elspeth said. "There are always other options."

Venser laid a hand on Elspeth's armored shoulder. "This is what must happen. You know that. I know it. In fact, I think I always knew it would happen this way. My life is almost done as it is. What runs its way through my body will not release me from its grasp. I've known since you and Koth came to my studio and brought me here. The moment I saw the first Phyrexian I knew Karn would be at the heart of this in some way. I had my fears that he would succumb to the black oil. This is something I have been thinking about—resigning myself to the possibility that I would maybe have to make this sacrifice. Imagine other planes with others people. I imagine that child in the bogs in Urborg, searching for his father. He had a chance, as must others in our time. You know as I do that the Phyrexians will take this place and move to another. They must be stopped. Here sits the one who, maybe more than any other, can stop their spread. And he is my friend. I will not let him fall like a dog to this sickness. You cannot ask me to let that happen."

Elspeth looked over at Karn. "I see the oil droplets on him again," she said. "You had better hurry."

Venser closed his eyes and turned to Karn. A second later the artificer's body crumpled to the floor. Released by his limp arm, Venser's dented helmet went rolling along the floor lopsidedly before clanking to a stop against Karn's metal leg. The silver golem's body gave a violent jolt and lay still.

CHAPTER
22

Elspeth's hand fell to the pommel of her blade. She looked down at the fleshling, who was watching the golem's motionless body on the floor. Behind, in the dimness somewhere, Koth tried to stand, but slumped back to the ground with a clatter.

Elspeth drew her sword. She held its crookedness out before her and let her eye travel down its notched edge. It was no wonder the blade was notched, with all the hacking of metal that had commenced. Hopefully there would not be a golem that begged hacking. She had her doubts as to whether she could match Karn, but she was not going to let him walk from the room with the black oil septic in his body. She had seen too much of Phyrexia to allow that.

If her sword broke on Karn, then she would stave in his face with her fist. If her fist broke upon him, then she would use her teeth. If her teeth were not up to the task, then the devils of Zarnic take him!

Karn's eyes snapped open.

Elspeth squared her shoulders and stepped forward. "If this starts to go badly," Elspeth said to the fleshling, "waste no time fleeing this room. Make for the settlement if you can. Do not waste time thinking to help me. This is the best place for me. Your people will need leading, and you are the person to do this."

The fleshling looked over at the huge door. There was a howl and the knocking of hundreds of metal feet on metal, and a group of Phyrexians surged into the door.

Karn rolled over and stood. The silver golem loomed taller than Elspeth. He looked down at her with dilated, metallic irises. The Phyrexians pushed through the door, wheezing.

"Venser, the artificer, has given you his heart," Elspeth sang out loudly. "What will you do with it, golem?" If Elspeth was nervous in the least, the fleshling did not hear it in her voice, which had a tone as though she was challenging an opponent to a tourney joust.

Karn put his arms out wide. Electric jags licked from arm to arm. "My dreams have been grim of late," he said. "My memories are as flashes of lightning. I dreamed of a throne that clung to my spine, of black blood in my eye, of the plane wrought by my hand pried from me by a tin-toy empire."

Elspeth turned to look behind. More Phyrexians had pushed their stinking way into the doorway. Hundreds stood hunched and dripping at the end of the room. She thought for a moment that she saw Glissa, but a moment later it was just another elf Phyrexian.

Karn's eye fell on the Phyrexians as well. "These dreams anger me," he said. He brought his arms down and the charge arcing between his fists branched out, traveling the distance of the room and striking one Phyrexian before jumping to all the others. They lit brightly for a moment before falling to the floor, smoking.

Karn looked back down at Elspeth and the fleshling, then down at Venser's dented helmet which lay next to his great foot. "And I grieve greatly that my friend Venser is no more."

Elspeth pointed the tip of her blade at Venser's body. "There is his body," she said. "What will you do with it?"

Karn looked from Venser's helmet to his body. "He will be wed with fire and made free. I will take him with me when I leave."

"Where will you go?" Elspeth said.

"I have traveled the planar byways spreading sickness. Now I must clean what I have dirtied. This is what must happen."

Karn started walking toward the doorway. His every step made the floor jiggle. More Phyrexians were collecting around the doorway, behind the piles of their dead comrades. Lightning crackled down Karn's bicep and jumped to one of their heads and branched. In a moment all of the Phyrexians lay smoking next to the others.

Karn stopped and turned. "I will collect Venser's body later when I have cleaned as much of this vermin as I can find." Karn sighed.

Elspeth glanced over at the golem and then back to Venser's body. "Don't wait too long, it's warm down here. You will not enjoy your trip with him if you wait too long."

But Karn had already turned his back. He stepped through the Phyrexian bodies and around some huge juggernauts bunched and smoking on the other side of the door.

"You will never be able to clear Mirrodin of Phyrexians," Elspeth said.

"I will kill as many as I may," Karn said as he walked. "But you are right. I will not be able to kill them all, I fear. You must all do your part."

"I will lead my people against the Phyrexians," the fleshling said. "There were Mirrans in the settlement we visited, but we should find more hiding."

Koth was quiet where he had propped himself against the wall.

"We will find all who wish to stand for their homes and fight this enemy," the fleshling said.

"Good and evil, there is never one without the other," Karn said. He stopped and gazed around the darkened corridor. "I forged this place when I was young. Bird and beast and flower were worrisome to me then. So I made this place where death was but a coincidence."

"Now it is a place of death, old machine," Koth said. He struggled to his feet and spat on the floor. "But the fleshling and I will clear this and all of Mirrodin of the scourge."

Elspeth could feel the heat radiating off of Koth. As she watched, slits of cherry red split his sides. His eyes began to take on the same rosy hue.

Karn continued speaking. "All has passed like rain on the fields, like wind in the mountain tops. My days seem gone with the sun at its set. But not yet! I have too much to put right." He walked faster, so the companions had to scramble to keep up.

"Are we ready for battle?" Karn said, striding even faster. "I have slept too long. Mirrodin has carried my pride and also my guilt. You all have fought my battles. Now, friends, we shall show these beasts of meat and metal the true nature of their Father of Machines."

"We will make this right," Koth said. He stood next to Venser's dented helmet. But the others had left, and his words went unheard in the gathering darkness.

EXPLORE THE MAGIC™ MULTIVERSE WITH THESE GREAT TITLES NOW AVAILABLE AS EBOOKS!

TEST OF METAL
MATTHEW STOVER

From the ashes of defeat, the Planeswalker Tezzeret will rise again. Beaten to within an inch of his life and left for dead by the psychic sorcerer Jace Beleren, Tezzeret must now turn to a former enemy for help: the dragon Nicol Bolas, perhaps the only being in the Multiverse powerful enough to get him back on his feet.

THE FIFTH DAWN
CORY HERNDON

In a world changed by the appearance of a new sun, the only ally Glissa knows she can depend on in the fight against Memnarch is the goblin, Slobad.

THE DARKSTEEL EYE
JESS LEBOW

Glissa, Bosh, and Slobad must flee across the harsh world of Mirrodin, running from an enemy who seems all-knowing. Within the deepest reaches of their world, the Darksteel Eye watches. And waits.

THE MOONS OF MIRRODIN
WILL MCDERMOTT

Across the harsh landscape of Mirrodin, an orphaned elf must make her way, seeking the secrets of her past, daring the perils of her present.

Find these eBooks and more at
www.wizards.com/magicnovels

MANY ROADS LEAD TO
 ™

RETURN WITH
G A U N T L G R Y M

Neverwinter, Book I
R.A. Salvatore

NEVERWINTER WOOD

Neverwinter, Book II
R.A. Salvatore
October 2011

CONTINUE THE ADVENTURE WITH
BRIMSTONE ANGELS

Legends of Neverwinter
Erin M. Evans
November 2011

LOOK FOR THESE OTHER EXCITING NEW NEVERWINTER RELEASES IN 2011

RPG for PC
Cooperative Board Game
D&D® Roleplaying Game

HOW WILL YOU RETURN?

Find these great products at your favorite
bookseller or game shop.

DungeonsandDragons.com

THE ABYSSAL PLAGUE

From the molten core of a dead universe

Hunger
Spills a seed of evil

Fury
So pure, so concentrated, so infectious

Hate
Its corruption will span worlds

The Temple of Yellow Skulls
Don Bassingthwaite
March 2011

Sword of the Gods
Bruce Cordell
April 2011

Under the Crimson Sun
Keith R.A. DeCandido
June 2011

Oath of Vigilance
James Wyatt
August 2011

Shadowbane
Erik Scott de Bie
September 2011

Find these novels at your favorite bookseller.
Also available as ebooks.

DungeonsandDragons.com